The Ice Out

Mina Myles

violet amin's playlist

Now that we don't talk – Taylor Swift
Burton St – OSTON
The Grudge – Olivia Rodrigo
Coffee – Chappell Roan
So Highschool – Taylor Swift
You're Gonna Go Far – Noah Kahan

mason hayes's playlist

Dial Drunk – Noah Kahan
Used To Be Young – Miley Cyrus
Paul Revere – Noah Kahan
Kaleidoscope – Chappell Roan
Castles Crumbling – Taylor Swift (ft. Hayley Williams)
Bloom – The Paper Kites

To those wondering whether they deserve better — you do. And to those struggling to heal and move forward, remember…

"Without your past, you could never have arrived so wondrously and brutally, by design or some violent, exquisite, happenstance…here."
— Taylor Swift

a note from mina

Hello Lovely Reader,

I can't begin to describe how much I appreciate you picking up a copy of *The Ice Out*. I love Violet and Mason will all of my heart, and I hope you do too.

Before you start reading, please note that this book contains depictions of emotional and verbal abuse, microaggressions, panic attacks, anxiety, and mention of alcohol abuse and housing insecurity (off-page). Additionally, this book contains profanity and descriptions of consensual sexual acts. As much as I want you to meet these characters, please prioritize your well-being.

With Love,
Mina

prologue

. . .

Mason

before

chicago

"ARE you sure you can't stay for the game? You're kinda killing my big surprise here." I try not to sound too upset with Monroe. About two hours after she had landed in Chicago, she got an emergency phone call from her boss at the PR firm she was interning at. Something about a reality dating show host catching her husband, and co-host, having an affair with one of the contestants during the live finale, which took place on a cruise ship. The PR team needed to be at the port as soon as the ship docked to control the scandal.

"And I thought you flew me out to Chicago because you

missed me. Instead, I was just some ploy to impress Violet. If she wasn't my best friend, I'd be very upset you know," she teased in the middle of packing up her carry-on.

"It's not that I'm trying to impress her, I just knew you two hadn't seen each other in a while and—"

Monroe snorted, giving me a pointed look. "You are aware that she's my roommate, right?"

"She *used* to be your roommate before you decided to move from Vermont to New York. Which I get, but now Violet's all alone and…don't look at me like that."

She held her hands up in mock innocence. "Who me? I'm just standing here minding my business. And pointing out that you talk to her more than I do."

"Are friends not allowed to talk?"

She raised an eyebrow, looking eerily like our mother when she caught me red-eyed and zombied-out in my room. "Sure, but I typically reserve making out for the friends who buy me dinner first. So, did Vi buy you dinner? Or was that one on the house?"

"I— she told you about that?"

"No, definitely not. Vi knows that news would have made me gravely ill. You two weren't exactly discreet."

Not a single day had gone by when I'm not reminded of that moment between Violet and me a year ago. *My senior year at Westchester featured a grueling game in the Hockey East Championships against our biggest rival from the other side of the Charles River — Bolton University. Every time I took a hit or scored a goal, Violet was right there, keeping me grounded. Less than three minutes into overtime and I had buried the puck into the back of the net. I was able to catch her standing in the crowd, her smile so beautiful and bright if the stars in the night sky could weep in envy, they would.*

Unsurprisingly, the party Bradon and Mikey had thrown in celebration was flooded with hundreds of students. Through the sea of people, I managed to find Violet and pulled her over to a semi-quiet corner in the apartment. On instinct, I moved a loose curl from her face, tucked it behind her ear, and let my hand rest on the side of her neck. I waited for confirmation. With one small nod I closed the distance between us and kissed her. A rush of heat filled my body as I dragged my tongue across her bottom lip, begging to explore her mouth. Violet parted her lips and let out a small gasp in response, one that I knew would forever be imprinted on my brain.

"Helllooo, earth to Mason." The sound of Monroe's voice snapped me back to reality.

I needed to change the conversation and get my head straight, given Violet and I were about to spend the next few days alone in this hotel room together.

"So what if we kissed at the party? The next day she laughed it off and said it didn't mean anything."

Really what she had said was, *"Don't worry about it. I know you were super drunk and probably not thinking straight. Let's pretend it never happened."* I wasn't sure why but, in that moment, all I wanted to do was let her convince me that was true — to force me to believe that the two beers I had earlier in the night were enough to affect my judgment. That the kiss wasn't the most sober I felt all night. I had figured it would make things awkward to tell her that truth, so we kept texting every day like nothing had happened. Eventually, I wondered whether I had made the whole thing up.

"Vi was just trying to protect herself, Mase. She probably wanted to know for sure that you really liked her." Monroe moved to sit down next to me on the bed.

"Of course I like her 'Roe. Our families are basically joined at this point."

She rolled her eyes. "What I *meant* was maybe she wasn't sure if she could trust you. Sure, you've been there for her as this pseudo-big brother, but your track record when it comes to girls is…lengthy in numbers and short in duration. You can't blame her for not wanting to be another one of your one-night stands."

I winced. "Harsh."

"It is harsh. And I'm not trying to shame you for it. But at the same time if it makes Violet nervous, I can understand why."

It felt relevant to add, "I haven't really hooked up with anyone since Violet and I kissed."

Monroe smiled softly. "I could see that winning you some bonus points."

I didn't have to tell Monroe that I was hoping it would. She knew how I felt. It was written all over my face.

"Is she just going to assume I orchestrated this whole trip so I could sleep with her? Now I really don't want you to leave."

"She won't think that, but as her best friend I am obligated to let you know that if you hurt her in any way, I will break your kneecaps."

"Noted. Any sisterly advice?"

"Mostly I just have threats..." She bit her lip, debating on how to say, "Violet will probably tell you this when she gets here, but she's currently deciding between two offers for the PhD programs she's been applying to. One's in New York and the other's in Boston."

She could be in New York soon. How the hell was I supposed to remain impartial to this information?

Monroe cocked an eyebrow at my perking up. "Listen, I know the last thing you want is your little sister sticking her nose into your love life, but just tread lightly, okay? She's about to make a huge decision and you're at the start of your pro career. I don't know if either of you are ready to jump into a serious relationship right now."

"Damn, and I thought the older sibling was supposed to be the one that offered all the sage advice."

"None of us were ever expecting you to be the smart one," she teased.

"What if I am ready for something serious?"

She seemed surprised by my counterpoint. "Well...then I think you guys could be really good for each other."

one

. . .

Violet

present day

THE THINGS I would do right now for an iced chai latte were unspeakable. I was heading into office hours sans caffeine which was unfortunate, both for my own sanity and for my students who were likely hoping for a coherent answer to their often incoherent questions. In an ideal world, their teaching assistant would have their life together. But this world was not ideal (see me spending the previous day fielding SOS texts from the undergrad research assistants I was mentoring, trying (and failing) to understand what was happening in my graduate statistics course, and catching up on grading papers for PSYCH101). In the aforementioned ideal world, I would have had time to finally make some progress on my thesis. Instead, after my hellish day I decided that I deserved a three-hour binge-watch of *Selling Sunset* and a pint of Ben and Jerry's.

I had no misconceptions about what a PhD program would be like when I started a little over three years ago. I knew it would be mentally exhausting, and some nights would be spent eating sleep for dinner (God forbid the university paid us a living wage). But no one had prepared me for the emotional turmoil that was my first year in the Developmental Neuro-science program at Westchester. When I started the program working for the top researcher in my field, who was also my hero at the time, I thought I was living the dream. That was until I got to see the true colors of my former mentor and the monster hidden behind a long list of esteemed awards, and ground-breaking publications. My second year was spent finding my footing in a new lab and slowly healing the wounds left from year one, wounds that I didn't even know existed until one would get pressed on.

I wasn't entirely sure how my third year would pan out, but I knew at the very least that I had nowhere to go but up. *A rare streak of optimism.* I may not remember the last time I got more than six hours of sleep, or when I'd had three full meals in a day, but I could at least put my past far behind me and stop crying over spilled milk (milk that ultimately ruined my laptop as I was coding an MRI task).

A clean slate. That's what this year would bring for me, Violet Amin — your favorite well-adjusted and somewhat mentally healthy graduate student. Though I still had my moments where the pressure would start to weigh down on me, I tried my best to not let it consume me like it had in the past. I would instead take ten deep breaths — in five seconds, out seven — and remind myself that this was my *dream*. This was all I ever wanted. Which meant it all would be worth it in the end. It had to be.

I made it halfway down the hall when I felt my forehead tighten — the start of an impending headache. I had entirely too much going on today to be taken down by a headache that was no doubt brought on by a mixture of sleep deprivation and caffeine withdrawals. *Maybe it wouldn't be the worst idea if you were a little late to office hours. The caffeine demon inside you is only going to get crabbier, and you rarely have students show up in the beginning.* It was later in the afternoon which meant the Beanery — my favorite campus café that made *elite* chai lattes — would likely be pretty empty.

For once, luck appeared to be on my side. I waltzed right up to the cashier and secured my delicious beverage in record speed, and it looked like I was going to make it back to my office in the nick of time. That was until I ran straight into a wall in my haste to exit the Beanery. A wall made of flesh and pectoral muscle. *Damn, what are they feeding these kids?* My eyes trail up to a muscular neck and finally, the stranger's face. As my eyes settled on his shaken expression, I realize he is not a stranger at all. Nor is he a student. The noise that comes out of my mouth is a horrid mix of a wheeze and a choke. It had been nearly three years since I had last spoken to *him.*

Three years since I made a vow to myself that I would never, ever, feel that type of pain again – pain that he caused. I'd tried my best to block out our last conversation. I didn't want his half-assed apologies or reasons as to why I was never good enough for him. *Why I was never good enough for anyone.* It wasn't the first time in my life that I realized I had cared a lot more about someone than they had cared about me, but I made a promise to myself that it would be the last. Up until now, I had thought I had moved on and fully forgotten that *he* had existed. But the twinge in my heart and the fact that I couldn't even bring myself to think his name told me how much I still had to get over. He didn't need to know that though. "Excuse me."

He stood frozen in place. For every bit of calm, cool, and collected I had hoped to appear, his face mirrored my true panic — eyes bulged wide, mouth slightly open, and cheeks flushed a subtle shade of pink. He looked as if he had seen a ghost. I suppose in many ways that's what I am to him. A ghost of his past, now haunting his present. He blinked a few times before getting out a "W— what?" He looked like he was about to pass out.

I took his moment of confusion to slide past him, bolting straight for the psychology building. I wanted — really needed — nothing more than to just huddle up in the corner of my office for the rest of the day. How could I possibly be expected to work, or even function, after running into *him* again? Except I had to; that was the promise I made myself. After spending countless days wondering where it all went wrong, I decided the best thing I could do for myself was to let it all go. Turns out I would also lose a part of myself when I let him go.

two

. . .

Mason

FOR TEN MINUTES I stood outside the café too stunned to move before I realized what had transpired. Years later I still couldn't get the image of her tangled in hotel sheets out of my head. Or all the promises that we made, but I knew we couldn't keep, that night in Chicago. She had responded twice to the dozens of texts that I had sent in the weeks after she left Chicago. The first text let me know she landed back home safely, and the second told me she needed space and time to think.

At the time, I hadn't realized she was cutting me out of her life. We had our fair share of fights before, the normal kind that are bound to happen when you've grown up with someone — fights over who got shotgun, who had the better taste in music, who had to tell our parents we broke their favorite vintage Tina

Turner vinyl. Usually, we'd ignore each other for a week, and then one of us (usually me) would realize they were being an ass, apologize, and we'd move on.

Chicago was completely new territory for us. I thought I was saving her, saving us, from future disasters. There was nothing that could keep us truly apart, or permanently sever so many years of friendship. We would survive this and be happier for it. Or at least that's what I thought when I tried to make amends a few months after Chicago.

I feel like I'm about to come out of my skin as I wait patiently outside Violet's home in Castle Harbor. This is probably the first time in my entire life I've rang the doorbell and waited for someone to let me in, as opposed to using my copy of the key and making myself at home. Something told me that wouldn't be appreciated now. I had sent Violet several text messages and left endless voicemails after she left me alone in Chicago. I respected her need to take some time for herself, and I also understood why she'd want to put that distance between us. That didn't stop me from hating the silence. The last thing I ever wanted to do was make Violet unhappy. I couldn't bear it.

Which is ultimately what led me here. When Violet's mom had invited me to her 'Congrats on getting into grad school' party, the thought of ruining another thing for her made my heart squeeze and I contemplated not coming. But regardless of Violet's current feelings toward me, I swore to show up for her. To always be there. So here I was, waiting outside for seconds? Minutes? Hours? Maybe no one heard the doorbell ring. At that thought the front door swings open and out comes the one person who has occupied every single inch of my headspace for the past three months.

Violet's vibrant smile immediately falls from her face as she realizes it's me. Her new default expression to seeing me was sadness. That was to be expected I supposed, but still hurt nonetheless. I tried to smile and make something intelligible come out of my mouth.

"Hey, you cut your hair." The curly mane that used to reach down to the middle of her back now fell to just above her shoulders. It's clear

she didn't expect me to start the conversation with that. "Yeah. I cut it last month. Needed a change."

"Well, it looks great. You look great." I'm speaking quickly so she doesn't have an opening to tell me to fuck off. "So will I be seeing you in New York over the next few years?"

"No. I decided to stay in Boston for grad school." She steps onto the porch and shuts the door behind her, making no move to invite me in. "What are you doing here Mason?"

"Your mom invited me. And I wanted to give you this." I move the large light blue gift bag from behind me and hold it out to her.

"Mason, I—"

"Please. Just take it." She makes no move to take the bag from me, so I step closer and extend my hand. "Open it."

She looks at me warily but relents. Digging through the endless amount of tissue paper I shoved into the bag, she pulls out the large metal tin inside. For a second, I wonder if I should've gotten her something more extravagant, but then I see the way her eyes light up while she tries, and fails, to stop the smile from coming over her face. "Is this—"

"Honeycomb Black Tea from the Old Barrel Shop. Your favorite." Violet's love for tea was no secret, she actually cried when the local tea company discontinued her favorite blend. I was with her in the shop when the cashier told her the news. I went back the next day offering up a generous amount of money in exchange for a four-year supply.

"I thought they stopped making this."

"They did, but I was able to persuade them into making me some more." Little did she know I had a whole other batch in my apartment stocked up for her. For each birthday, graduation, and National BFF Day until she forgives me. I watch as the smile on her face falls back into a frown. "What's wrong?"

"I just realized that every time I drink this, I'll think of you. And it's just too much. This is all too much."

She sets the bag down in front of me and steps toward the door, primed to leave.

"Violet. C'mon. Can't we just go somewhere and talk?"

"I don't really have much to say." She takes a deep breath before delivering her final blow. *"I wanted something more from you, and I thought you wanted the same. I misread the situation, and now I'm trying to move on. And I can't do that if I'm constantly reminded of you."*

"So that's it? You promised me we would be okay."

"And I wanted to keep that promise, Mason. Trust me I did. But I need more time. Can you give that to me?"

Time. 'I need time' wasn't exactly a 'I never want to see you again', so I suppose that was a win."Yeah. I can do that. Just please...come back to me at some point. Don't shut me out forever."

"I'm sorry." She retreats inside immediately after, leaving me dumbfounded and absolutely gutted.

"I'm sorry too, Vi." I whisper to myself, as I pick up her gift and head back to my parent's home.

Three years later I was still waiting. I hadn't heard from Violet since that night. Now here I was, watching her run away from me again. Over time I realized she had meant a lot more to me than I ever did to her. Why else would it be so easy for her to cut me out of her life?

After I crashed Violet's party, I tried to get my younger sister —who also happened to be Violet's best friend— to help me. And while I know Monroe loves me, she made it very clear that she would never break Violet's trust. I understood why Monroe wouldn't tell me about what was going on in Violet's life, but a heads-up about potentially running into her again would've been nice.

I pulled my phone out of my pocket, dialing Monroe. A few seconds later, her voice rang over the speaker.

"Wow. A call from my older brother, who I haven't heard from in *weeks*. To what do I owe this pleasure?"

In the background I can hear a car blaring its horn. During her senior year, Monroe started a year-long internship with one of the best PR firms in New York. After putting out a few fires, she'd secured herself a full-time position with the firm once she graduated.

"Bad time to talk? I can call you back—"

"Nope, just heading back to the office after a lunch date with Jacque."

"So, we're still with the douchey art bro?"

Monroe had met Jacque Loui (whose real name was John Levinston, but apparently that name doesn't sell you paintings or make you interesting in New York City) about eight months ago at some art gala her firm was promoting. I could practically hear her eyes roll through the phone.

"Yes still with Jacque, and no I don't have any plans to break up. I still don't know why you and Mom don't like him."

"Yeah, that one's a real mystery…" It's not like I didn't try to like the guy at first. But whenever anyone disagreed with him, he immediately shifted into defensive mode where he had to name-drop the Ivy League school he went to and count off how many of his uncles ran hedge funds in the city. My mom and I both have an ongoing bet on how long Monroe will tolerate his bullshit and for all our sakes (and my $100 on the line), I hope she calls it quits soon (like in the next month).

"The city misses you. I found this hole-in-the-wall deli in midtown that has *the* best everything bagel. I'm also like ten-ish minutes away from work before I have to go, so what's up?"

"Why didn't you tell me Violet was at Westchester?"

"Violet…" Monroe trailed off as if the name was foreign to her. As if *she* had been the one Violet blocked out of her life.

"Violet. Violet Amin. Practically lived with us growing up. Your best friend. Hasn't talked to me in like two years."

"I actually think it's closer to three, but I suppose math was never your strong suit—"

"How come no one told me she was a grad student at Westchester?"

"I thought she told you she would be in Boston."

"Yeah, and there are at least ten different schools in Boston.

Last we talked she chose Bolton. Now suddenly I see her at Westchester and am so dumbstruck I can't even process what is happening before she's running away."

"In all fairness, you never asked me *which* school she decided to go to. Besides, Westchester has a massive campus. How was I supposed to know you would run into her the one time you went back to visit your old coach? Evidently, the universe has jokes." Her faint laugh comes through the speaker.

"A heads up would've still been nice."

"What does it matter? It's not like you'll be seeing her every day."

"I might."

"Mason. Stalking is illegal in the state of Massachusetts," Monroe warns.

"That's not what I meant." I bite my lip debating if I should tell her the news. "Coach Jameson offered me an assistant coach position here. I accepted."

If you had asked me four years ago where I thought I would be today, my answer would've been something along the lines of, 'gearing up for another great season with the Rangers coming off a Stanley Cup win' or even 'riding out another year on my multimillion-dollar NHL contract.' Instead, I spent the morning begging my former coach for a job because I had somehow managed to blow through all the money I earned before I was forced to retire, and these medical bills weren't paying themselves.

"Mase, that's amazing. I'm so glad you're back on your feet again." Monroe's voice is laced with relief.

"It's a provisional position for now. I have until the end of the season to prove I can handle this, or I'll have to figure out a Plan B. Or I guess Plan C. This is my Plan B."

Maybe I should've cared more about school when I was still a student here, or maybe I should've listened to my doctors more when they warned me to take it easy before my last concussion that left me permanently benched, but alas here I was.

"Well, if anyone can get that team into shape, it's you. I know it."

"I appreciate it 'Roe. Now…how do I handle this Violet situation?"

"Not sure."

"Monroe." The frustration coated my voice and hopefully clued her into how desperate I was to get an answer. "I went from talking to Violet almost every day for fifteen years, to her not even acknowledging my existence over night."

"Well, maybe if you had come home a few months ago for the Summer Festival, you could've seen her. You know it's her favorite time of year."

The last week in June featured Castle Harbor's annual three-day Summer Festival — created to pay tribute to Castle Harbor's longstanding history as one of America's first fishermen's towns. The spectacle involved everyone in the small town and was also a major tourist attraction. Many of them came in not quite knowing what they walked into and left wanting to come back every year. Crowds flock to the beach early Saturday morning to see which family will get the honor of placing first in the boat races. Violet's favorite event (to spectate) followed the boat racing, which featured a 50-foot telephone pole covered in grease and suspended 10 feet above the harbor. By Saturday afternoon, every male between the ages of 18 and 25, brave and drunk enough, lined up for a chance to catch the flag at the end of the pole and secure bragging rights for the rest of the year. I'd managed to sneak in when I was 17 and nearly broke my neck falling off that pole. The glee on Violet's face, mixed with the subtle hint of concern as she and Monroe fished me out of the water, had all been worth it.

"Coming home wasn't an option. And no, I don't want to talk about it. Just…tell me how I can fix things with her. Or at the very least, not make things worse."

She paused for a second. "Honestly Mason, Violet never really told me what happened. She just said some things went down between you two that night in Chicago, and she needed some space. She kept insisting that I didn't need to worry about it, and I didn't want to push so…"

"Alright well, thanks I guess…I miss you, by the way."

Monroe snorts at that, her tone turned teasing. "Yeah, yeah, I miss you too. Do me a favor? Don't back down okay? Keep working until things can at least go back to normal, ya know, before Chicago. I feel like a child of divorce having to decide who I want to spend my holidays with and it's exhausting."

"I would if I could, 'Roe."

"Just try. It can't get much worse."

Apparently, Monroe isn't privy to hockey superstitions. Now I'm definitely fucked.

three

. . .

Violet

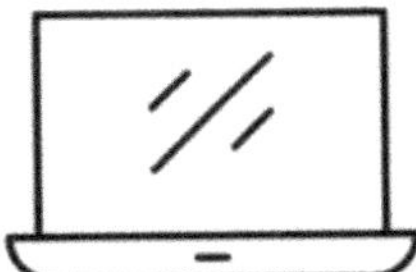

BY THE TIME I made it to my office, mercifully, no one was standing outside. All I had to do was hope that for the next hour, it stayed that way. My hands were still shaking from my run-in with *him*. I took a huge gulp of my chai latte as I settled into my slightly broken desk chair. I took ten deep breaths — in five seconds, out seven — and when that did little to calm my racing heart, I defaulted to my other coping mechanism— burying myself in my work.

I manage to answer five emails and write a line of code when there is a knock on my office door. I turn to see a 6'4 blonde sporting a 'Westchester University Men's Hockey' t-shirt. *I make it three years without a single hockey player in my life and now they are popping up all over the place.*

The blonde clears his throat. "Hey it's Jake. Are office hours still going on?"

"Yes! Come on in and feel free to take a seat." I gesture to the other chair I'd struggled to fit into my broom closet-turned-office. "What can I help you with?"

"I've gotten Ds on the past two homework assignments, and I was wondering if we could maybe figure something out." He pulls two crumpled worksheets from his backpack and hands them over to me.

I reach into my bag and pull out the answer key to the assignments, then take a few minutes to scan through his responses. Immediately I notice a pattern of misunderstanding key concepts discussed in lecture, which often happens in large classes like PSYCH101. I start to delve into the difference between correlational and experimental studies, when Jake says, "Coach has really been on my ass lately about my grades, and I was thinking maybe you could just take a second look and bump me up to a C, or even a C+. I know it would probably look shady if I went from a D to a B, so I'm willing to compromise."

I blink a few times, needing more time to process what he just asked of me. "I'm sorry?"

"I know that's not my finest work, but I'm sure if you read it again you'll notice places where you were a little harsh with grading and give me some points back." He nods back to the papers I'm holding and flashes me a smirk. A smirk that's filled with such entitlement I know this isn't the first time he's asked for a grade change.

"I'm looking at the answer key right now. Unfortunately, I don't see any places where you were mistakenly penalized. I am happy to walk you through these different concepts though and answer any questions you may have."

It's a struggle to keep my tone level. Calm. Nothing to hint at the building irritation slowly forming. The cocky grin on Jake's face widens, and his tone is unmistakably condescending.

"Are you sure? There's really *nothing* you can do?" He gestures again to the papers in my hands as if that would clear up my eyesight.

"You're more than welcome to take it up with the professor if you would like and ask her to regrade it. However, I try to be lenient when I grade these assignments and I can't promise that Dr. Grant will do the same. You risk lowering your grade by asking her for a regrade."

As I hand him back his papers, I brace myself for his last-ditch effort to woo me. *Don't curse at the student Violet. Just a few more minutes and this will all be over. Soon you can go home and see if Mary secures the deal for that beach-facing property.* The smirk on Jake's face fades, and irritation fills its place.

"C'mon Violet. Can't you cut me a little slack? I had two big games the night before these assignments were due."

"Again, any grade changes are going to have to go through Dr. Grant. If you're worried about your grade in the class, I'm happy to talk to her about a make-up assignment for you to earn extra credit."

Having worked as a teaching assistant for Darcy for the past two semesters I knew she was willing to give her students second chances if they were trying their best. Can't say that Mr. Hockey here was trying his best, but I desperately wanted this moment to be over. "We've offered that a few times to students in the past and they've all been able to recover their grades with the additional points."

"I barely have enough time to do the homework as it is." Jake rolls his eyes, crumples up his assignment and throws it inside his bag. "Well, if you can't change my grade, can you at least give me an extension for the next assignment? It's due the night after our game at Bolton which is honestly just unfair. The whole school is gonna be at that game."

Westchester University had always been a hockey school, which wasn't entirely surprising given the thick hockey culture that ran through Boston. The best players from all around the US and Canada were recruited to come play here, and very few turned down the offer given the institution's stellar track record of getting players drafted to the NHL. Student sections for home games were always packed, and tickets for big rivalry games, like Bolton's, could get as expensive as seats to see the Boston Bruins. The hockey players knew their value to the university and had no issues taking advantage of that fact.

"We don't typically grant extensions unless it's due to extenuating circumstances, and previously scheduled games that you were aware of do not count." My tone comes out clipped, but I can't feign sympathy for his situation. Once you've seen one college jock begging for grade inflation, you've seen them all.

"Whatever, this was clearly a waste of my time." He throws his backpack over his shoulder and slams the office door shut. Now I am not only on edge, but the tension headache I'd fought off is back. Fabulous.

four

· · ·

Mason

LYING IN BED THAT NIGHT, my mind couldn't help but remind me how much control over my life I had lost the past few years. I thought I'd always have hockey, but even that reality was almost unrecognizable from the dream it started as. When I had first signed a deal to join the Rangers in New York I was over the moon. Getting an NHL contract was a dream come true, but what I had been looking forward to the most was finally moving out of Massachusetts. Sure, I may have spent my college years in Boston, but Westchester was close enough to home that I found myself commuting back most weekends. I never really had a chance to get away. It's not like I didn't love the small town I grew up in, but I had lived there for most of my life, and I couldn't help but wonder what I had missed out on by staying close to home.

My first venture living outside of Massachusetts was when I moved to Connecticut, spending a few months playing for the Rangers' farm team. Admittedly there wasn't much to see out there, but it didn't take long before word got around to the coaching staff in New York about the rookie who had a slap shot most goalies couldn't see before the puck hit the back of the net. Before I knew it, I was living in a place that was filled with life and always buzzing with something new — New York City.

The first time I entered Madison Square Garden, I swore my heart was about to take flight. I'd played on many teams before, but no one really knew whether or not a team was going to click until the players actually got on the ice. Teams had spent millions of dollars and traded some of their most loyal players to bring in flashy names to their roster, and it backfired. In my case, it had been a storybook run from the start. Within my first three games in the NHL, I had three goals and two assists, and the rest of the season was uphill from there. I was riding an all-time high, leading the league in goals, when I got my first minor concussion. I'd shrugged it off and was back on the ice in a week — getting injured in a hockey game is a given — so I hadn't thought much of it at the time.

Being one of the hottest players in the league came with a lot of fun, like late nights going out to clubs or hosting parties in my apartment, and a line of girls wanting to 'help me celebrate my wins.' Who was I to turn down a little celebration? I never stopped to consider why I had so many new friends, or whether they would still be here if my career was suddenly taken away from me. Never stopped to think about all the calls from my loved ones back home that I had failed to return.

It wasn't until my most recent injury that I realized how much I had fucked up. Initially, I got lots of messages from my friends telling me that they'd be 'waiting for me on the outside' (apparently getting released from the hospital was like getting released from prison). But then my headaches kept coming back, and I couldn't skate around at full speed for more than a few minutes before my stomach would turn. The texts, phone calls, and invites started to drop off, and when my symptoms continued for the months following that…well, let's just say things were bleak.

Connor, my closest friend on the team — the *only* friend from New York who still kept in touch— tried his best to be there for me when he could. But Connor's busy work schedule left me alone more often than I would've liked. Left me to think about how things would've gone differently if I hadn't gotten hurt. Those thoughts had mostly stopped once I moved back to Boston, but on some nights, like tonight, those thoughts crept into my mind and plagued my dreams, turning them into nightmares.

My restless night left me wide awake at 6 a.m. I decided to go to the one place where my mind was always still. As I entered the arena, I breathed in the silence. It had been a week since my meeting-turned-impromptu-job-interview with Coach. He must have pulled some strings to get me onboarded as soon as possible because a few days after, Coach handed me the keys to my new office and told me to get to work on the dozens of game tapes stacked on top of the desk. Reality sunk in at that moment, and I realized how much I didn't want to fail Coach. Or myself.

Walking into the locker room, I couldn't help but think back to the last time I'd been in these halls. The boys had come off a 3-2 win in the Hockey East Championships which secured our place in the Frozen Four. We had gone on to win that tournament, and that final home game victory against Bolton has secured a core spot in my memory. The game had been an all-out war from the start, and nothing felt sweeter than being the one to bury the puck into the net and send my team off to the NCAA championship. I barely had time to process that goal before Brandon and Mikey — my two alternate captains — had jumped on top of me in celebration. Most of my big wins were a blur; my mind would black out in the minutes before and after a huge win. But that game had been different.

I still remember scanning the crowd and seeing my family screaming their lungs out. I remember seeing *her* — the way her face always revealed too much. She had a smile that lit up her entire face and the way she blinked away her tears made me finally realize how much more we could be. I had never thought she'd wanted to be more than just friends, but the way she had looked at me that night told me all I needed to know. Unfortunately, that same beautiful face had kept me up many nights since leaving the NHL, but the smile was turned down, and the eyes flared with contempt. As much as I wanted nothing more than to forget it, to forget how much I hurt her, she still had a hold on me all these years later. That face was etched into my memory as if to say, 'I'm still here Mason, and I still hate you.' So much has changed since I'd last been in this arena.

"Didn't expect to see you here so early. I'm usually the first one."

The sound of Coach's voice snapped me back into reality. If Coach noticed how dazed I was he didn't say anything. Instead, he entered the locker room and dragged the whiteboard over.

"Figured I should start showing up early given that I have a lot to catch up on." I grabbed a marker from the bottom of the board and started drawing up a play I wanted to run by him.

He nodded his head silently while looking at the drawing on the board. "How far did you get with the tapes I left you?"

"Got through almost all of them." I shrugged. Not like I had anything better to do these days. Might as well get a head start on this job.

"I gave you nearly 40 hours of footage."

To a stranger, Coach's words would've given away no emotion, he always had an uncanny ability to be impossible to read. But after training under him for four years I picked up on the subtle hint of shock in his tone. He didn't think I would take this seriously. I tried to ignore how much that stung.

"I am familiar enough with the roster to see a few strengths and weaknesses in each player." I nodded my head toward the whiteboard. "I think this new play could fill in the holes we have on defense."

"Walk me through what you're thinking."

———

After an hour of going back and forth with Coach about potential line changes, we decided to table it until staff meeting on Wednesday. The next hour was spent in my office discussing the off-ice logistics I was now expected to handle — my first real test as assistant coach. The quiet of the arena this morning was long gone and replaced by chaos and buzzing energy from the team as they got dressed for practice. I walk into the locker room and immediately notice two players wrestling over the last roll of stick tape (adding "order more stick tape" to my to-do list). As I mentally prepare my 'knock that the fuck off' comment, a wave of silence hits the room. I peek over my shoulder, waiting for Coach to walk up behind me — the man always knew how to get a rowdy crowd to shut up by his mere presence — when I notice I am all alone.

A tall blond is the first to speak. "Holy Shit. We got Mason Hayes back in Westchester. You back to see the new golden age of college hockey?" A sly grin takes over his face as he throws an arm around my shoulders. "Listen man, any chance you can get me two glass seats to the next Rangers game? There's this absolute rocket in my marketing class that I've been trying to take out and—"

"Get your ass over here Jake before you say something that will get us all skating suicides after practice." A brunette who was shorter than Jake by a few inches, but significantly more built, rolls his eyes at his teammate before turning his attention back to me, giving me a nod.

"Adam Reed, right wing, and team Captain."

"And he never lets us forget it, that's for damn sure."

The quip from Jake earns him a laugh from the rest of the players in the locker room, but Adam appears unfazed as he continues to get dressed. It felt like I had walked into a time capsule. The team may not have been filled with my old friends and teammates anymore, but the locker room itself hadn't changed at all. I suppose I shouldn't be surprised given the high amount of superstitions hockey players had. The centermost cubicle had always belonged to the team captain, and while I had opted to cover my locker in photos of my favorite pro players back in the day, it appeared Adam had photos of his family instead. The cubicles to the left and right of the Adam's typically went to the two alternate captains and I school my surprise as I note one of them belongs to Jake.

Before I am able to introduce myself to the remaining players, Coach Jameson enters the room. "Alright everyone, we have some important announcements. As you may know, the process of finding a new assistant coach after Coach Whitney retired has been a shit show. Mason will be filling in the spot until we make our final decisions."

A series of cheers echo throughout the room. "While I understand all the excitement, I'd like to remind everyone that Mason is here to be a *coach*. And not your friend."

Coach continues with a breakdown of goals for practice today before he ends the team briefing. As he shuffles out of the locker room, he casts a glance at Jake and then directs a pointed look at me as if to emphasize what he had said earlier. I was here to be a *coach* and not their friend.

"Hey Jake. Let me talk to you for a second." I nod toward the hallway connected to the locker room and walk far enough to ensure the other players won't be able to listen in.

"What's up coach?"

In addition to watching tapes, I'd been tasked with checking in on players whose GPAs were on the verge of probation. I hesitate for a second debating on how to drop the news without causing a full panic. Coach had already warned me that Jake had a bit of an attitude problem, especially when it came to respecting authority, and the last thing I needed was him going off on me.

"We need to talk about your PSYCH101 grade. You know the University has a strict policy on benching players that have any grades lower than a C-. We're going to have to take you out of the next few games if you don't get your grade up."

Jake blinked at me a few times as if I had spoken in a different language. "Are you serious?"

"I don't like this any more than you do." It was true. I'd lost count of the number of times I'd had this same conversation with Coach Jameson when I was on the team. If anything, it makes me feel like a massive hypocrite as I attempt to lay down the law. "But the rules are the rules." Jesus I'm bad at this. Given the expression on Jake's face he feels the same.

"We're going up against UCONN and Bolton soon. All the scouts are going to be there man, I *need* to be on that ice…It's not even my fault I have a D in that class. The TA took off all these points on my assignment for no reason, and when I tried to ask her about it, she just blew me off."

Ah, the 'blaming the teaching assistant' defense. I'd pulled that one out of my back pocket before too, one too many times… "C'mon Jake, be real with me here and I'll do what I can to help get you out of this—"

"I'm being dead serious! I'm not saying I would've gotten an A+ or anything, but I definitely should've gotten a C or something. I went into office hours to check what I got wrong, and I noticed I got marked off for answers I shouldn't have. When I asked the TA if she could fix my grade, she just said that all grades were final. I even asked if I could do some extra credit, but she shut that down too. I'm really trying, she's just unreasonable."

A feeling of guilt filled my chest as I took in the sincerity and defeat on Jake's face.

"How about I talk to her? Maybe she'd be more understanding of your situation if it came from your coach."

"You'd honestly be saving my ass. Maybe you can drop by her office hours?"

This is what coaches did right? Advocate for their players and make sure no one is left behind. "Yeah, that sounds like a plan. I'll let you know how it goes."

The sound of the whistle reverberated against the walls, drawing players back into practice. "Why don't you get your ass on the ice and show me— what did you say earlier? The new golden age of college hockey?'" I couldn't help but roll my eyes.

A smug grin replaced the somber look on Jake's face. "You got it Coach."

five

. . .

Violet

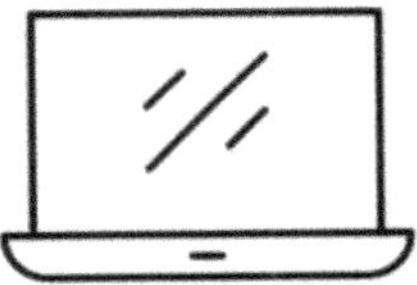

"DON'T HATE ME, but I think we need to recruit more participants."

I did my best to hold in the groan I was dying to let out while my advisor stared at the puzzling set of graphs and brain images on the screen. I'd finally found a few hours of free time last night to run some preliminary analyses on the data I had hoped to use for my third-year project. After spending the entirety of the summer practically living at the MRI center on campus scanning moms' and babies' brains, I had hoped I would be done with data collection by the time the semester started. I had a feeling that I may have bit off more than I could chew when I initially pitched tracking how infants' brains develop during the first three months of life. Working with infants meant tons of messy and hard-to-distinguish brain scans, not to mention how difficult it is to recruit busy caregivers in the first place. But Bethany gave me the green light and well…I was never one to back down from a challenge.

Dr. Bethany Coleman was the psychology department's leading expert on all things babies, brains, and caregiving relationships. In addition to being a top researcher in the field with a lab booming with productivity, she still manages to chase her two twin boys around. In addition to having her career and personal life together, Bethany always looks like a runway model. Though she was only 5'8 in heels, her blonde hair was styled in a cute shoulder-length bob, and she had a capsule wardrobe that would make Michael Kors jealous. When I first met her, I wasn't sure what I wanted more — to work with Bethany or to *be* her.

"I had a feeling you were going to say that." I rubbed the sides of my temples, feeling a headache coming on. "We had forty families come in, but only thirty babies managed to stay asleep long enough for us to get a good scan."

Bethany had the decency to look sorry for me. "The downside of working with cute, tiny humans — it's so hard to get them to lay still! I think if we can get maybe fifteen more families in, we'll be all set."

"I can probably move some things around for the next few weekends and also schedule evening scans at the imaging center to get this done by January—" Goodbye sleep and my ill-fated attempt at a work-life balance. Though I suppose you can't say goodbye to something you never had.

"Mmm…why don't we aim for November? I think it'd be nice to have data collection completed and a draft of your paper before winter break."

I know I should push back. Between my teaching schedule, coursework, and the other parts of my dissertation I hadn't touched yet, there was no way I'd be able to recruit fifteen additional families and analyze their brain scans in two months. It's not like my other lab mates weren't constantly asking for extensions. They had warned me from the start that Bethany's perception of how much time it takes to run projects was…idealistic and that she usually never had issues with moving deadlines around. But I already owed Bethany so much for what she'd done for me this past year. So instead of setting boundaries and asking for what I needed, I did the thing I always do.

"Yeah, that makes sense. I can make that work."

———

Staring at my laptop I know one thing for certain — my calendar is an absolute nightmare. If you listen closely, you can hear a 16-year-old Taylor Swift singing 'Should've Said No.' My people-pleasing tendencies had failed me again, and now I had somehow managed to double my workload. In an attempt to get a head start on things, I went straight to my office after my meeting with Bethany. Not too long after one of my research assistants texted me about our computer freaking out in the middle of a participant session. The hour I would've used to get ahead faded away along with my hopes of this semester being less stressful than the last.

By the time I get everything sorted out and return to my office, I'm interrupted by a faint knock on my office door. Setting out a small plea to the universe that this time the person behind the door wouldn't be an entitled student yelling at me for a grade change, I call out.

"C'mon in. How can I help y—"

The words die in my throat, along with all the thoughts in my head, as a familiar scent of pine and soap washes over me and goosebumps trail down my entire body. Please no. It can't be *him* again. I had barely recovered from our last run in. And this time I had no place to escape to. *It's okay Violet. You're okay. Just pretend he's a stranger whose dropped by your office hours.* Easy enough.

I debated how long I could keep up this facade of pretending to not know him. It's not like we hadn't grown up in the same small town together, or that his younger sister wasn't my best friend. Or that he once knew me better than anyone else in the world. Before he can respond, Maya, a data scientist in my lab, walks through my door looking equally as flustered as I feel.

"So sorry to bother you Violet, but the computer in the lab crashed again. We need to get it up and running before the family arrives in 10 minutes. Do you think you can take another look?"

Talk about perfect timing.

"Absolutely!" I gathered up all my belongings with the full intention of never returning. It's not that I was particularly attached to my broom closest-turned-office, but I would miss the private space. Now that he knew I was here, I simply couldn't come back. Ever. I politely shove him out of the office and slam the door shut behind me.

"Sorry, looks like you'll have to come back another time", I bumble out. I run off with Maya in tow before I even register what just transpired.

———

After finishing up in the lab, I realize I left my laptop charger in my office. I start to browse the internet for used MacBook chargers as I step into the elevator, committed to never returning to my office, when a memory floods my mind.

I was six years old when my mom woke me up in the middle of the night and told me we were going on a road trip together, just the two of us, as she loaded her SUV to the brim with our stuff. I had always wanted to go on a road trip after hearing a few of my classmates talking about the family trips to Disney World they took over the summer. But once we drove straight through Florida without stopping, I realized this trip would be different. We made a stop somewhere in Virginia where I experienced fall for the first time. The motel we stayed at had a row of trees in front of it, the leaves shades of bright red and yellow. I managed to shove a few of them in my pocket as we checked out. As we continued to drive up the coast my mom finally clued me on this big adventure. We were officially moving to Castle Harbor — a small beach town just outside of Boston — but my dad would be staying in Florida. She paused for a moment, probably to see whether I would be upset. Instead, I just asked her if this would mean we didn't need to hide in the bedroom anymore because Dad was angry. She turned around for a moment to look at me and say, *'You never have to hide from anyone again.'*

The elevator dings as the doors open to the first floor. My mother's words are ringing in my head, serving as a reminder of how far I had come and how hard I had fought to be here. Though this situation is entirely different from my childhood road trip, the thought of hiding from a man, and evacuating my home (or broom closet) to avoid him makes my blood boil. I *will not* hide. I shake my head as my finger jabs the '3' to take me back up to my office.

six

. . .

Violet

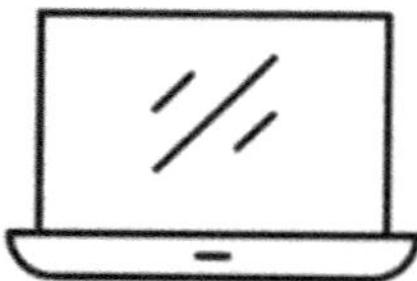

THE HIGH OF returning to my office space and getting my charger (and confidence) back is overshadowed by the nightmares I have that night. Or memories, really. Most people underestimate how much your childhood fears follow you, even subconsciously. Though the exact memories have gotten a bit fuzzy as I've gotten older, they never really go away. No matter how much I want them to. Tonight, my dreams take me back to when I was five. My dad had just gotten home and was already upset about something, which he handled by pouring himself a drink. We sat down at the table to eat dinner, and my dad was immediately displeased with what my mom made. His slurred words turn into hateful screams, and suddenly I'm in my mom's arms as she slams the bedroom door shut. While we could no longer see the rageful fit he was having, the door was not able to block out the sounds of plates being shattered and a slew of curses on the other side.

Self-preservation from what came next jolts me awake, my entire body covered in sweat. The time on my alarm clock reads 4:55 a.m. and my heart feels like it's about to jump out of my chest. In a feeble attempt to slow it down I take a series of deep breaths — in for five seconds out for seven, in five out seven. It's been at least two years since I've had a nightmare like this. I had finally built enough confidence to start moving on from my past, but one visit from *him* sent that wall of confidence crumbling like a house of cards.

After two hours of tossing in bed, my alarm goes off. I groan as I drag myself out of the bed and head into the bathroom. *Lovely.* I look about as good as I feel. I force myself to take a quick shower hoping to jostle myself awake, but the exhaustion is settled deep into my bones. I feel like a zombie as I head out of my apartment and board the campus bus. I realize too far into my journey that I forgot my to-go cup of tea on my kitchen counter which means I will be hauling my dead body to the Beanery.

I make a beeline to the cafe as soon as I get to campus and let out a sigh of relief when I see the line consists of only five people. Soon, so soon, I will have my hands on pure caffeinated bliss — nothing like a warm cup of tea to soothe all my problems. The door behind me chimes as someone walks in and joins me in line. A chill runs down my spine as cool air from outside rushes in, followed by a waft of pine and soap. Fucking Mason.

I hadn't seen him since last week. I tried to block out my poor attempt at seeming unphased in my office. I hoped he saw 'twenty-five, flirty, and thriving' and not a tortured soul looking at the last person who had owned her heart before letting it drop to the floor and shatter into pieces like it was made of glass. Did his body feel as thrown off its axis being in the same room with me as mine did? I suppose I should be thankful he didn't speak.

The remains of my heart would turn to ash at the deep silk of his voice.

"Hello Violet. Are you finally going to talk to me today?"

Shit. His deep voice was as chipper as it was smug. I feel goosebumps rise on my neck as he leans down and whispers into my ear. "Or do you want to keep pretending like we've never met before?"

While I may be an ash pile on the floor, the good news is I'm incredibly stubborn. And my sleepless brain has no words.

"Hmm, seems like you're still feeling quiet today. I am curious how long you think you can keep this up."

I keep my eyes forward and groan internally as the person at the front of the line requests a large, iced caramel macchiato with almond milk, no whip, light ice, and 2 pumps of toffee nut syrup. While I was sure my stubbornness knew no bounds, Mason had a knack for finding my limits...and pushing them. And if the patron in front of me had any say, Mason would have all day to do it.

I could feel him shift his body back away from my ear. Presumably, he had his arms crossed as he quipped.

"At first, I thought 'That can't be my Violet.' Same height, same curls, same addiction to chai lattes, but you're up and running at 7:30 a.m., and she would never. Not a morning person at all. But now, I see her. The Violet I knew really hated confrontation. So much so that she decided to cut me out of her life, even though she promised she wouldn't. Just *poof,* excom-municado. Like I was nothing to her."

The absolute *nerve*. As if he wasn't the one who decided he couldn't handle being in a relationship.

Mason continues to search for my limit. "You seemed to move on fairly quickly if my memory serves me."

Congrats Mason, you found it. Now I'm pissed. I whip my body around to face him and whisper-yell.

"What are you talking about?!" If he was happy that he had gotten me to crack, he certainly didn't show it.

This was the first time we had truly looked each other in the eyes in three years. We seemed to both take the opportunity to peruse one another. Mason's classically clean-shaven face is long gone and is now covered in a short beard that's a few shades darker than the medium-brown strands of his hair. Speaking of his hair — Mason had grown it out slightly, though it still sat on his head in that classic windblown-but-not-quite-messy kind of way. And though he may be retired from the NHL, it's very apparent that he keeps up with his workout regimen. His dark gray Henley clings to his arms and chest, accentuating every muscle and leaving little to the imagination. Not that I'd have to imagine what was underneath, I had seen it with my own eyes. Who would've known a long-sleeved shirt could look so obscene on a person? From the corner of my eye, I see a hint of ink peeking out from under his sleeve, though I can't quite make out the shape. Another part of him that's new to me. A part I have no business being curious about.

I pull myself together to respond only to realize we had made it to the front of the line. Jesus, how long had we been staring at each other?

"She'll have a medium iced chai latte, half sweet, and I'll have a small americano." He says this as if it's three years ago, and ordering my favorite drink is something I would expect he do. He's reaching out to hand the barista his credit card when I intercept it.

"What do you think you're doing?"

"Buying us drinks. You have to pay for these ya know."

"Well maybe I want something else." I do not.

"Do you?"

That was entirely beside the point. I can't tell if I'm irritated because of how predictable I am or because of he knows me so well even after all these years. Regardless, I want to wipe that smug look off his face no matter the expense. *Goodbye my precious half-sweet chai latte, you will be missed.*

"I was actually hoping to get a cold brew instead. With milk and sugar."

The barista exchanges a look between the two of us, decides whatever is happening is of little interest to them, shrugs, and takes the card from Mason. I accept defeat and walk away toward the pick-up area. Mason follows.

"You know this could be considered stalking."

"It's considered stalking to get a coffee at the cafe closest to my office?" He nods his head toward the hockey stadium.

My jaw finds residence on the floor. I was so thrown off by his drop-in a week ago that I hadn't thought about why he showed up during my office hours, or even why he was here now. I look at him dubiously.

"You work *here* now?"

"Well, no. I don't work at the Beanery. New assistant coach for the men's hockey team. Provisionally, we'll see what happens at the end of the season."

The sheepish look on his face catches me by surprise. I don't think I've ever seen Mason look self-conscious about anything in his life, especially not something related to hockey. I think that was the aspect of him that had attracted me the most. As a pathological people pleaser, I'd spent most of my life trying to fit myself into whatever box would make the people around me happy, often at the expense of myself.

Mason was the complete opposite — the wildest hurricane paled in comparison to his confidence, strength, and unwavering ferocity. He never let anyone tell him how he should feel or act or be. In a way, his energy had been contagious. There were few moments when I had stood up for myself when I was younger, and those moments were almost always connected to Mason.

"Oh. Cool." I cringed slightly at my inability to string more than a few words together in response. Trying to have a conversation with someone who used to be the most important person in your life, who I now know nothing about, is one of the most uncomfortable and out-of-body experiences. It's like, "Hey you've seen me naked. What are you doing for work these days?"

It seemed Mason was equally unsure of how to proceed now that we couldn't pretend the other person didn't exist.

"Since when do you drink cold brew instead of tea? I thought the extra caffeine gave you heart palpitations."

"I had a rough night and it's going to be a long day, so." He didn't need to know that the cold brew would be given to Maya, and I would sneak back to the Beanery afterward to right the wrong.

"Are you still getting nightmares?"

Gone was his usual happy-go-lucky expression, his eyebrows now scrunched together in concern. A few years ago, having Mason's full attention was all I could have ever wished for. Now I wanted nothing more than to get as far away from him as possible before I found myself getting wrapped back into the storm that is Mason Hayes. I had already drowned in him once, and I had no intention of drowning in him again. And sharing vulnerable information was not going to do me any favors.

"They've stopped, for the most part." I turn away from him and let out a visible sigh of relief when the barista places our drinks on the counter. I toss a quick wave over my shoulder as I exit the café. "Thanks for the coffee."

Mason won't take a hint. He trails behind me as I head to the psychology building.

"What are you doing?" I snap.

"Well, I just feel like we have so much to catch up on, don't you?"

"I can't say that we do. You can go now."

"Wow. I'm crushed, and also not that easy to get rid of. "

"You know you're not as charming as you think you are. You're actually quite annoying. Like a pest. Or a cream-resistant rash."

Harsh, but necessary. I swear I had used the same words back in high school when we got in a fight over him scaring one of my boyfriends away.

"Charming. I really missed your sense of humor." He deadpans.

"Is there a point to this, Mason?"

"I mean if it wasn't clear already — I miss you. And I'm a little upset about the fact that you said everything would be fine between us one day when you never meant it."

His words freeze me in place, and suddenly, I find myself interested in the cracks on the sidewalk. Was that hurt in his voice? It couldn't be. Not when he found it so easy to push me away. I knew at the time that asking him for more than his friendship meant I would never be able to go back to being his friend again. It would hurt too much knowing that I loved him and he couldn't love me back. But he did, or at least he said as much, but not enough to want to be with me. I didn't want someone's half attempt at adoration, I wanted to be their every-thing. And Mason couldn't give me that, so I was done giving pieces of myself to him.

"I have to head to class soon. Is there anything I can *actually* help you with, or are you just here to rehash the past? Don't you have some...coaching to go do?"

"Ah yes speaking of, I was hoping to talk with you about one of my players, Jake. That's why I dropped by your office hours last week," he offers.

Of course, that's what all of this was about. It all made sense now. Mason was always very good at charming someone before asking for a favor. Remembering my latte order and pretending to care about my recurring nightmares were all part of his plan to butter me up so I would go easy on his players. For a moment, he had me convinced that he cared about repairing what was he broke. *Fool me once, shame on you. Fool me twice...*

"I remember Jake. He came by my office to grade grub a few weeks ago."

"Yeah, he told me all about that."

Mason pauses, realizing we're standing a few feet outside the building. I turn to face him, curious as to what his request would be. Will he ask me to put together an extra credit assignment — which I had already offered to do — because he told Jake that grade grubbing is insulting? Or will he ask me to give the little shit an A+ because hockey players don't need to understand research methods?

He lets out a small breath and bites his lip like he's nervous. "I was hoping maybe you could take another look at his assignment?"

Aaaand we're done here. "You can't be serious."

"Well Jake mentioned that he accidentally got marked off a few points more than he should and that he tried to get it fixed but his teaching assistant…"

Mason's choice not to finish that sentence likely means he realizes how absurd it sounds. I take the opportunity to berate him anyway.

"'His teaching assistant' what? Why don't you go ahead and tell me what I did, Mason? Misgraded his paper, and when it was brought to my attention told him 'Too fucking bad'?"

I wasn't proud of my anger in this moment but after all the challenges I had to overcome during grad school, I'd become particularly sensitive about how I was perceived professionally. I care about my research and my students. I was sick of feeling like everyone around me questioned my judgment and decisions. Unfortunately for Mason, he was just a drop in the bucket.

"I just…" He opened and closed his mouth a few times like a goldfish. "He's one of our star players, but we have to bench him if he doesn't get his grade up. And I'm his coach so it's now my responsibility to help him out. I'm trying to help him—" I put my hand up to stop him.

"I tried to help him too. I double-checked to make sure the points he got off weren't done mistakenly, and I even offered him extra credit to bring his grade up, but he turned it down and said he didn't have the time for it. There's only so much I can do to help my students, especially if they're not willing to help themselves. It seems you and I have very different ideas of what 'helping' means."

Mason's pained expression matches his voice. "Vi, I didn't know. I wouldn't have asked you to take another look at his assignment if I did."

The remorse I see in his eyes makes me want to believe him, but I have learned the hard way how persuasive he could be. How easy it was for him to lie to me to get what he wanted. Putting our history aside, Jake was not just 'our star player'; he was *my student,* and I cared about my students.

"Listen, maybe it's best I set up a time to meet with Jake and the head coach so we can figure out what the next steps are together. Steps that don't include me changing his grade just because he feels entitled to it."

"Sure, that works. Except Coach Jameson put me in charge of handling Jake's academics so it looks like you're stuck with me."

"Are you serious?" This comes out aghast, and for the sake of maintaining my angry exterior, I am grateful for that. But really my surprise comes from the *teeniest* bit of pride. He's managing his players' professional and academic careers. I never thought I'd see him in this leadership role. It looks good on him.

"I'm afraid so." He gives me a sheepish smile.

"Fine. Whatever. I'll send you and Jake an email later today."

I manage to enter the building and make it down the hall when I hear Mason calling my name. He jogs up to me and stands in front of me, blocking my path. "Violet, wait up for a second."

Hello god, the universe, or whatever else is out there. Please put an end to this torturous conversation and I'll never be lazy about dividing up my recyclables again.

"Yes Mason?"

"You didn't get my email. You need my email to set up the meeting."

"I was planning on just looking it up in the Westchester staff directory."

"Oh right. That makes sense." He makes no move to get out of my way.

I raise my brows as if to say, *'anything else?'*

"I was hoping we could…um." He looks down at his shoes for a minute before looking back up at me as he shakes his head.

"Actually no. That was it. Just wanted to make sure you had my email."

"Great. See you around."

seven

· · ·

Mason

I SPEND the rest of my morning in my office, staring at the current roster list while only thinking about Violet. I had planned on coming up with new plays to accommodate the change in lines I proposed, but after my run-in with her, everything felt off. So much time had passed, and I expected our interactions to feel stunted, but I never expected to feel fully disconnected from her. I had thought I'd at least recognize the person that I knew before our fallout, but she was so distant from who she once was. Or at least from how she used to be around me. Maybe it's because we both still harbor some resentment from the past. I have tried to be a bigger man and get over the fact that she wasn't willing to be in my life if she couldn't have everything. But I can't ignore the resentment I feel at how fast she was able to move on. To be so hardened and resistant to the fact that I wanted to fix things when she just wanted to throw the whole relationship out. I knew we still had something worth saving, and now that life was different for me, I was still holding out hope that one day we could be something more than friends. Or enemies. Or whatever we are now.

I had come up with a whole plan after our awkward encounter in her office. I would gently confront her and finally clear the air. I would tell her that I had so much time — painful, lonely, self-loathing time — to reflect on what matters in this life. And it is her. She matters. And whatever she wants from me, I will give. And she would tell me that I was only saying this because I had nothing left after my retirement. No girls, no dream job, no support. Because she is Violet and she never lets me off easy. And I would tell her that only an idiot realizes what he has once he has nothing. And I am an idiot, a big one who hopes she can find it in her huge heart to take pity on me. Then she'd smile, walk over into my outstretched arms, and I'd kiss the top of her head and breathe in her delicious curls. After that we'd go out to dinner, and I would suggest dessert at my place. And, with her permission, I'd have her panties around her ankles before the cab pulled away from the curb.

All of that went to shit the second I saw her at the Beanery. She came off as the epitome of unaffected. Rather than being flooded with emotions of remorse and regret to fuel my apology, the second I saw her all I felt was hurt. From there I forgot my well-rehearsed pitch to convince her to hear me out. Instead, all I wanted to do was get a reaction, of any kind. An acknowledgment that I was a living, breathing man and not some ghost haunting her favorite coffee shop.

So rather than telling her how much I missed her and how my life hadn't been the same since she cut ties with me, I started resorting to my old tricks from when we were kids — teasing her and hoping it would bring some level of familiarity back. I tried to channel the days when we would bicker then end it with a final sarcastic quip or an eye roll, knowing things were fine between us. But this wasn't like our normal conversations, and she appeared to genuinely want nothing more than to get away from me. I didn't want to bring up Jake, but I did need to clear that up before our next game. I knew she wouldn't love me asking for a favor, but I certainly didn't expect the contempt. Nor did I anticipate that I was pouring fuel on the dumpster fire that was our relationship (or lack thereof). It's as if my brain short-circuits whenever I'm in a room with her.

Ugh. I really should've listened to my gut when it came to Jake. I had a feeling his story was off, but it's my first week, and I want my players to trust me. And I hoped he was telling the truth. Coach's most important task was to get the guys' grades in order, and now I feared Jake was going to make this task very hard for me. I suppose I could manage Coach's look of disproval when Jake is inevitably benched for his D, but the look of hurt and rage in Violet's eyes is more than I can bear.

As if thinking about her was enough to summon her (years of unsent texts have proved this theory wrong), an email notification from Violet pops up on my computer.

Today, 2:13 p.m.
To: Jake Keeley (keeleyj25@westchesteru.edu)
cc: Mason Hayes (mhayes@westchesteru.edu)
From: Violet Amin (aminv@westchesteru.edu)
Subject: PSYCH101 Follow-Up Meeting

Hi Jake,
After speaking with Coach Hayes, we decided it would be best for the three of us to meet to discuss your current grade in PSYCH101 and how we can get things back on track. I've attached a Calendly link for ease of coordinating. If any questions arise in the meantime, please reach out.

Best,

Violet

--

Development Psychology PhD Student
Westchester University

I shouldn't have expected anything beyond a professional email, but something about the rigid formality made me feel like an outsider. Just another university colleague. I had worked very hard to be an insider with Violet once upon a time. Violet had always struggled with trusting people and letting her guard down. I couldn't fault her for it, given all the awful shit she and her mom went through with her dad before they moved to Castle Harbor. Over time, Violet shared bits and pieces of the life she and her mom lived before moving. The many nights her father would come home drunk and lose his temper, her and her mom hiding away in her bedroom until he managed to fall asleep or fully blackout. I couldn't imagine the courage it took for her mom to pack up their whole life in the hope of a new beginning.

Their first few years in Castle Harbor weren't exactly easy either. Violet's mom was spread thin, working as many jobs as she could to provide for her and Vi. My family and a decent number of others had been welcoming and offered whatever help we could, but there were some locals who harbored resentment for any 'outsiders' that moved into town. Some of the not-as-friendly locals felt like Elaine, Violet's mom, had to prove she wasn't a tourist in disguise just there to purchase land in Castle Harbor and take up real estate but contribute nothing to the town. Elaine put those concerns to bed over time with how involved she was in the community, building up a coffee shop a few years after moving in. As for the very small remainder of locals who would make microaggressive comments about their Middle Eastern heritage, well they knew better than to open their mouths when I was around.

Despite Violet's cageyness, she's one of the most vulnerable and caring people I have ever met. I was drawn to her immediately and couldn't help but feel protective over her. Little by little she let me in, and I found that to know Violet was to love her. To love the ferocity she had when it came to supporting those she cared about, and the compassion she showed whenever someone was going through a hard time. She would never admit it, but all she ever wanted was to let her guard down and love without abandon.

I never imagined I'd be on the receiving end of her ice out. Maybe this was for the best. Perhaps keeping things professional would force me to face the fact that after three years of ignoring me, she no longer wanted me to know her and therefore, love her. The thought of finally letting go of someone who no longer wants you is supposed to come with sorrow but also a feeling of freedom (or so my NHL-required therapist used to say). Instead, I felt like I was going to be sick.

A knock on the door snaps me out of my pity party as Jake walks into my office. How timely.

"Sup Coach. You got a minute?"

"Definitely. I was just about to see if you were in. I had a chance to talk to your TA, Violet— "

"Yeah, I saw the email. So, you got her to reconsider?" He sprawls out in the chair in front of my desk, a shit-eating grin taking over his face. A part of me wonders how I didn't see this side of him earlier. I feel a wave of shame as I think back to all the times in the past when I had acted similarly. That aura of confidence and self-assured ego had been my default response to anyone who tried to suggest I care about anything that wasn't hockey. I wish I'd had the foresight to consider how fast an NHL contract could go away and leave you scrambling to figure out what's next.

"We had an honest conversation about how your grades have been slipping."

You're here to be their coach, not their friend. "Well, slipping would imply you were excelling in the first place. She mentioned how you asked her to change your grade even though the answers were incorrect—"

"C'mon man, she's lying. I'm not the first player she's done this to. She has a thing against hockey players. Maybe one broke her heart back in the day and now she's taking it out on the rest of us."

If only he knew the full story. "So, she didn't offer you an extra credit assignment that you turned down because it was 'too much work'?"

Silence, the closest thing to a confession that I would get. "It appears some wires were crossed—" I gave him a pointed look, "— so for that reason, we decided the three of us would have a meeting and decide what the best course of action would be. With the goal of getting you back on track so we don't have to pull you off the ice."

That manages to get a reaction from him. "Pulling me off the ice?! I thought you were fixing this not making it worse."

"This *is* part of fixing the issue. I can't say for certain I know exactly what her plan will be, but I'll be there too. I am on your side, Jake. Even if it doesn't feel like I am."

I wanted to support him in more ways than he realized. Just because I made the mistake of putting all my eggs in a puck-shaped basket doesn't mean he had to.

Jake appears vulnerable and small as he softly asks, "So I'm officially banned from playing then?"

"Not yet. But you will be soon if you don't take this meeting with Violet, and whatever plan comes with it, seriously."

"Shit. Alright. You sure she'll be reasonable about this?"

If he was as persistent on the ice as he was now, we'd be locked in for the championship this year. "I'm sure. Should we figure out a date to meet then?"

"Yeah, I guess so."

eight

. . .

Violet

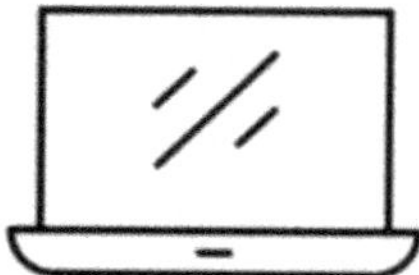

THERE IS one place in the world I know I can go without any chance of running into Mason. The irony was it happened to be the same place we met so many years ago, a place we once both called home. Despite living only an hour train ride away from Castle Harbor, I hadn't visited in several months. According to Monroe, Mason hadn't visited in years and every time she tried to broach the subject, he made up some excuse as to why he couldn't come back. I wanted to pry into why he suddenly stopped visiting home, but those are things friends know, not ex-'will they won't they's.

As soon as my feet step off the train, I am heading toward my first stop— a small park lined with rows of trees, settled on the outskirts of town. The trees, once covered in gorgeous leaves in shades of red, orange, and yellow, are now bare, the leaves piled on the ground. Soon this place will be covered in a beautiful cast of snow, and from afar, the scenery will look like it belongs inside a snow globe. While the temperature was the type of cold that made you want to stay inside burrowed under a cozy blanket, the park is still filled with parents trying their best to keep their kids bundled up while chasing them around the park. I manage to find an open bench toward the edge of the park. Across the street, I can see my old elementary school, a small rectangular building covered in faded blue paint, almost as old as the town itself.

Teachers born and raised in Castle Harbor would tell us stories about the library that many believe is haunted by the ghost of a former U.S. president. At first, I was convinced it was an elaborate story the librarians concocted to scare us into turning in our books on time, until one day in the second grade. I finished my classwork early and asked my teacher if I could go to the library to continue reading a book I had been hooked on. I was nose-deep in a whodunit mystery when, out of nowhere, a stack of books fell from the shelves one by one. I initially thought one of my classmates had snuck in and was trying to scare me. Until I realized the only two people in the library were myself and the librarian who was standing on the opposite side of the room and had a look of pure fear on her face. We locked eyes for a second before we both ran out of the library and never spoke of that day again.

I always feel a mix of emotions when I think back to my early days in Castle Harbor. I had been thrilled that my mom and I were able to start something different, something new and hopefully happier, now that we were away from my father. But I also felt so out of place. All my classmates had lived there their entire lives, along with their parents and grandparents. They seemed to distrust out-of-towners and made no room for me in their friend groups. Luckily, none of that mattered to Monroe.

I was by myself at the end of a long wooden table when she took one look at my Lilo and Stich-themed lunch box, sat down next to me, and declared we were best friends. I was in no position to turn down friendship, and frankly, her forceful approach scared me a little, so I simply nodded my head. The rest was history. We'd spent the rest of lunch talking about our favorite Disney characters, and for the first time, Castle Harbor started to feel like a place I could call home.

A few weeks after that day, Monroe stayed home sick with a stomach bug. Not wanting to be alone again, I sat down next to a group of kids from my class whose names Monroe had mentioned to me when she was giving me a run-down of the playground rules. Things started off okay until I pulled out my Tupperware from my lunch box. My mom had packed me leftovers from dinner, a traditional Iranian beef stew filled with cooked spinach, beans, and rice. It was my absolute favorite food in the world, but as I went to dig in the kids around me squealed in disgust. I felt myself getting smaller and smaller as they made comments about how gross my lunch looked, how bad it smelled, and how my mom must not love me if this was what she fed me. That last comment earned a laugh from everyone sitting around me. I realized that without Monroe I was an outsider in my own hometown.

I did my best to blink away my tears, not wanting to give my classmates another reason to make fun of me. A tall boy from the grade above threw his bag down on the floor and sat down next to me. He had soft-looking brown hair and kind green eyes as he glanced between me and my lunch. That brown hair and those green eyes belonged to Mason Hayes. He looked at my face, then at the food sitting in front of me, before taking the spoon from my hand and taking a large bite.

"Tell your mom I said thanks for making my favorite. Those PB&Js were getting boring."

He placed his sandwich in front of me, as if trading lunches was our everyday routine. A wave of silence washed over the table as everyone watched Mason finish the stew and all but lick the container clean in a matter of minutes. He angled his eyes toward the tinfoil-wrapped sandwich in front of me, prompting me to eat, and spent the rest of our lunch period talking to me like we were old pals. I mumbled a soft 'thank you' to him as I passed him on the bus. He walked me home after and didn't leave until he saw my mom and told her he loved the food she had made me for lunch. She sent me to school the next day with two Tupperware, which Mason gladly accepted. No one teased me about my food after that.

I let out a deep breath as the memory faded away. The hurt always manages to linger, despite my best efforts to move on. Though he wasn't physically here, the longer I stay in my favorite places in Castle Harbor the more I feel Mason's presence. I hate how coming back to this place means I can't ignore how deeply Mason Hayes was embedded in my life. I suppose that's what happens after nearly twenty years of friendship. Even when they hurt you, they remain a part of you forever.

"Violet Amin, did you think you could sneak into town without seeing me first? Just wait until I tell Elaine."

My eyes snap up to a familiar set of green eyes— Mason and Monroe's eyes. The older woman heading toward me is Melissa Hayes, my second mom. Her platinum blonde hair had faded slightly over the years, now a more subtle shade mixed with strands of gray.

I stand up from the bench and throw my arms around her squeezing tightly. She lets out a melodic laugh before returning the hug.

"Don't think you're not still in trouble missy. It's been entirely too long since I last saw you."

"I know. Things have been so chaotic with school and work and just life." I shrug. "But I'm here now." My smile feels a bit forced.

"I was just heading over to your mom's. Care to join me?"

After five years of working odd jobs, late shifts, and scrambling to make ends meet my mom finally saved up enough to buy the rundown bait and tackle shop and turned it into the town's most popular coffeeshop and bakery, Rise N' Grind. The cafe was a twenty-minute walk from the park, located in the center of downtown. If you can call a street with a knickknack shop, two bars, an ice cream parlor that was closed for half of the year, an apothecary, and a coffeeshop "downtown". Still, it always managed to be the one spot where you can expect to run into almost anyone, from your favorite elementary school teacher to your ex-boyfriend's cousin who you were convinced always had a thing for you. Which is why I had initially planned to avoid it like the plague. But I could never say no to Melissa.

"I was just heading down there myself."

We spend the first few minutes of our walk catching up about the latest town scandal and I gasp in delight when Melissa tells me the town's newest headline is about Maria De Luca — the last person I would ever expect. As far as anyone in Castle Harbor was concerned, Maria was a modern-day saint, running every single holiday charity event you could imagine, from the St. Patrick's Day Shamrock Shake Sale to — my personal favorite — the annual Summer Festival. Despite her status as a town celebrity, most of us knew very little about Maria besides the fact that she had married her high school sweetheart, Gene, with whom she raised two children.

It turns out that twenty-five years ago, two months before the wedding, she and Gene got into a huge fight and temporarily called the whole thing off. During the brief period Maria De Luca was single, she booked a two-week trip to Italy to visit her great-grandparents. It was there that she met the second-greatest love of her life, Marco. The two had spent every second of her trip together. He took her to all his favorite places in Venice, and on the last day of her trip, he professed his love for her on a romantic gondola ride. As the rumor goes, they spent the rest of the night together as well, but when Marco woke up the next morning, Maria was nowhere to be found. She had come back to Castle Harbor to make up with Gene and the rest was history. Only Marco hadn't moved on and had spent the past twenty-five years trying to track down his American sweetheart. Two weeks ago, he finally did.

Marco showed up with a bouquet of pink lilies — the national flower of Italy and coincidentally Maria's favorite flower — and an engagement ring. Imagine his surprise when, instead of Maria, it was Gene who answered the door demanding to know what the hell was going on. All hell broke loose when Maria had come downstairs, and Marco proposed to her then and there. Some neighbors claimed they saw Gene De Luca hit Marco over the head with a pot of planted roses. Others say they overheard him demand a paternity test for their eldest son. Though no one has seen Maria around town since the confrontation, Marco refuses to leave until he gets to speak with her. He is currently shacked up at Jolly's Bed and Breakfast.

Melissa wipes tears from her eyes as she tries to stop laughing. "And to think this only happened a few weeks ago. Imagine how much you've missed in the months you haven't dropped by."

"We'd need to start a whole podcast to keep up with all the town gossip. 'Keeping Up with Castle Harbor: The Tales and Tribulations of your Favorite Fishermen's Town.'"

"Hmm that title needs work, but I think you're on to something." Melissa pauses for a moment to open the door to Rise 'N Grind, when I'm hit with the incredible scent of ground coffee beans, spices, and baked goods. A few of the cafe's regulars spot me immediately and give me a wave. I scan the room for my mom when she pops up from behind the counter, her apron covered in flour.

"Hey Elaine! Guess who I found on my walk through the park."

My mom's eyes widen as she realizes I'm here, and she practically shoves her employees out of the way as she comes from behind the display case and squeezes the oxygen out of me with a hug.

"Violet? Why didn't you tell me you were coming? Oh, it's been so long."

It didn't matter if I was gone for a day or a year, my mother would always act like I had returned from war whenever I came back home. "Mom, it's only been a few months and we talk all the time."

"We text. Like that's the same thing as getting to see you." My mom looks over my head to her best friend. "It's truly a shame, Mel. We put all our best years into raising these kids and they can't even give us their time of day anymore." She waves us over to the stools closest to the cashier, so we can continue to chat while she preps the chocolate croissants behind the counter.

For a moment, we sit in silence, my mom and Melissa staring at each other and doing that incredibly annoying thing where they hold an entire conversation without even speaking. Just stares, blinks, and subtle eye movements. Their own Morse code. Melissa is the one to break the ice, pausing for a moment and giving me a look that tells me I'm not going to like whatever comes out of her mouth next.

"So, I heard you ran into Mason at Westchester."

How would they even know that?! I'm fairly certain Mason has limited almost all his contact with his parents which meant. "I'm really going to need to have a conversation with Monroe about girl code. It's a sacred and honored tradition in which things said to your best friend don't also get shared with said best friend's family tree."

"Meddling is an honored tradition among the Hayes' women. Practically runs in our DNA. You can't fault her, or me, too much." A flash of mischief sparks in her eyes. "I just figured with the two of you working in the same place now, maybe it could be time to make up?"

"Unlikely," I snap. I immediately regret it as a flicker of hurt comes over both of their faces. "I mean just because we're both in Westchester doesn't mean we'll be seeing each other all that much..." Except for when he inevitably comes back begging for more As for the other hockey players taking my class for their gen-ed requirement. "…or that he even wants to be friends again."

Melissa takes a sip of the coffee my mom sets in front of her.

"Oh honey, that boy would sell his autographed game-worn Patrice Bergeron jersey from their last cup win if it meant fixing things with you."

"Doubtful. He's seems pretty unphased by the fact we don't talk anymore." Me on the other hand…

This time my mom decides to interject. "He's not okay. The first six months after your fight he didn't talk to anyone."

"Yeah, and after that he seemed to move on just fine—" I was suddenly hit with the reminder that I did not, in fact, need to be having this conversation. Hence why I didn't come home more often, nosey women.

"—wait whatever happened to privacy? And boundaries. I am twenty-six, ya know."

My mom clicks her tongue in response. "I'm a Middle Eastern mother. I don't know what either of those words mean."

I press my forehead to the cold marble bar in front of me and wish that I could magically teleport out of this conversation. I cave in to their silent stares that I can feel burning a hole in the top of my head. I turn my head slightly to look at Melissa who is biting at her lip the way Mason does when he's nervous.

"Is what he did really so unforgivable?" The question comes out as a whisper.

The broken look on her face makes me want to keel over. I hate seeing her this upset, and how this fallout between Mason and I has caused a rift between our two families. We'd all spent the last few years clinging to a facade and pretending like nothing had changed. Still, I don't think I had the courage, or the strength to confront Mason. Removing him from my life broke me, and I spent all my energy healing myself after the turmoil and disaster that was my first year of graduate school. I had no reinforcements left for my Mason-related wounds. Melissa and my mom didn't need to know that though. Nor did they need to know why things fell apart and shattered so quickly. They just needed to believe we would try.

"No. You're both right. We probably just need to sit down and talk things through." *Which is never going to happen.*

"So, you'll talk to him then?" The hope in Melissa's voice following my lie makes my stomach turn.

Even if I wanted to, I couldn't let myself go back to how things were when we were just friends. It would hurt too much. "Sure. I'll talk to him."

nine

· · ·

Mason

YOU WOULD THINK my distress tolerance would be much higher after years of playing in the NHL. Yet here I was, unable to stop fidgeting with the watch around my wrist or the zipper of my bomber jacket, leg bouncing up and down restlessly. Turns out, staying levelheaded when you have a one-point lead with sixty seconds left in the third period to defend your net doesn't translate to staying calm before my weekly check-in meetings with Coach Jameson.

Today we decide whether to follow through with some of the ideas I proposed to him. It was a risky move to pitch switching up the lines that had managed to keep Westchester a top playoff contender for the last two seasons. I knew better than most how hard it could be to build chemistry and trust between players.

The longer you stay on a line with certain people the more you pick up on their subtle quirks and tells. You start thinking, moving, even breathing as one. That's what it felt like when I was playing alongside Connor, or even with Mikey when we were both playing for Westchester. *Jesus when was the last time I'd spoken to him?*

Like me, Dalton Michaelson— or Mikey to those who were close to him — was born and raised in Castle Harbor. We'd met at a peewee hockey tryout when we were 10 years old, instantly clicked, and bonded over our love for the Boston Bruins. It felt almost poetic that our two favorite players, Bergeron and Marchand, were not only linesmen but also best friends. When we both received offers to play for Westchester, it felt like a dream. The various championship wins and parties after were just the icing on the cake. Not many people got to spend their college years playing hockey with their best friend. After graduation, Mikey opted to move back to Castle Harbor instead of trying his shot at the pros. It was one of the few times in my life where I didn't understand what he was thinking, why he wouldn't at least try to secure a spot on a minor league team. I'd confronted him a few times about it, but each conversation was met with a shrug and a few words about how he loved hockey, but he loved being close to his family more.

When I got injured, he came to visit me a handful of times and reached out a few times after that. I could never bring myself to respond. It wasn't fair, but I was in such a low place that every time I saw Mikey, I felt a pang of resentment. He was perfectly healthy and able to play for the NHL at any given moment, yet he never wanted that. I was willing to give up anything, and frankly did sacrifice more than I should've, yet I was stuck in recovery and forced to retire.

Once the resentment faded, the guilt suffocated me. Mikey was a hot head on the ice, but he was always the more responsible and practical one. He never once waivered in his morals or his beliefs nor did he turn his back on his family as I had.

Monroe assumed I wouldn't step foot in Castle Harbor because of the fight I had with Dad when I was still active on the Rangers, but other ghosts of my past haunted me. Ghosts I wasn't ready to face yet.

"We're still good to meet now, Mason?" Coach Jameson came barreling in with his clipboard and Dunkin' iced coffee in hand.

"Yup, I was just waiting for you." More nervous fidgeting. "So any consensus on what lines we're going with against UCONN?"

The game was a little over two weeks away, and the more time we had to test out the new arrangements, the better. Just because I had a hunch that certain players would be good together doesn't mean it would pan out on the ice. Better to test that out during practice than against one of our toughest opponents.

Coach says nothing for a few minutes and instead flicks his eyes between his clipboard and me. Over and over again. The suspense is going to send me over the edge.

"The other coaches are split on whether changing up the lines is a good idea. On one hand, we clearly need to ramp up our game if we're going to stay alive against teams like UCONN and Bolton this year. On the other hand, splitting up guys who work well together is a risky move."

"And what do you think?" It was Coach Jameson's decision that mattered the most in the end. Both when it came to implementing my changes and whether this job turned into something more permanent.

"I think that I brought you in so you could shake things up, so I'd be a hypocrite to not give you the chance to do that. We're gonna run these new lines starting today." He stands to exit my office. "And you get to be the one to break the news to the players."

I can't even contain the groan. "I'm going to piss off a lot of people, aren't I?"

"Definitely. Better you than me though." He lets out a soft chortle. "Welcome to the joys of being a coach."

———

If looks could kill, I'd be dead five times over. I knew moving some of our star players down to the third and fourth lines wasn't going to do me any favors, but they didn't need to be so hostile about it.

"Listen, I know a few of you are upset right now—" That garners a few eye rolls and snorts. I look around the room for Adam, our team captain. If I can get him on my side, I know everyone else will follow suit. At least for today. He gives me a look that tells me he's almost convinced so I keep going. "But we need to do something that's going to up our game and give us an edge. We can't keep playing like we have for the past few seasons and expect to make it past the first round of playoffs."

Adam gives me a small nod before backing me up. "C'mon boys he's right. We've been coasting for the past two seasons and I'm sick of it. Don't we want to be something more than the team that's good but not good enough?"

"That's easy for you to say Cap. You're not the one who's losing his first line spot for no reason other than 'let's try something new.'" Jake retorts against his best friend, and the locker room, unsurprisingly, turns against me again.

A part of me hoped Coach Jameson would speak up and tell them they could either follow my instructions or keep the bench warm, but as I felt his presence hovering behind me an even bigger part of me wanted to show him I could handle this. I knew all too well how line changes can sour relationships. Kallum Donovan and I had never been best friends, but once I took over the veteran's spot when I joined the Rangers, anytime we were on the ice together, it felt like we were playing against each other.

I try to think back to that time, to how my coaches had handled the often-one-sided tension between Kallum and me.

"Do you want to know what sets apart a good team from an elite team? The difference between a team that makes it to the Stanley Cup finals and wins, versus one that gets close enough and chokes in the end?" A wave of silence covers the room at the shift in my tone. "On the elite teams, no one cares about what line they're on. They set their egos aside and focus on two things: how to stay on top of their game and how they can help build their teammates up. You think Patrice Bergeron or Brad Marchand cared that they weren't on the first line when they were hoisting up the Stanley Cup?"

I wish I knew whether my words resonated. Most of my players look less upset, but I can't guarantee they don't hold some resentment toward me. Maybe they always will, and I will just have to deal with that.

Coach Jameson finally steps up from behind me. "Alright enough wallowing. We're running the new lines today in practice, and from there, we'll figure out what to do next. Boys, I want all of you on the ice in 15."

He says nothing to me as he heads down the tunnel toward the ice, but I manage to catch his lips twitch upward slightly. It's enough to settle my heartbeat for the remainder of practice where we put my plans to the test.

ten

. . .

Violet

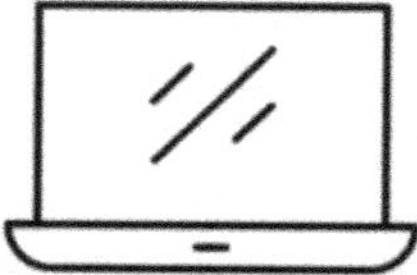

"EXCITING NEWS. I think I figured out a way to get you out of having to TA." Bethany exclaims, taking a sip of coffee from her mug. While most PhD students worked as teaching assistants so they could have some source of income, teaching often came at the expense of sacrificing time that ideally would be dedicated toward our research and completing degree milestones. In my program, labs with more grant money could pay students directly so they could stay focused on their research, which created an uneven playing field.

"The department just received a very generous donation and the faculty have decided to take some of that money and use it to fund a fellowship program. If you get the award it should cover you for about three years and allow you to focus on your research."

If you get the award. Academia was a constant cycle of applying to things, getting rejected, dusting yourself off, and trying again. I'd become more or less numb to the rejection, but it's also made me much less optimistic about things working out in my favor. "Do you know what the application process will look like?"

"Yes! Students will be asked to draft a personal statement and research proposal, very similar to the other fellowships you've applied to before." *And didn't get.* "Each year the department will choose a specific area of research they give priority to. This year they want to focus on the relationship between maternal mental health and infant development."

Wait a minute. "That's literally what my dissertation is going to be on." Is this what hope feels like?

"I know! Violet, I really think you have a good chance at getting this, and you know I'm not the type to just say that."

It was true and one of the things I appreciated most about Bethany. While she was always very supportive, she also did a great job at tempering expectations. A lot of people are super qualified in our field, and most don't get the grants they apply to.

"So, you really think I have a shot?"

"Beyond your qualifications, you're one of the only students in the department with an active project that focuses on all aspects of what they're looking for. Also, when the fellowship topic was revealed, a few faculty immediately brought your name up and mentioned you should apply." Her eyes lit up the way a proud mother's would. "Obviously I have to recuse myself from voting as your adviser, but I have a good feeling about this."

"Amazing. Do you mind sending me the official details?"

"Absolutely." She glances at the clock hung up on the wall. "I have to run to another meeting, which frankly really could've been an email."

"The day people learn that most meetings could just be an email will be the day in which the universe truly heals."

We both pack up our belongings and head off in different directions. Waiting for the elevator, I debate whether to go down to my office or to the Beanery to get some work done. Given the Beanery has windows and lattes whereas my office has neither of those things, it was the clear winner. The ding of the elevator brings me back to the current moment. I'm suddenly face-to-face with the one person I want to avoid more than Mason. The one person who brought me to such a dark point my first year that, had it not been for Bethany I would have dropped out. Would have given up on all my dreams that I had worked so hard to achieve.

Dr. Darlene Atkins was one of the most senior faculty in the psychology department and the impact of her research on our field couldn't be understated. It was both her seniority and her reputation that allowed her to get away with years of mistreatment, exploitation, and the verbal and emotional abuse of her students. For decades, a handful of professors had a vague sense that her behavior was problematic but kept it hidden from the heads of the department. They never wanted to address how one of the most influential scientists in the world, in a field dedicated to helping people, could be so cruel to her mentees. This fueled a long cycle of hopeful candidates accepting offers to join her lab and then realizing soon the truth behind the saying "Never meet your heroes." I had been one of the naïve and hopeful candidates.

In the beginning, I thought it had been just me. Figured I was an imposter among my classmates and that everything she had said about me was true. Until one of her former students reached out to check in on me, and I realized how far back her mistreatment stemmed. No one had ever been brave enough to report Dr. Atkins to her superiors, until me. To this day I wasn't sure if it really had been bravery or just plain stupidity.

"Violet." The sound of my name coming out of her mouth

was enough to make me wince. "I haven't seen you since…well since you quit my lab." She purses her lips. "A true shame that whole ordeal was. I hope you're not causing as much trouble for Bethany as you did when you were with me."

She walks away with her nose held high before I can think of a response. My heart is pounding so hard I swear it's a few beats away from jumping out of my chest. I try to take a few deep breaths to center myself, but my throat is a vice, constricting my breathing. I didn't even realize how badly my hands had been shaking until I entered the elevator. It takes me a few attempts to press the button for the first floor. I knew at some point I would run into her again, I just didn't realize how visceral of a reaction my body would have. Didn't think I'd be on the verge of a full panic attack. I'm brought back to how often I would have to fight them off when I was working for her. They used to happen daily back then.

Walking outside always helped. I take the long way to the Beanery, letting the shock of the cold air hit my face and cool my body. Eventually, I calm my heartbeat down enough to enter the cafe, but I have a feeling I'm going to be on edge for the rest of the day. *You're okay Violet. You're okay.* I repeat the words in my head like a mantra, hoping it will drown out the memories of my first year. Every meeting we had where she tore me apart, every late-night email filled with threatening language, every idea of mine she stole and claimed as her own.

The first few months her criticisms and demands started off subtle enough that I had defended her behavior. *'This is what happens when you work with someone who is very established. Of course, she's going to be hard on me.'* The following months it became more and more apparent how wrong I had been. The second I fulfilled one of her demands, tasks that no one else would think to ask of their first-year graduate student, the more liberties Dr. Atkins took with her role as my adviser.

I think to survive, even for a little bit, I had to convince myself that it was all normal. That I was supposed to leave every meeting in tears, or only sleep three hours a night to meet my mentor's unrelenting demands. Even though she never really was a mentor to me. No matter what I did, it was never good enough. Day by day my resolve was chipped away until I was just a shell. Over time I lost so many pieces of myself I forgot who I was before I was broken.

eleven

. . .

Mason

I FEEL like I'm having an out-of-body experience as I walk through the familiar halls of UCONN's hockey arena. How many games had I played here with Westchester? How many grueling losses and epic wins were tied to this building? Deja vu isn't sufficient to explain the emotions I am feeling. It feels like I am watching my past, as if someone recorded my memories and is playing them back to me. The bus ride on the way here felt equally disconcerting. Gone were the days when Mikey and I would dick around in the back and plot what local bars we were hitting up after the game. I sat in the front with Coach Jameson discussing arrival and check-in times, UCONN's roster, and whether we should risk using my lineup for this game. Our practices had gone well enough to warrant testing at least some new plays, but I know things don't always translate from practice to games, and UCONN is one of our biggest threats.

It is early enough in the season that we can recover from a loss on paper, but hockey isn't just about the game played on the ice. It's also about the games that you play in your head. This whole season UCONN has been touted as some unbeatable force, with many journalists declaring every other team should pack it up and call it a season. If we lose tonight, college hockey fans will say that we lost to an elite team, nothing to be ashamed of. But I know what it will do to the psyche of my players. I've seen too many of my past teammates get in their heads that certain opponents were unbeatable. It didn't matter whether those teams actually *were* better. All that mattered was the confidence you had in yourself to not only play the game but to play it better than the person skating against you. And though Coach didn't explicitly say it on the bus, I know he and I are on the same page. We need this win.

In a blur we check in, go over plays in the locker room, and leave the players to get dressed and prepped for warm-ups. Somewhere in between all the chaos, Coach Jameson announces that we won't be changing up the lines for tonight's game. I try to keep my face stoic as my chest deflates. If he can't trust me to add a few changes to the roster tonight, how will he ever trust me to fully coach the team? I do my best to push down that thought and focus on the task in front of me. I still have a job to do, whether I agree with Coach's decisions or not.

The ringing buzzer fills the arena, signaling to the players to head back to their respective locker rooms for one final check-in with the staff before the game begins. I lead the meeting, reminding the team of which UCONN players to look out for and how to identify and isolate their weaknesses. Adam and Jake come together to lead a final chant to hype up the team as Coach Jameson and I head out of the locker room.

"It's weird how things can be so similar and still so different from when I was on the team."

Coach rolls his eyes. "How nostalgic, Hayes."

"Just trying to make conversation here." *Trying to ignore the fact that I'm about to coach my first game and I still feel like I scammed my way into this position.*

"Do I need to give you a pep talk too?"

"No." Yes.

"C'mon, you'll do fine. Worst case scenario you just shut up and do what I say."

He leads me down the hall toward the ice and settles in behind our bench. The perfect view to oversee every angle of the rink in front of us. The familiar chill of being this close to the ice hits my bones and settles me. From across the rink, I can see the UCONN players start to skate out and I send our first line out to follow. The next few minutes are spent announcing the refs and players, and watching a dramatic but albeit well put together montage of UCONN's best plays and hardest hits this season. When I look down from the video to my players, I see them hyper-fixated on the jumbotron, Adam nervously toying with the bottom of his stick. Shit. Of all the players on the team, I need him locked in the most. The second a captain loses his cool everyone else starts panicking too.

As the starting ceremonies end, I watch as Adam and UCONN's captain, Luke Anderson, skate up to the center line; their respective linesmen taking their positions as well, awaiting puck drop. I can't hear what's being said on the ice but from the bench, I can see Adam's face tighten up as Anderson starts running his mouth. It's a cheap tactic to start chirping at your opponent before the game even starts. Cheap and effective having done the same a few times myself. Both players lower their sticks, coming close enough that I wonder if they're going to brawl it out as soon as the play starts. *Stay in it, Adam. Stay in it.* A second after the puck drops, Adam scoops it over to our side and sends it to Jake who starts heading down our offensive zone. He gets a small opening and sends the puck flying through the air, but the shot goes wide, rebounding off the glass.

UCONN's goalie snatches the loose puck and stops the play, giving his teammates time to regroup.

The next play starts in UCONN's zone, but we can't get control of the puck. Anderson sends it flying down center ice to his alternate captain, who comes barreling down the ice for a breakaway attempt that soon turns into a goal as the puck hits the back of our net. 1-0 UCONN. It feels like all the oxygen has been sucked out of my players as the entire bench looks down in defeat. We're an absolute disaster after that. Though we're only down one goal, with most of the game left to play, the boys are acting as though we're already beat. We get fresh legs on the ice, keeping to Coach's original lines, but it's no use. Miscommunications are happening almost every play, and when our players are on the same page, they forget to keep track of their surroundings. This results in them either getting body checked into next week or having the puck stolen from under them.

We end the first period down 3-0 with little hope for a comeback. As the team shuffles into our locker room, I pull Coach aside for a second.

"We need to try something new. UCONN's not doing anything special out there, the boys are just too rattled to take possession of the game."

If he's upset about my demands, he doesn't show it. "What do you suggest?"

"I think we try the new lines out."

His face remains expressionless. "You said it yourself the team is already rattled. You think changing the lines up in the middle of a game is a good idea?"

"We need them to get out of their heads and locked back into the game. Maybe this will force them to think about the new plays and less about who we're playing." This could also be the final nail in the coffin for this game, but I wasn't about to tell him that.

"Agreed. Let's regroup in the locker room."

Shit. I guess we're doing this. Coach barrels into the room

and starts yelling about getting their heads out of their asses and how they can decide now whether they want to forfeit the game and put us all out of our misery, or if they're going to try to play hockey. Having been on the receiving end of many of Coach Jameson's "Get your shit together" speeches, I take a moment to appreciate that for once, it wasn't being directed at me. Although if my plan fails, I'm sure I will get my own version of this 'pep talk' soon after.

While he takes some time to cool down, I announce that we're going to try out the new line arrangements in the second period. I expect to receive tons of pushback and disgruntled quips, but all 20 pairs of eyes are locked on me, ready to listen. I guess being down three goals will make you desperate enough to try anything. Good. That's where I need them. Desperate, disappointed, and angry enough to turn this game around. We spend the last ten minutes of the break ensuring everyone is on the same page before making our descent down the hallway and back toward the benches.

Adam takes the lead, and this time instead of his usual linesmen flanking him, Dylan and Tristan follow him on the ice. I see UCONN's coaches debating for a moment who to send out in response, clearly thrown off. The ref signals them to skate out soon or they'll risk a delay of game penalty. UCONN's captain and the rest of the first line trail out. Dylan and Tristian are our strongest, and frankly cockiest, freshmen on the team this year — both rocking matching smirks to back it up. They add a layer of energy and unpredictability to Adam's game. Importantly, I knew those two would be chomping at the bit to prove themselves and show they deserved more ice time.

UCONN wins the first puck drop of the second period, but the energy and response from my players feel completely different from the first period. Our defense is immediately on top of them, blocking a few goal attempts before sending the puck to Adam. He sets up for a shot that hits the goal post, but Dylan's right in front of the net and ready for the rebound which he slides between the goalie's legs. The players on the ice go wild. Dylan's first goal since he joined the team. Adam grabs the puck from the net and brings it back to the bench for Dylan. A moment he won't forget, I'm sure.

"Attaboy Dylan, that's the exact type of focus we need out there." I pat him on the back as he files back onto the bench and a different line of players get ready to head out. Before Jake can fully hop onto the ice, I offer a few words to light a fire under his ass. "You gonna let the rookies have all the fun tonight, Keeley? Looks like I made the right decision bringing Dylan up."

Jake brushes me off and instead takes his anger out on some of UCONN's largest defensemen. In a matter of minutes, he shoulder-checks someone on center ice, steals the puck, and hits a few other players as he rushes up to the goal. He can't get a good enough angle to take a shot, so he passes it over to his linesman, who aims for the top right corner of the net, but the goalie has it spotted. It's not until the last five minutes of the second period that Jake's antics finally start to pay off. In a fit of rage, UCONN's captain slashes Jake right in front of the ref, sending him into the sin bin. We head for a power play.

We lose the first face-off, costing us a solid 30 seconds of the power play – UCONN icing the puck to kill time. It's a brutal moment watching my players struggle to get control again, but once they do, I can see their focus is unwavering. Unfortunately, the same can be said for every member of the opposing team. I watch as we pass the puck back and forth on the ice hoping to find one small opening with no luck. I let out a small groan of frustration as the timer reaches zero. UCONN's players are so focused on adding another player back onto the ice that they don't see Jake has slowly edged himself to the left of the net and slid the puck through. This brings us up to two goals before the end of the second period.

Coach takes the lead as the team huddles together in the locker room.

"I want you boys to listen. Two goals. That's it. That's all that separates us from winning. You just scored two in the last period. All we need to do is keep that same momentum going for another twenty minutes. That's it, that's all."

There's not much more that needs to be said so we leave the locker room and let the boys spend the last few minutes strategizing among themselves.

While our players have done a near 180 from the first period, it seems UCONN's have as well. Their coach has always had a notorious reputation for dealing out the worst punishments after a loss. It's clear he gave them a talk to inspire fear, but UCONN is slowly falling apart at the seams. They're giving up way too many passes and missing too many goals for a team whose leading their division right now. *Good. We're in their heads.* I watch as Adam intercepts a pass and starts skating down the ice like a madman. No one's able to catch up with him and I hold my breath as he lifts his stick and sends the puck soaring in the air. Their goalie dives, and for a moment, I'm convinced the goal's been blocked until the goalie comes up and reveals an empty glove.

A chorus of loud boos fills the arena as we tie the game, followed by a wave of silence so heavy you can feel the despair from the crowd. From across the ice, UCONN's coach signals to the ref for a time-out, giving my players a few seconds to cool off. Scanning the bench, everyone looks like they're on their last legs. Playing against this team was always going to be a battle, and forcing a comeback wasn't easy.

"Just one more goal boys. One more. Let's wrap it up here in the third, we don't need this game going into overtime."

The ref skates by our bench to let us know we can get back on the ice. No one ever warned me I'd feel more nervous as a coach than as a player. It takes everything in me not to cover my eyes these last five minutes, only peeking through my fingers like that will somehow calm the tension. UCONN drives the puck up the ice toward our zone. In a desperate attempt to cling to their lead, UCONN pulls their goalie out of the game to add an additional man on the ice. My stomach is in knots as I watch them take shot after shot at our goal.

Through sheer force of luck —*or maybe I willed it*—one of UCONN's players breaks his stick in half during a pass attempt. Dylan is right there to pick it up as he dashes down the ice, his linemates right behind him for backup. With a few seconds left in the period, Adam screams at him to shoot the puck. With no goalie to stop it, the puck soars right in the center of the net. Our bench erupts into absolute pandemonium. I took a moment to appreciate the scene in front of me, the utter joy on my players' faces, and the rush of emotions filling me. The feelings of exuberance, pride, and adrenaline that I only thought I could experience as a player, I now felt ten-fold.

It's only me and Coach Jameson left standing near the stalls as he claps a hand on my shoulder. "Now *that*...", he points to Dylan as he celebrates with his teammates on the ice, "...was some pretty solid coaching, Mason."

twelve

. . .

Violet

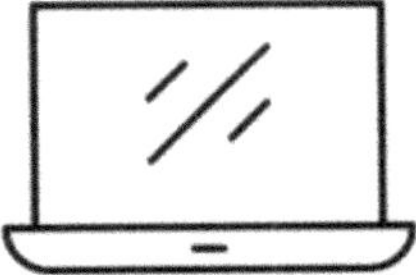

IF STARING at a blank Word document was a job that paid well, I'd be a millionaire right now. The research proposal for my fellowship application was drafted and emailed to Bethany for her feedback. However, writing a personal statement about adversities I'd overcome and my personal motivations for the research I wanted to do…that type of writing was its own kind of hell. I'd never been great at talking about myself or what I went through growing up. It took me almost a decade to find the courage to talk to Monroe about my dad, and that was only because she had overheard our moms speaking about what things were like before we left him.

I can still feel Monroe's arms wrapped tight around me as she told me she was so sorry for what I had gone through. That and the feeling of embarrassment that ran through my whole body, as I realized she knew one of my deepest secrets. It's funny how that works. You can be the person someone takes all their anger out on and still feel embarrassed about it, while they continue on unaffected.

"Violet, I know you hate talking about yourself, and I don't want you to feel pressured right now…but if you need someone to talk to, I'm here." Monroe gives my hand a small squeeze of reassurance probably sensing that I need another reminder that I'm here. Safe.

"I know, and I'm sorry I didn't tell you this before I just — " I won't cry. This is going to be hard enough, but I refuse to cry, "I was just so…embarrassed."

"You have nothing *to be embarrassed about."*

"I know it sounds dumb, but growing up I always blamed myself. I always assumed it was my fault. It was the only thing that made sense. My dad was so nice and charming to people at his job and in public. He only got really drunk and angry and upset at home, so I figured…I figured I was the problem."

The sadness in Monroe's eyes turns to rage as she takes in my words and engulfs me in a hug. "Vi, you did nothing wrong. Nothing."

Over the years my default state was to push my emotions down and bury them as deep as I could. It served me well. Except for the moments when I had to write stupid essays that asked me to rehash a past I wanted nothing to do with. I had camped out at the Beanery the past three hours, hoping the smell of coffee and general anxious energy being emitted by the other students would rub off on me. Instead, I managed to achieve absolutely nothing. Unless you consider doom scrolling on social media an achievement.

"Rough day, Vi?" I lift my head to see Carlos, my favorite barista and manager of the Beanery, setting up fresh pastries in the case. While I was on a first-name basis with all the baristas, Carlos and I had become especially close over the years as I spent many late nights camped in the back corner. As the manager he'd usually be the last to leave, letting me stay way past closing. On those nights he'd walk me to the bus stop to make sure I got home safe.

"Eh, I've had worse. I'm more annoyed at myself than anything." I turn my screen so he can see the blank document. "I've been here for three hours, and this is all I have to show for it."

"That's tough, but I think I have an idea of what might cheer you up." He heads to the back, and I have a sneaking suspicion it's to make my regular order.

I open my mouth to tell him it's not necessary, but who am I to turn down my favorite drink? Accepting defeat for the day, I shut my laptop as he brings the glass over to my table. "Do you want to take a seat for a minute?"

"Sure, I'm due for a break." He sets my chai latte down before claiming the seat across from me. "So, what's new this week?"

We spend the next fifteen minutes catching up. I vent to him about how much I hate having to share my feelings knowing my mentors and other faculty will be reading it. He tells me about how he's convinced his roommate, who refuses to do laundry more than once a month, has been stealing his underwear for the last few weeks. The look of horror on my face is then followed by a devious smile from Carlos as he tells me about his plans for revenge. He's hidden away all his underwear except for one pair that he rigged with itching powder. If his suspicions are correct, Carlos's roommate will have a very rough time soon. I'm wiping away tears of laughter when I notice the familiar scent of pine and soap surrounding me.

"I was just looking for you, Violet." Mason's tone is unreadable, which sets me on edge. He's normally an open book when it comes to his emotions.

"Well as you can see, I'm busy." I gesture toward Carlos. "Carlos made me a drink and we're catching up. Now's not a good time."

"Did you forget our meeting today? We agreed on 3 p.m. right? I know I'm a few minutes early but—"

"We agreed to 3:30. And we decided to meet in your office."

There was no way my broom closest would be able to fit myself, Mason, and Jake.

"Are you sure? Let me check my calendar." Mason grabs a chair from a nearby table, plops in right between Carlos and me, and takes a seat as he pulls his phone out of his pocket.

"Back to drinking chai lattes I see." He gives me a small wink before turning his attention to Carlos. "Is it half-sweetened?"

I watch as the tension starts to form on Carlos's shoulders. "Excuse me?"

"Violet likes her chai lattes half-sweetened. The extra sugar hurts her teeth and leaves a bad taste in her mouth." Mason tries to come off as genuinely curious and concerned for me. Nobody is buying that crap, buddy.

"I think I'd know her order by now." Carlos bites out.

When Mason was still playing hockey, he was one of the biggest pests on the ice, always knowing exactly what to say to set someone off. Right now, he seemed perfectly in his element.

"Why? Is that because you're her barista? Or you're something else?"

"Careful. I think your jealousy is showing. And that's never a good look." It seems Carlos wasn't so easy to rattle. I didn't expect to enjoy this dynamic so much, but I just sat back and enjoyed my tea and a show.

"What we are is none of your business."

"Oof. Caught in the friend zone, huh? That's tough." I swear the smirk was permanently etched onto Mason's face.

"At least Violet considers me a friend. I doubt you can say the same." Carlos was more perceptive than I thought.

Carlos's cutting words leave Mason speechless and clenching his jaw. The movement is so subtle I doubt Carlos even noticed it. But I did. I knew all of Mason's tells, including those that signaled he was losing an internal battle and was about to go off. And from the tension in his jaw and the way his hands were balled into fists, I gathered it was time to close the curtain on my entertainment and head to this meeting.

I push my seat back from the table and stand drawing their attention. "As fun as this has been, Mason and I do need to head to a meeting." Mason looks up at me, the little storm clouds in his eyes settling as he registers the seriousness on my face. He gets up and puts some distance between us as I pack up all my things. Turning to Carlos, I feel a flood of guilt wash over me at the look of hurt on his face. "We'll catch up more later C, I promise."

"Maybe over dinner soon?"

We'd never really hung out much outside of the Beanery, but I sort of relished in the bold offer directly in front of Mason. I gave him a soft smile. "Sure, sounds nice. Talk to you later?"

"Definitely."

With that I throw my bag over my shoulder and exit the café, Mason right beside me. Neither of us say anything as we begin our walk to the hockey arena, his silence only fueling my irritation. We are almost at the rink when I can't contain myself anymore. "Care to explain what the hell that was back there?"

"Not sure what you mean Vi."

"Seriously? Did I just hallucinate the dick-measuring contest?" I give him a pointed look so he knows I'm clued into his little games.

"Don't be so dramatic." He rolls his eyes as he holds the door to the arena open gesturing for me to walk in first. "I was just getting to know your friend."

"No, you were actively trying to provoke him."

"Oh, was I?"

"Yes. Your infamous 'I'm Mason Hayes. I'm so much better than everyone. I wonder how long I can keep pushing before this guy snaps, and I can feel better about myself' face was in full force."

"Wow. You got all of that from looking at me? Who knew you were so perceptive."

I feel myself regressing back to when we were teenagers. "You can be such a dick sometimes."

"Yea, I'm a real asshole. Makes sense why you cut me out of your life."

I nearly trip over my own feet at his words. He halts abruptly and turns back to look at me. "Oh, nothing you want to say now."

It was a statement more than it was a question. Or really, an accusation. One that I didn't feel the need to address.

"I didn't think so." He mutters more to himself than me as he continues to stalk down the hall, where we see Jake propped up against the door.

The tall blonde hockey player steps aside as Mason unlocks the door and huffs inside. Jake raises his eyebrows at his coach's clear irritation, and shoots me a look that says, *'What's his problem?'*. When he realizes I'm equally upset and unwilling to talk, he rolls his eyes and lets out an exasperated sigh before entering the office. "This should be fun."

thirteen

. . .

Mason

THERE WERE many parts of the nearby streets surrounding Westchester's campus that were unrecognizable to me now. Nearly every old restaurant or bar I had spent my nights in as a student here had been torn down and replaced by either a trendy brewery that only served IPAs or fusion restaurants most students couldn't afford. The one staple that remained was Cornwhall's, an old family-owned pub established in the late sixties, beloved by students and most locals. Walking into the pub and over to the bar I'm immediately met with the familiar scent of burgers and beer. The wall farthest back in the room is still covered in a shrine of newspaper articles detailing massive championship wins from Boston's professional and college teams.

It takes me a few seconds to spot the photo of me, Mikey, and Bradon propping up the Bean Pot trophy. Of course, that would be the picture they decide to hang up. Not the one of our NCAA win, or even the night we became Hockey East champions. Instead, they memorialized a moment from a tournament based solely on bragging rights and school pride. Every year TD Garden, home of the Boston Bruins, would open its arena for two weeks to some of the biggest college hockey teams in the area. Tickets to the games would sell out months in advance as old alumni flew in from across the U.S. to attend. We'd won the whole thing my sophomore year after nearly a decade of losses and the entire arena exploded. The first place we brought that trophy was Cornwhall's.

"I wonder whatever happened to those kids."

The comment snaps me out of a daze, and I turn around to see Mikey standing behind me, a huge grin on his face. Damn, I didn't realize how much I missed him until now. "Thanks for taking the train down." Our hometown is only an hour away and I know driving into Boston could be a nightmare.

"You know I love this place." He claps one of his massive hands on my back and slides into the bar stool right next to mine. "Glad to see you finally remembered how to use your phone, Hayesy."

The nickname from the days we played hockey together takes me back. "I don't even remember the last time someone's called me that."

He signals to the bartender who sets down two beers in front of us before turning his attention back to me.

"Damn you went to New York and everything changed, huh?"

"Yeah. It was like another world out there. Now I'm back here and everything feels different too."

"Eh things aren't that different."

"You have a mullet now." The last time I saw Mikey he had a

buzzcut. Now brownish blonde hair was hanging at his shoulders.

"The ladies love the long hair."

"You sure about that?"

A wicked grin takes over his face as he tugs down the collar of his shirt to reveal a hickey. "Positive."

"Jesus." I let out a laugh while I sip from my beer. "Still a fucking menace I see."

"You're one to talk. Back in the day, I could have used noise-canceling headphones when we lived together."

"I plead the fifth." I guess I deserve that. Both of us took being bachelors in college very seriously. "I do really appreciate you meeting me here. And I'm sorry it took me so long to reach out."

Talking to Mikey had always been so easy. After spending a few minutes here, the weight of all the chaos in my life already felt lighter. That lightness is quickly replaced with a feeling of guilt. I never should have shut him out of my life. No matter how embarrassed or ashamed I felt, Mikey would've understood. Would've been there for me. Plus, I knew all too well how much it hurt when someone you cared about stopped talking to you without warning. "I was just in a really bad place after I had to retire and…and I couldn't face you. Couldn't face anyone really."

He toys with the pint glass in front of him, eyebrows scrunched together like he needs to think about how he wants to respond. "I get it, man. I just wanted you to know that I was here for you if you needed it."

We both take large gulps of our beers, needing a moment to work our way back from our unexpected heart-to-heart. Mikey clears his throat like he's clearing the air. "So, what's this I hear about you coaching at Westchester now?"

"Dude, it's literally insane. All I know is I went in ready to beg Coach to let me clean the locker rooms or wash some jerseys, and the next thing I know I'm an assistant coach."

"What the hell do you know about coaching?"

"Literally nothing."

"Damn. He really must be desperate."

"Fuck you." I laugh, shoving his shoulder. "It's a provisional position. Meaning if I fail, I'm back to square one."

"You're not gonna fail, Mason."

"It wouldn't be the first time." The words come out of my mouth before I can stop them.

Mikey looks at me like I've grown a second head. "What are you talking about?"

"Well, I mean. Not exactly playing for the NHL anymore, so…"

"Because you got injured. After some of the best seasons we've seen from a player in decades."

He wasn't the first person to remind me of all I had achieved in such a short time. But being reminded of the glory doesn't really ease the sting of the fall like people think it will. It serves as a reminder of all you had left to achieve. Now I have nothing to show for my efforts beyond a couple of healed scars and some old highlight tapes. And the lingering pain that comes with getting the one thing you always wanted and having it taken away from you in an instant. *For the second time in my life.* Unable to say anything, I just shrug in response.

"You've always been way too hard on yourself, Mason." Realizing he had walked us back into a heart-to-heart, he switched gears. "Anything else going on in your life?"

Why is the only other thing I can think of related to Violet? "Violet's at Westchester now, for her PhD. She's also working as a teaching assistant for one of my players."

"Oh." Mikey was the first person I reached out to for advice once I realized Violet had ghosted me. He'd also spent many nights in New York with me as I drank my way through the rejection. He's probably wondering why I just responded to his question about my life with an update about hers. *Why did I do that?*

"The first time I ran into her it was like she didn't know me." *That fucking sucked.* "And the times where I've tried to confront her about what happened between us…haven't gone well." It felt good to finally talk to someone about this. Is this why girls are always drinking wine and complaining about their boyfriends? There might be something to that…

"That sounds about right." He lets out a small laugh. "The only person I know who is more stubborn and better at denying their feelings than you is her."

"Every time I say something to her now, I feel like I'm putting my foot in my mouth. In my head I'm just trying to go back to the times where we would bicker and tease each other, but knew that it was all innocent."

"Maybe that's the problem. Maybe you're too focused on trying to talk to the old Violet that you're not hearing what current Violet is saying."

What the fuck Mikey? Now it was my turn to look at him like he had grown a second head. "That is awfully profound. When did you learn so much about human relationships?"

"When I decided to grow out my hair. Puts me in touch with my feminine side. The beer also helps." He holds up his empty pint glass and waves it in front of my face.

"I'm pretty sure current Violet wants absolutely nothing to do with me."

"Well, if that's the case," Mikey waves over the bartender, "we're gonna need a lot more drinks."

———

The rest of my night at Cornwhall's is spent catching up on the things going on in Mikey's life that I'd missed out on. He is still very single— hence the hickey— and hellbent on staying that way. Mikey claims he's too busy to really settle down, especially now that his parents are retiring, leaving their restaurant in his hands. For as long as I've known Mikey, he's always floated around finding new jobs, hobbies, or even girls every couple of months. I got the sense he has commitment issues. The only thing he ever stuck with for long was hockey, and a part of me always wondered if he stuck that out for me more than himself.

He brings up Castle Harbor, and he's generous enough not to mention my parents. Though it was hard not to think about them whenever I heard about the town I grew up in. Maybe that's yet another reason I avoided speaking to Mikey. He knew so much about me and my past that he served as a permanent reminder of my failings as a son.

He was a model child — making his parents proud with his immense physical talent and endless potential but dropping everything to return home and run the family business when they needed him. Me? I had slowly started shutting people out of my life the moment I landed in New York. It wasn't something I had done intentionally; I just took so many people in my life for granted and assumed they would always be there for me regardless of my actions. And though I know my parents still love me, I hate the idea that they might be disappointed in me or, worse, ashamed of who I had become. I still check in with my mom here and there, but my dad and I still haven't spoken since our fight. *'You moved to New York and turned your back on us.'*

It had been a while since I relived those words, and when they came back into my head last night, I immediately ordered our third, and then fourth round of drinks. I was so exhausted — and inebriated — by the time I got back to my apartment I fell asleep on my couch. In addition to the pounding headache I woke up with, I also couldn't seem to get Violet's face out of my head. It's like the more I wanted to forget her the more I couldn't let her go. After trying to force myself back to sleep, I decided to carpe diem this shit. I chug three cups of coffee and head to the one place I know will quiet my mind.

Unsurprisingly the arena is pitch black and dead empty on a Sunday morning. It feels strange getting dressed again in my old locker room, seeing it decorated now with pictures of the current players and their loved ones. I'm not sure I'll ever get used to the feelings of this place both belonging to me, but also moving on from me. I take a deep breath before stepping onto the ice, bringing a few pucks along with me. Though this isn't my first time running drills mildly hungover, I am grateful to be alone as I settle into my skates. I set a pace for myself, circling around the boards a few times.

Eventually, I'm warmed up enough to switch to shooting drills. My first few wrist shots either bounce off the post or go completely wide. I repeat my movements over and over again until I get into a rhythm and the pucks start hitting the back of the net. Entering a meditative state, I lose track of the number of pucks I line up and send flying into the net. It's not until I begin to feel my soreness turn into a more painful sensation that I decide to take a break.

I reach over the bench for my water bottle, splashing some water on my face before chugging the remaining contents when the sound of footsteps catches my attention.

"Your slapshot was always a thing of beauty." Coach Jameson stands a few rows behind, now walking down the steps toward me. "Didn't expect to see you here today."

"Guess I could say the same about you."

"I like coming in when I know no one else will be here. Something about the stillness of this place when it's empty. It…"

"Clears your mind?" I offer.

"Exactly." He gestures to the bench next to him and we sit. "You've done good with these boys so far Mason."

"I'm trying, Coach."

"I can't believe you convinced Jake to get a tutor."

"It was more of an ultimatum. Also, more of his teaching assistant's call than mine." Violet made it clear Jake could start attending tutoring and work to bring his grades up or he could spend the rest of the season on the bench.

"Fair enough." He lets out a small chuckle. "Listen, I need a favor."

"Of course. Anything you need."

"I was hoping you would say that."

fourteen

• • •

Violet

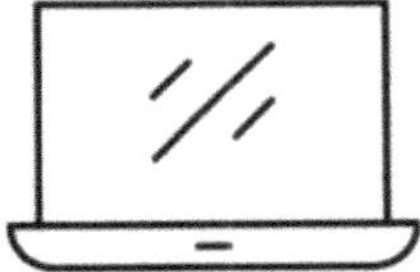

I HAVE ALWAYS LOVED WINTERTIME. If I could start decorating for Christmas in October without being judged, I would. To me, there is nothing more magical than going to bed and waking up the next morning and seeing the entire street covered in a soft layer of snow. When I was a kid, my mom would often scold me for staying out too late making snow angels and haphazardly building snowmen that fell as soon as a mild breeze blew. My love for winter remained even as I got older and was forced to help shovel the driveway every morning before school.

After spending most of my life in Massachusetts, I was almost certain there was nothing that could make me hate winter — until today. I'm woken up in the middle of the night by an awful noise, like violent teeth chattering. My own teeth, apparently. I am a New Englander — raised to have iced coffee even when the high outside is 20 degrees and feels like 10 with the wind chill— and I refuse to set the thermostat higher than 70 in November. Growing up we'd do anything to save a few extra bucks on the monthly utility bill, including sleeping with mittens on. But I can currently see my own breath, so I concede and get out of bed to turn the heat on. Or at least that is my plan until I see the thermostat is broken.

Maintenance can't help me at this hour, so I pull my winter gear out of my closet and dress for the Arctic. I wake up in a sweat the next morning, curled up in a blanket while wearing my winter coat, an extra pair of sweats, and thermal socks. I call maintenance and they promise it will be fixed before I get home today. Though no one is surprised when I get home from the lab and find the thermostat still broken.

Given how old these university buildings are, I wouldn't be surprised if several tenants were experiencing the same issues I was, which meant I was likely one of *dozens* of faculty, staff, and grad students who had filed a complaint. Maintenance left an orange note on my door saying that they would try to swing by again in the next few days, but for now, their "hands were tied." I would ask to stay with Maya, but she's attending a conference and visiting some of her family in Korea this week. My situation was less than ideal, but this was not the first time I had to get crafty during the winter.

When my mom told 6-year-old me we would be moving to Castle Harbor, I remember looking out the window and smiling, imagining the kind of home we would have. It would be like a Hallmark Christmas movie, made of dark red brick, the front yard covered in snow, with a fireplace where Mom and I could make indoor smores while we drank hot chocolate. My 6-year-old illusion shattered when we arrived at the small fishermen's town and began unloading our things into a renovated attic in someone's family home.

Not too long after moving to the small New England town I realized the sacrifices we would have to make to start our new life. My mom had no job, no friends or family, and no way of paying the bills. When the fall breeze turned into winter chill, my mom would crack the oven door and let it run for a few minutes after she finished cooking to spread heat through the apartment.

As I head over to the kitchen and preheat my oven, I hear a faint noise coming from outside my back window. Perched on the fire escape, I see a small tabby cat shaking.

"How did you even manage to get out here?" I open the window and bring the cat inside, snuggling it in my arms. The fluff ball responds with a deep purr, dragging its head up and down my chest. "Unfortunately, it's probably not that much warmer in here than it is out there, but don't worry. I've turned the oven on so this place should warm up soon." The cat stares at me intently as if agreeing to wait patiently for the room to warm. Perhaps this little refugee was fleeing their own freezing apartment. The small collar around its neck includes a name tag that reads, 'Penny'.

A loud, panicked knock comes from the door, causing me and Penny to jump. We weren't expecting guests. I settle Penny back in my arms and open the door. Isn't it funny how you can do so well avoiding someone in public and yet run into them in the most unlikely of places, like your own doorstep? Mason's face is flushed, and his hair is tossed in a dozen different directions as if he'd been running his hands through it. Underneath his winter coat is a red flannel that looks remarkably similar to the one I bought him for his birthday four years ago. Mason had worn it nearly every day for two weeks straight until his dad told him it was a Christmas gift and not an engagement ring and begged him to throw it in the wash. When I lock eyes with him, he appears dumbfounded, as if I'm the one intruding.

"Violet?"

"Yes." The word comes out sharp, sharper than I intended as I recognize the irony of my situation. I was starting to have that Christmas Hallmark movie moment, with snow on the ground, my little makeshift heater, and my new snuggle buddy. It felt so quintessential that I guess the powers that be felt obligated to send me a sexy flannel-wearing companion to round out the fantasy. But I was not interested in said companion. Nor the nasty gut feeling I got at the tick in his jaw or the way his green eyes dimmed slightly at my tone. "What are you doing here?"

Mason's eyebrows crease together as if confused by my question. His eyes widen as he notices Penny curled up in my arms. I look down at Penny, who is looking at him like she has never seen him in her life, jumps down, and saunters down the hall. Damn, that is what I should have done when I saw Mason. *Maybe I can just turn away and* — Mason slides passed me while muttering 'stupid demon cat' and heads in the direction of Penny.

"Hello? I did not invite you in." I cross my arms and stand right in front of him, momentarily blocking him from advancing toward my room. "This is trespassing."

Mason is undeterred as he gives me a tight smile, steps around me, and begins walking down the hall. I grab his arm and tug, keeping him from proceeding to my room. *He will not be ruining that space for me as well.* He stops, turning to face me. Only a few inches apart and my nose is filled with the scent of him — subtle hints of pine and soap that reminded me of a cozy winter day. The smell that was so addicting I once hoped to bottle it up and turn it into a candle. He smirks, and I wonder if he can tell I am smelling him. He takes a few steps forward, inching me backward down the hall.

"You literally held the door open for me."

"No, I opened the door because some *asshole* kept knocking on it like he was seconds away from being murdered." I attempt to keep my abrasive tone, but my voice shakes. Since Mason came back into my life he has felt like a stranger. But at this moment, he feels familiar, and it's freaking me out. Flashbacks of our night in Chicago run through my head. *Now that's a dangerous thought.*

"'Asshole' huh? If I had been someone about to be murdered, you would think my knocking was asshole behavior? I must say, if I am ever about to be slaughtered I don't think I will be coming here first."

I scrunch my nose in annoyance and rack my brain for a cunning response, but all I can come up with is, "Don't be a smart ass."

"Wow, more mean names. Is this always how you treat your house guests?" Mason deadpans while making another attempt to walk around me.

I slam my hand on the doorway, physically blocking him from entering my room. The slap of my palm on the doorframe gets his attention. He looks as though he is just now realizing I might not want him here. Sure, it was a little dramatic, and my hand was stinging, but I needed to make a point. He was not welcome in this apartment, and I was not just going to let him push me around. I narrowed my eyes at him and gave him my best "fuck around and find out" face. I could've sworn a flash of pride came over Mason's eyes as I continued to stand my ground. Pride mixed with something else, something that I refused to acknowledge despite that look causing a small shiver to trail down my spine.

He holds his hands up in surrender and puts some distance between us. "Alright Vi, I won't move any further. But that orange demon in there is Coach Jameson's cat. And because my life has become a series of cosmic jokes, I'm in charge of watching it over the weekend."

"*You're* cat sitting? Coach Jameson asked *you* to cat sit? I'm taking it he doesn't know about the time you killed Marge Preesley's cat?"

His cheeks flush red. "I did *not* kill Mr. Noodles. He was perfectly fine when I watched him that week. It makes perfect sense that a cat that old would have a heart attack the day his owner returns. His poor heart couldn't take the excitement. It happens." Marge Preesley had spent the rest of the month sobbing outside her porch every day, holding onto a small sweater she had knit for Mr. Noodles as a Christmas present. Mason has never been able to walk down her street since, and I never let him forget it.

"Seriously Violet, please just let me get the demon cat back to Coach's apartment and then you can get back to..."

He looks me up and down, seemingly just now noticing my parka, mittens, and beanie. Before he can comment on my ensemble, I step out of the doorway and gesture for him to proceed into my room.

He walks up to my bed and crouches on all fours. "Heeere demon kitty." He sticks his arm under the bed, and quickly yanks it back, spewing out a string of loud curses. Claw marks cover the top of Mason's hand and down his forearm. I kneel beside him and gently extend my hand. Within a matter of minutes, I coax the orange tabby out from under the bed.

I move to hand the little menace to Mason and find his attention now fixed on my mouth. I immediately have a fever.

"Jesus Violet. Why's it so cold in here?" *Shit he must be able to see my breath.*

"My heat is broken. I put in a maintenance request but apparently a lot of people are having issues, so it could be a while before they get to mine."

"A while? It's literally supposed to hit record lows tonight, there might even be a snowstorm." He walks back into the hall, toying with the thermostat as if pushing the buttons over and over again will magically fix it. *Men.*

"It's fine. As you can see, I am dressed for a snowstorm inside this very apartment, and if I get really cold I will just sleep in my oven," I joke, trying to make light of this damsel-in-distress scene he is trying to depict.

"Why don't you come stay with me? Or um, us." Knight In Shining Armor, right on cue.

"Us?"

He points toward himself and the cat that is very clearly

digging its claws into his arms in a feeble attempt to get him to release her. "Us. Me and the demon cat. It's blistering hot in Coach's apartment, so you'd defrost in no time."

Defrosting sounds incredibly tempting. Still, a weekend with him alone was out of the question. "Thanks but—"

"C'mon Violet, I can't go back knowing you're at risk of freezing to death here."

"I'll be fine. My oven's already heating up the place."

"Oh yea your lips are only slightly blue now, as opposed to when I first got here." He raises an eyebrow, a challenge. I make no move to collect my things. "Well, if that's how you are going to be then I guess we're staying." He walks into the living room and sinks down onto my couch.

"Hey, no. What do you think you are doing?"

"I told you; Coach's apartment is super hot. I had to open a window to let a breeze in and that's when the demon cat got out. If I go back, I'll have to crack open a window, and we wouldn't want Penny to get loose again now, would we?" He shakes his head. "I guess you're stuck with us here."

"So my options are freezing my ass off with you here, or sweating it off in Coach's apartment?"

"Precisely."

Maybe it's time to reconsider Violet. One of those options ends in hypothermia, which I hear is hard to come back from. I rack my brain for any excuse to stay in my apartment *alone* but came up with nothing. "Fine. Just give me a few minutes to get ready."

fifteen

. . .

Violet

three years ago

night before chicago

MASON

All set for your flight tomorrow?

> Packing as we speak! Can't wait to see you. You have no idea how BADLY I need this trip

Oof all caps. Sounds rough. Want to talk about it?

> Saw my dad today. For the first time in like…14 years. He is still as awful as I remember.

Jesus Vi, I'm sorry. If you weren't on your way,
I'd fly out there and beat his ass

Now that I would pay to see

You say the word and I'll square up

Seriously though, if you need to talk tonight let
me know

I'm fine. I just want to get to Chicago and let
this whole day go

When my mom moved us to Castle Harbor to escape my dad, I truly believed I would never see him again. Aside from finalizing the terms of their divorce, I had assumed my mom cut off all communication with him. I was wrong. Apparently, he had been sending her letters throughout the years. Evidently, it's not that hard to track down your ex-wife when the law office grants him access to files with her address. The thought that my dad knew we were in Castle Harbor this whole time makes my skin crawl. Even worse that he's now stepped foot in the town that's been my safe space away from him.

"Violet, honey. Can we at least talk before you head out to Chicago?" My mom's broken whisper hits me, and it takes everything in me to hold the water works back. There's nothing I hate more than fighting with her. The woman who has been my rock, and my hero, so many times in my life. But right now, I can't even look her in the eyes without wanting to break out in tears.

"I really don't have it in me right now to hash things out, Mom. And I don't want to say something I'll regret." I throw an extra pair of leggings into my suitcase and dig through my drawer for my favorite hoodie but come up empty.

My mom shakes her head and takes a seat on the bed so she's staring right at me. "Just tell me what happened. What did he say to you?"

"What do you *think* Dad said to me?" I spit, hearing his cruel words rush back in my head. *'I'll never know why she chose you over me. We had a good life until you came around and ruined every-thing…No one ever wanted you.'*

Unshed tears fill her eyes and she blinks them away. "He promised me things had changed. That he just wanted to make amends."

"And for some reason, you believed him? Or I guess you didn't really have a choice, did you? Not with all the money you've been taking from him." It's a low blow, and I know it. One that I regret the second it comes out of my mouth, and I know I will never be able to take it back. "Mom, I—"

"I had no choice, Violet. I know that's not the answer you want to hear, but it's the truth." She closes her eyes, takes a deep breath, and pats the empty space on the bed next to her. I drag my feet but sit down anyway, not having it in me to fight with her anymore. "I know how awful your father is, both when he's sober and especially when he's drunk. That's why I packed up our lives and brought us here. But I don't think I need to remind you of the shoe closet we used to live in. Or the fact that I couldn't afford to pay for the damn heat in the middle of the winter." She lets out a sob.

"Mom, I'm sorry. I shouldn't have said—"

"No. You are right to be upset with me. I just want you to know where I'm coming from." She grabs my hands and squeezes it. "Despite our rocky start I have never regretted our move here. But this past year has been so *hard* on me, Vi. First, it was the espresso machine breaking, then the winter storm caused a pipe to burst and the whole cafe flooded…and I couldn't exactly serve customers with no machine and a flooded room."

"You never told me any of this."

"You were away at college. I didn't want you to worry. The bank rejected my request for a loan…" She finally opens her eyes, filled with tears, and looks at me. "I hated doing it. I hate him. But I refuse to lose everything I've built."

I cup my face with my hands, not knowing how to respond. I understand why my mom felt so stuck in that moment, but what I still didn't understand was—

"Why *him*? Why couldn't you ask Melissa for help?"

"Melissa is like a sister to me, but the Hayes's have helped us enough. I couldn't have them help me with this too." She shakes her head. "That wasn't the first time he had offered me money, but it was the first time where I felt desperate enough to take it. I just remember thinking to myself, 'This is the least he could do.' I felt he owed it to me. Owed it to *us*, for all the hell he put us through."

"Why did he have to come here though? Couldn't he just mail you a check?"

"He said he would only hand over the money in person. I should've known his kindness came with conditions. It always did."

"So he asked to see me as another one of his conditions?" From the side of my eye, I see my mom hesitating. "What am I missing?"

"He asked to see *me*. And I told him I wouldn't unless he apologized to you first. I wanted you to get closure."

"Oh." Of course. That made much more sense. He didn't want me when I was a child; why would he want me now? "Well, that explains why he was in such a pissy mood."

"I am so, so sorry Violet. I should've known better. I always tried to protect you when you were little. I am still trying to protect you, *aziz*." The term of endearment rolls off her tongue. She wraps her arms around me as I sit next to her, limp from the emotional rollercoaster of today. "But you are an adult and deserve to have all of the information."

"I'll be okay. *We* will be okay" I give her a small squeeze. "We always are."

She places a kiss on my temple before moving to stand. "My sweet, strong girl. I love you so much."

"I love you too, mom." No matter how mad I am, that will never change. I stand and head for my closet. "I really need to finish packing for my trip." I nod to the half-filled suitcase on the floor.

"Oh yes. You're trip *with Mason*." She perks up, winking at me. "So, what do we think? Is it finally time to tell him about how much you love him?"

I stop in the middle of sorting through my closet. *Seriously where was that damn hoodie?* "I don't know what you're talking about."

I can practically hear my mom's eyes roll. "I am talking about the time I came home only to find you sobbing on the floor blasting 'White Horse' by Taylor Swift because you found out Mason had a girlfriend."

"I was twelve years old, and on my period. Plus, he was the only boy who was ever nice to me, and he was older. That's all it takes for a crush to form. I've moved on since. This trip is just two friends hanging out." At least that's the lie I had been telling myself.

"So, nothing happened when you went to visit him last year? During the Hockey East championships?" she pries, the question a little too on the nose. Of course I shouldn't be surprised. Persian moms are super nosy when it came to their children's love lives, and mine was no exception. The trick was figuring out the balance between providing enough details to keep them satisfied without landing you on the receiving end of a lecture and deeply unsettling look of disapproval.

"Did Monroe say something?" I stall.

"No. Was there a story worth sharing?"

I would not talk about the time Mason and I kissed. I refused to. She would also never know that I replayed that kiss in my head every night since. "Nope. Nothing that comes to mind... ugh why can't I find my hoodie!"

"All of your laundry should be there. Which one are you looking for?" My mom stands up to help me look through my closet.

"It's the one I got from our trip to Mount Greylock."

"Ah. You mean the same one that Mason has?" She has a mischievous look in her eyes.

"Does he? Well, at least we know he has good taste in outerwear."

"Oh Violet. For everyone's sake, I hope he makes a move soon and puts us all out of our misery." She chuckles to herself before heading to the laundry room to search for my sweater.

Though she was no longer in the room, her words swam around in my head. *I hope he makes a move soon…*

sixteen

. . .

Mason

three years ago

chicago

AIRPORTS ARE the 10th circle of hell which is why offering to pick someone up from the airport is a love language. Hence me now sitting in bumper-to-bumper traffic on my way to pick up Violet. I'd been wired all morning; pregame jitters are what we will call it.

Sometime between Monroe leaving earlier this morning and Violet texting me how much she was looking forward to spending time with me this weekend, I realized Monroe was right. I wanted Violet. I think it took me so long to come to this realization because I couldn't pinpoint the exact moment when our friendship turned into something more.

You always hear couples saying things like, "And that was when I knew she was the one!", but I couldn't narrow it down to one specific time when I was with Violet and thought, "Damn, this is it for me". I am too inexperienced with love to pinpoint a monumental moment like that, but I can recall dozens of little moments over the past sixteen years that felt significant in hindsight.

I can remember how natural it felt to welcome the shy little kid who had just moved to our small town when she was six years old. I can remember holding her while she cried because her mom had to miss Christmas for a new temp job at the local hospital. I can remember the sense of pride that filled my chest when she published her first research paper. I had read it at least five times and still couldn't figure out what it was about. My girl wrote it, and that was enough.

On my way to practice this morning, it became clear that the reason I couldn't figure out the exact moment I fell for Violet was because I couldn't remember a time when I *didn't* love her. And I supposed it was about time I told her that.

I make it to Violet's gate before she sends me a text saying she'll be out soon. Every romance movie tells me the guy should wait outside of the car so the girl can run into his arms, so I do. But shit, the March wind in Chicago is absolutely brutal. I check my reflection in the side mirror and run my fingers through my hair a few times as if good hair will help Violet realize she's in love with me too. Romance movies also tell me chicks fall all over a guy rocking a backward ballcap. *Maybe I have a cap in the car...* I search my backseat for a baseball cap when I see her walking toward me. I shut the car door and turned to face her. I take in her long, curly black hair that's currently being grounded by the beanie on her head. Shit, so hats are hot on girls too. Her face is flushed from the cold, and a smile takes up her whole face as she sees me. She's so stunning when she looks at me like that. Before I have time to overthink it, I wrap my arms around her waist and bring her into my chest for a soul-crushing hug, praying she doesn't notice how fast my heart is beating.

A small laugh leaves her lips, and she wraps her arms around my neck and buries her head deeper into my chest. "Well hello there. That is quite the greeting."

"Can you blame a guy for missing you?"

"No, I'm pretty fantastic. I'd miss me too."

We break apart and I grab her suitcase. I place it in the trunk and circle the car to open the door for her. "Shall we?"

I watch her face in anticipation, as she sees the small bouquet of flowers on the seat.

She looks pleased, "I feel like I should be the one getting you flowers. It's your game day after all."

Smiling like an idiot, I close her door and round the car to the driver's side. I pull out from the curb and head toward I-490.

"Yeah, but it's your first time seeing me playing for the Rangers and instead of going somewhere warm and tropical for the rest of your spring break, you chose to come to the frigid cold of Chicago." *You chose to spend it with me.*

"Well, you are on the first line. I had to see it with my own eyes to believe it." She teases.

"Yeah, it's been pretty insane. It's still a temporary thing as far as I know. During practices they'll still switch me and Kallum in and out of the lines and it's usually a game-day decision whose starting."

A few weeks ago, the coaches pulled me aside and let me know that they'd decided to move me up to the first line for our game against the Bruins. It was a ballsy choice given the guy I was replacing was Kallum Donovan — one of the most popular and established guys on the team and my alternate captain. A part of me wanted to turn it down. I had only been with the Rangers for a year and didn't want to start any tension. But a bigger part of me knew that there wasn't a point to any of this if I didn't bet on myself.

"So, I have to warn you…I was only able to book one room since the hotel was basically sold out." It wasn't an entirely true statement. I had initially booked two rooms, one for my sister and Violet and one for myself. But then one of my teammates, Connor Marshall, realized he booked a room in a hotel an hour outside of the city, so I let him take my room and figured I'd sleep on the couch or something.

She raises an eyebrow at me. "Well when you bring someone home tonight, can you point me in the direction of the closest Motel?"

My face flushes bright red and my stomach vacates my insides and plummets to the floor. I felt sick about the woman I loved thinking about me in bed with someone else. Even though I had earned that quip.

"I wouldn't do that to you. Especially not after the week you just had." I am looking at the road ahead, but I can see her head hanging down as she begins picking at her fingernails. "Do you want to talk about it?"

"About my dad?" I nod. "Nope. He's taken up enough of my time. And I won't let him ruin this weekend too."

"Fair enough. One fun-filled weekend coming up." I tease. "You excited to share a room with me? It'll be like when we were kids and you used to climb into my sleeping bag when you swore our house was haunted." I shoot her a wink.

She looks at me out of the corner of her eye, a smile forming on her face. "Yep, just like old times when Monroe and I would paint your nails while you slept."

Her mention of Monroe reminds me that we will be alone this weekend. Shit maybe she is uncomfortable with this arrangement. "I can probably stay with one of the guys if you want? I wouldn't mind at all." I would be a *little* upset, but "I don't want you to be uncom——"

She places her small hand on my shoulder and squeezes gently. "It's fine Mason really. Though if you are anything like your sister and start hogging the bed we may have a problem.

So, what's on the agenda for the next few days?" I chose not to address the bed-sharing comment…for now at least.

"Are you saying you don't have a three-page, single-spaced, bulleted itinerary mapping out all the hidden gems and tourist shops in Chicago that you want to go to? What the hell did Vermont do to you, Vi?"

"Hey, I can be spontaneous and go with the flow. Spring break is a great time for me to get work done but I am being so chill and laid back. Look at me, I'm literally in Chicago!"

"We've been planning this for months. Down to when you could fly in so you wouldn't mess with my morning practice, but also be able to make it to the game without getting stuck in traffic." Violet was probably one of the least 'go-with-the-flow' people I'd ever met. Not one single Hayes-Amin vacation took place without extensive planning and preparation. She ran all of our trips like a drill sergeant, and no one was safe from her wrath if they managed to get off schedule (see the time my parents got lost in Rome because they woke up hungover and Violet refused to be late for our tour of the Vatican so she left them behind. It was their wedding anniversary trip).

"Well, I guess this just shows that I trust you so much, I'm willing to let go of my calendars and itineraries."

I know she's teasing but my heart races anyway. Violet had confessed to me before that her need for planning largely stemmed from her hate for the unexpected. Likely a result of all the shit she and her mom had gone through before they left her dad. I didn't know how to respond knowing that she felt comfortable enough to let me take the lead this weekend. To avoid spilling my guts about all the things I'd been feeling lately, I clued her into what the rest of today would entail.

"There's honestly not a lot of time between now and when we have to get to the arena, so I was thinking we could drop off your stuff at the hotel and then grab lunch at Catering. I can introduce you to some of the other…" I'm not sure how to label

Violet. *Friend* feels derogatory now, "...friends and family of the team. They can take you to the box."

"Ooo box seats. I feel so special."

"You are special, Vi." Shit, I hope that sounded casual. "I mean, if the Hockey East Championships are any indication, you're definitely my good luck charm."

A faint blush forms on her cheeks. "Alright let's reel in any talk of good luck before your teammates catch wave. Last thing I need is to be forced to follow the team around for the next few months because of some superstitious hockey players."

My laugh fills the car. Not a bad idea, Vi.

seventeen

. . .

Mason

three years ago

chicago

"LOOKS like Hayes has someone special with him here today."
Kallum nods to the suite where Violet sits alongside the wives,
kids, and family members of the team. Warmups were always a
great time to stake out the crowd before all the fans rolled in.
"The sixth something special since he joined this team. The
ladies really will do anything for box seats."

From across the rink, I see Connor passing a few pucks with
his fellow linesmen. He must hear the jab and skates over to me.

"Should we expect a Mason Hayes hat trick tonight now that
your girl is here?"

"She's not my girl." Not sure why that was the one comment I chose to address.

Connor raises an eyebrow as if to say, 'You could've fooled me' before coming closer to me and lowering his voice. "You want her to be though. Don't you?" Connor's one of my closest friends on the team and knows the most about my personal life. He never explicitly asked me if I had feelings for Violet, though I guess he, like Monroe, managed to see the signs I didn't even know were there.

"I think tonight might be the night where I tell her how I feel." *Tell her how I feel.* Hell, I don't think I have ever said that phrase. It sounds so corny.

Connor lets out a howling laugh. "You're looking a little green man, you sure you're good to play?" I shove him, and he changes his tone. "Listen, I'm just teasing. I think it's great that you're gonna put yourself out there. Just remember no one wants to date a loser, so maybe try to get your head into the game?"

"Yeah, yeah I got it, don't worry."

Violet wouldn't care if I had a fat "L" tattooed on my forehead; it's what's on the inside that matters to her. But she very well might not appreciate my choice(s) of "bedmates". I skate over to the bench and tell myself a quick lie built on wishful thinking. *Violet won't care about your past once she hears how much you care about her and want her to be your future.*

It feels like slow motion as I watch the first puck drop, hit the ice and get scooped up by a Blackhawk's right winger. I'm quick on his back, stealing the puck and sending it flying across the ice to Connor. He attempts to bury it in the goal, but it ricochets off the top of the crossbar and deflects into the crowd. We reset and I take the face off. The puck drops and I move my stick over, sending it around the boards and behind the goal to Rowan, who scoops it up and buries it in the back of the net before the Blackhawks goalie even realizes what's happened. A chorus of 'boos' fill the arena as we lead the home team 1-0.

In the final two minutes of the first period, we are still leading while Connor skates up the ice and makes a move to shoot when he gets cross-checked from behind and goes down hard. He gets up on his own, but he's not fully there and our trainers pull him into the locker room. The Blackhawks score and we're tied 1-1 at the end of the period. Tensions run high during the second period when Kallum shoulders their captain into the boards, dodges two defensemen, and sneaks the puck right between their goalie's legs. The Blackhawks' captain skates up to Kallum and starts mouthing off about a tripping penalty. A few seconds later a full-on brawl breaks out. The refs break it up and we make it through the second period with no ejections. We manage to hang on to our lead until halfway through the third period when a miscommunication between two of our defensemen costs us big time. Tied at the end of the third we head into overtime.

This is one of the most physical games we've played all season. My shoulder's still aching from the body check that sent me flying into the boards, and my jersey is soaked through with sweat. My teammates are looking battered. Coach's shouts and commands are barely registering in my head as we set off on the ice. The game clock ticks down as the Blackhawks winger takes a shot at our net. The shot goes wide, and Connor scoops it up and sends it across our defensive zone over to Rowan. He's bustling down center ice in a matter of seconds and finds himself wedged between two Blackhawk players in their defensive zone. Their defensemen are preoccupied, trying to disarm Rowan, as I skate behind them and wait for the perfect moment to take the puck. I settle the puck with my stick and move toward their goalie. We lock eyes as I fake going left before switching the puck over to my right, and send it barreling into the net.

After a win like this, I'd be one of the last players off the ice, soaking it all in as the arena empties out and the lights start to shut off. Tonight, I'm the first to skate off into the locker room.

Our coaches texted us to meet in the hotel lobby at 10 a.m. tomorrow for our post-game debrief and discussion of our schedule for the next week. As I start heading out, a few of the players on the team do their best to convince me to bring Violet out to hit the clubs with them, but I have no intention of sharing her with anyone tonight.

I head straight to the friends and family suite, finding Violet, dressed in my team jacket. She's practically swimming in it and I can't deny that seeing her in my clothes awakens a possessive side of me. After a quick goodbye to Rowan's wife, Violet starts heading toward me.

"You take care of my girl, Tanya?" I shout from across the room as I wrap an arm around Violet's waist and bring her to my side.

"She's welcome back anytime!" A few of the other hockey wives nod in agreement.

It's not like I needed anyone's stamp of approval, but a warmth fills my chest knowing that she fits in so easily with my new life here. I turn my attention back to her. "You ready to head out?"

If she notices my possessive hold on her, she doesn't mention it. Instead, she intertwines her fingers with mine and gives my hand a squeeze. "Ready."

———

I've spent the last ten minutes sitting on the bed in my hotel room fidgeting with my hands. Violet is in the shower and I can't remember the last time I'd been this nervous. My M.O. is casual sex and ghosting anyone who asks me for more. Now, the one girl I do have feelings for is naked, less than 20 feet from me, and I have no idea what to do or how to move us out of the friend zone. If I keep it PG, will she think I'm not interested? If I push for more, will she see it as just another hook-up? Or worse, a gross come-on by her best friend's creepy older brother? Fuck, I have no idea what women want emotionally.

"You look like you're gonna be sick." Violet steps out from the bathroom dressed in an oversized t-shirt, and I am suddenly very interested with the hairs on her head and not the bare chest under her shirt.

She tosses the towel she was using to dry her curls on the bed, before pulling out a bunch of different products from her bag. I have no idea what they all do but the room fills with scents of coconut and vanilla as she runs the different gels and conditioners through her hair. I realize I'm staring at her getting ready for bed, so I look away. That feels too intimate. Instead, I take in her legs that look so soft and silky, I would give anything to get my hands on them. Fuck nowhere is safe to rest my eyes. This comforter is nice. Oh look, a loose thread.

"Is everything okay?" She looks over at me curiously.

"Yup. Just checking out this thread count." God that was pitiful.

"Ooo big NHL player cares about thread count now." She lets out a small snort and sits next to me on the bed, nudging her knee against mine. "After the win you just had, I'm surprised you're not hauling your ass to the club to celebrate."

I consider deflecting but decide to just be honest. "I wanted to spend more time with you." I ignore the tiny voice in the back of my head telling me this is a bad idea. Fuck you tiny voice. I take her small hand into mine and rub my thumb against her palm. "I missed you."

Her brown eyes soften, and I can feel her pulse start to quicken as I trail my fingers up and down her forearm.

"We text like, almost every day." She's smiling curiously at my hand on her arm. This is definitely not how I typically interacted with her.

"Yeah, but it's not the same as having you here with me." A loose curl falls in front of her eyes, and I wrap it around my finger before tucking it behind her ear. Okay, I think I am officially freaking her out. Pivot to normal conversation. "So, what's this I hear about you potentially moving to New York?"

"Ah, I take it Monroe told you? I have a couple weeks to decide whether I want to do my PhD at NYU or Bolton."

Bolton? Monroe had failed to mention that little detail. "You can't go to Bolton. That's actually sacrilegious."

"Mason, c'mon. You don't even go to Westchester anymore."

"*And?*" The rivalry between Bolton and Westchester's hockey teams was almost as old as the city of Boston itself.

"Isn't it time to let the rivalry go?" She says with mock seriousness.

"Nope. I can hold a grudge like it pays the bills. I'm surprised you didn't apply to Westchester."

"Actually, that was my top choice. I got waitlisted after the interview though. And the professor I applied to work under is like, super famous, so whoever she extended an initial offer to is probably going to take it." She shrugs. "Bolton and NYU both have really amazing psych programs either way so wherever I end up I know it's going to be great."

"Yeah, but if you move to New York you could be with me."

"Sure, but Boston's only a few hours away, so I'll still be close by. We could meet up for—"

"No Vi. If you move to New York, you could be *with me.*"

She blinks a few times and lets out a soft chuckle. "What?"

Her eyes are frantically searching mine, looking for the joke I wasn't telling. Needing to clear my head I let go of her hand and put some distance between us. "I have a confession to make. After the Hockey East Championships last year, I didn't kiss you at the party because I was drunk. I care entirely too much about you to ever treat you like that. I know we agreed to pretend it never happened, but I can't Violet. There's not a day that goes by when I don't think about it. About you."

The room is so quiet the only thing I can hear is the sound of my heart racing before Violet finally breaks the silence. The words are so faint coming from her mouth as if she's unsure whether she should voice them. "So you don't want to pretend it didn't happen?"

"No. That's not what I want at all."

She looks at me with such seriousness. "Then what do you want?"

"You. I want you."

eighteen

. . .

Mason

three years ago

chicago

I KNOW it's typically three little words that change people's lives but, in my case, it was four.

"You. I want you."

One second, I'm wondering how badly I've fucked this up and whether I can convince Connor to let me stay with him these next few nights, and the next, Violet's sitting in my lap. Her arms are wrapped around my neck and she's looking down at me shyly, like she'd been waiting for the permission my words gave her. "Is this okay?"

This is heaven. It has to be. "You're so perfect, Vi." I suddenly felt the urge to let out all of the loving thoughts I'd been having about her. A faint blush starts to form on her golden-brown skin. "Can I touch you?"

"Yes." She leans her forehead against mine as I move my calloused hands to her waist on top of her oversized t-shirt. While I was itching to explore what was underneath, I wanted to make sure we were on the same page.

"Vi, look at me. When I say I want you, I don't mean just for sex. I want to stay up until midnight watching those 90s rom-coms you love so much and wake up in the morning knowing you'll be the first thing I'll see. I want you at my games cheering me on and I want to be the first person you tell all your big wins to." I press a small kiss on her forehead. "And when the weight of the world feels like it's too much to carry, I want to be the first person you call to lean on. When I say I want you, I mean I want all of you."

A smile that could light up the whole city takes over her face and I swear time stops as she kisses my neck and whispers, "I've had this dream so many times before, it doesn't even feel real now."

"You're mine." I cup her face in my hands and close the distance between us, kissing her with every ounce of intensity I have. This draws a moan from her. *Fuck I need to hear that again.* I want that noise to be imprinted on my brain forever.

I drag my tongue across her bottom lip, begging for her to let me in as I caress her bare thighs. My cock is already hard and begging, but I intend on dragging this out. I want her so wet, aching, and desperate for me that she will never want to leave this bed. I trail my fingers up her thighs, toying with the sides of her underwear. She weaves her fingers through my hair and tugs, earning a small groan from me.

"Mason, why so coy?"

I break apart our kiss and take in her brown eyes, now filled with lust, and her soft lips that are starting to swell. Licking my own lips, I drag my gaze down her body. Violet's nipples are now fully peaked through her shirt, asking me to give them the proper attention they deserve. As I reach for the hem, I feel her stiffen slightly, causing me to pull back. "Everything okay?"

Violet removes her hands from my hair and starts toying with her fingers anxiously, avoiding my gaze. I tilt her chin up with one hand and cup her face, drawing soothing circles on her cheek.

"You're in full control here, Vi. We don't have to do anything if you don't want to." She was so confident a minute ago.

She turns her head to place a kiss on my palm before removing my hand from her face and placing it on her racing heart. "I want more. Trust me I do. I'm just feeling a little nervous…and maybe a bit insecure."

Insecure? Does this girl not see what she's doing to me? "You have nothing to be insecure about, Angel. It's taking all of my self-control not to strip you bare and fuck you right now. And if you need additional evidence of how turned on I am…" I tip my head down at my cock, fully tented in my sweatpants.

A faint blush covers her. "It's just crazy because it's you, and it's been a while since I've been with someone, and you have a lot more experience than I do."

"Are you slut shaming me?" I tease in an attempt to lighten the mood.

"No! I'm just nervous that I won't live up to what you've had in the past…" She closes her eyes and leans her forehead against mine. She sighs deeply, releasing all of her feelings into the air.

I'd never given a second thought to my relationship history (or really lack thereof) until this moment with Violet. It made my stomach pinch knowing how much it was bothering her. "I'm grateful that you trust me enough to share your insecurities." I move my hands back to her thighs and place a small kiss on her nose. "And, just so you know, I am basically a virgin. I also haven't been with anyone in a while. Not since we last kissed." I throw in a wink to play off my humiliating revelation. If she didn't know I had been pining before, she does now.

"That was almost a year ago."

"I know."

She looks awfully gleeful at my discomfort. I'd be offended, but the glee has replaced the tension as she steers us back on track. She covers my hand, the one still placed on her beating heart, and moves it to the bottom of her shirt.

I toy with the hem before smiling up at her. "Yes?"

"Yes." She sounds so definitive now, pupils dilated and locked on mine.

I strip the fabric off her and toss it across the room, hiking her closer to me. I am now face-to-face with the most perfect pair of tits I've ever seen. I press my face to her chest, dragging my hands up to cup her. I take her nipple in between my thumb and index finger, applying a bit of pressure until she's grinding on my thigh with abandon and panting my name. Her fingers find their way back into my hair, and this time, instead of pulling she's guiding me over to her unattended breast. Her wish is my fucking command. My tongue starts tracing the faint pink of her nipple before placing a kiss on the underside of her breast. I repeat this a few times before her nails are painfully digging into my scalp. I finally give in, taking her breast into my mouth and sucking hard.

"That feels so good, Mason." She slides one of her hands down my chest and starts clawing at the fabric of my sweats. "Off. I need these off."

"Such a needy little thing." I reluctantly pull away to remove my sweatpants. Violet moves her hands to tug my boxers off, but I pull away and bring her back on top of me. Without my sweats, I can feel how soaked she is through her panties.

"Fuck you're so damn wet." Before she can make another move, I take both her hands into mine, trapping them behind her back. She huffs in annoyance as I silence her with a kiss. "I have so many plans for you, Angel. So many ways I want to make you feel good. Will you let me show you?"

She grinds against me in response. "I'm happy to see some of my planning has rubbed off on you, Mason."

"I love that smart mouth of yours." I let go of her hand and move us down onto the bed. "I'll love hearing it beg." I bring my lips to hers, drawing out the kiss as I tease my hand lower and lower down her abdomen. I decide she's been teased enough and sit back up to slowly slide off her lacey underwear. I flick away a fleeting thought, wondering if she planned for this or if she always wears underwear like these. I sink to my knees in front of her and my cock throbs as I watch her thighs spread for me instinctually. Turns out I'm the one begging here. Never have I been so eager to please someone. My tongue dips out to lap up the wetness that's already trailing down her thighs.

"I haven't even touched you and you're already dripping for me." I continue my relentless teasing, kissing up and down her thighs. Coming so, *so* close to her pussy but never quite there.

A small whimper leaves Violet's throat. "Mason, I can't handle all this teasing. I need you."

*Well when she says it like that…*I grab one of her thighs and drape it over my shoulder while holding the other still. I slide my tongue up her hot slit, groaning at how good she tastes. Violet lets out a moan so loud it fills our room. I can hear how badly she needs this. I am both upset and thrilled that someone else hasn't been pleasuring this woman like she deserves. I drag my mouth up to her swollen clit, circling it with my tongue as she claws at my hair. She's a writhing mess. I place a small kiss on top of her center before teasing a finger up and down her entrance.

"Yes Mason. Yes."

My eyes are glued on hers as I slide a finger in and out of her core, my cock twitching at the obscene noises coming from her mouth. "Does that feel good, Angel?" I move my mouth to her clit, this time sucking on it hard. She bucks her hips into my face, my finger continuously thrusting inside her.

"So, so good," she purrs, sparking a sense of pride. Her

breaths became more and more hurried. I want to see her face as she comes, so I bring myself up, hovering on top of her and running my free hand through her curls.

"You're so beautiful." I place a soft kiss on her forehead before sliding another finger inside of her. I can feel her clenched down on me. I curve my fingers ever so slightly inside her until I rub against a spot that draws out a string of curses. I adjust my hand so my thumb can toy with her clit and move my lips to her ear. "Let go for me Violet. Let go." And with those words, I watch as pure euphoria takes over.

She watches me with her mouth wide open as I pull my fingers out of her gently and bring them to my mouth, moaning as I suck them clean. God, she has no business tasting this good. My eyes stay on her face as she starts to come down from her high. We hold onto one other for a few minutes before Violet skims her hand slowly down my chest to the top of my boxers. She laughs to herself like she almost can't believe the last 15 minutes. She looks up at me questioningly, like there could be a chance I'd deny her. "You own me, Violet. I'm yours."

She hums in delight as she finally takes me into her hands and my body vibrates with pleasure. Her grip on me tightens slightly as she strokes me, and I swear I see stars.

"Is this okay?" The words are barely a whisper.

"Let's just assume everything you do is okay. It's all fucking perfect." There's something so incredibly sexy about how determined she looks as she's working to get me off. The tip of my cock starts to leak, and I watch in awe as she leans her head down and licks me from base to tip. There's no way I'm going to last if she puts her mouth on me again. And I have no intention of ending this night with a blow job, regardless of how good it may be.

I drag her body up to mine, moving one hand to her nipple while the other slides down and parts her lips, giving me perfect access to her swollen clit. My thumb flattens against the bundle of nerves which I follow by a series of small circular strokes. My touch is much gentler than before.

Violet had kept her hand on my cock, but she falters when she feels me back between her legs. "W-what are you doing?"

"Taking care of you." The words are a promise. "Do you want me to stop?"

"No, I just...I've never..." She lets out a frustrated noise as I wait patiently, thumb still circling her clit. "I've never come twice. It might take awhile..."

A small chuckle leaves my mouth. "Is that a challenge, Angel? Because you know how much I love a challenge." I cup her face in my hands and place a punishing kiss on her lips, nipping and biting. I move to her jaw, then to a spot on her neck that draws out the prettiest little moans. I leave her on the bed as I pull my bag out of the closet and riffle through it for a condom. When I come back, she's on her knees waiting for me.

"I need to be inside you Violet. Need to feel you wrapped around me."

I sit back on the bed, leaning on the headboard, on full display for her. I slide the condom on and notice how antsy I feel, like I haven't done this tens of times before. My patience wears itself thin as she crawls toward me at a slow, tortuous pace. She licks her bottom lip, taking me in. She looks as hungry as I feel. But as she reaches me, she stays seated on my thighs.

"Don't go shy on me now, Angel." I lift her up and rub my cock on her clit for a few seconds before lining her up, so the tip is teasing her entrance. "Ride me."

Violet places one of her hands on my shoulder, and I watch as she uses her free hand to slowly slide me inside of her. She's so fucking tight it makes my head spin. I trace her chin with my thumb and whisper a few words of encouragement as she pauses to adjust herself. "You're doing so good. My girl looks so fucking good taking me."

She responds with a throaty moan before fully sinking herself on me. "Mason, I need you to...take me...I can't..."

"I got you, Vi." Bringing my lips to hers I leave one of my hands on her waist to move her up and down my hard length, the both of us groaning together as my cock hits her g-spot and she clenches around me. My other hand moves up her chest to tease and tug at her nipples. Her nails dig into my shoulder.

"Fuck that feels so good baby." The sound of our bodies coming together fills the room and she squeezes her eyes shut like she's trying to fight off the orgasm. I refuse to have any of that. "Violet, open your eyes."

She shakes her head in defiance, so I stop moving inside of her. Violet's deep brown eyes pour into mine and I grab her chin with my thumb and index finger bringing it down to where she can see us joined together, "Look at how good you're taking me." I feel her clench around me as I start to thrust into her again. "Such a good fucking girl." Releasing her chin, I slide my thumb back down to her clit drawing quick small circles that make her hips drive into me.

"Mason, I'm close. So close."

I knew exactly what she needed, knew that my girl needed my permission to come. She loves to boss me around out there but here, in this room, she wants to give up control.

"Come, Violet. Come right now." My demanding words are her final undoing as she lets out a low moan and clenches me so tight. I lose my own battle for control, shooting into the condom with one final thrust. I leave a trail of kisses down Violet's neck as we both come down from our orgasms, and I gently pull out of her. "You're so perfect," I mumble. To her? To myself? Who knows. I just needed to say it. Needed her to hear it.

"You're not too bad yourself." She yawns, fully spent, and wraps her arms tight around me. "I think I'll keep you… forever."

Good, I think to myself. Because she's stuck with me as far as I'm concerned.

Reaching over to the nightstand I grab one of the hotel water bottles, unscrew the cap, and bring it to her lips. I don't let go of the bottle until she's had a few sips, and I swear I hear her mumble something like 'protective asshole' under her breath. Damn right I was. Laying back down I tuck her into my chest and idly draw my hand up and down her bare back. "I never want to leave this bed."

She lets out a small laugh before lifting her head from my chest. "I'm pretty sure your pay is directly tied to you playing games."

"I guess I'll just have to bring you back to New York with me then."

"Unless I decide to go to Bolton."

"Please don't ruin a great night by saying such awful things." I tease, earning an eye roll. This feels normal. There is an ease that comes with falling in love with someone you already know so well. "You know I'm just messing around, right? I know how hard you've worked for everything and if you really want to take the spot at Bolton, I'd cheer you on the entire time."

"I know you would. You've always been there for me." Violet brings my hand, which is entwined with hers, to her mouth and presses a kiss to the back of it. "I think it's time to give the Big Apple another shot."

"Really? You hated New York every time we would visit when we were kids." I may want nothing more than to have her as close to me as possible, but I also don't want it to come at the expense of her happiness. Long-distance would suck, but Boston's only four hours away. We'd make it work.

"I'm sure. I've never been more sure of anything in my life."

nineteen

· · ·

Mason

three years ago

chicago

THE INCESSANT BEEPING of my alarm pulls me into consciousness the next morning. Violet lays sound asleep, using my arm as her personal pillow. I gently slide her off me and fail at not staring at how beautiful she looks, her curls splayed across the pillow. The girl could truly sleep through anything, and it was an ability I was always incredibly jealous of. I quickly throw on a pair of sweats and a hoodie, placing a small kiss on her head before leaving. I warned Violet last night that I would have to step out for a bit in the morning for our team meeting.

Kallum and Connor meet me in the hallway. Connor looks like the fucking Cheshire cat.

"So I take it you had a goodnight?"

"Of course he did. He scored that winning goal, didn't he?" I can't tell if there's a slight edge to Kallum's voice as he interjects, or if I'm reading into things. Though he's never vocalized it, if I was in his position I wouldn't like me much either.

"That's not the only way he scored last night." Connor lets out a howl of laughter followed by a grunt of pain as I smack him hard on the back of his head.

"Watch your mouth, my guy." I don't care if he is my closest friend on the team, I have an extremely low tolerance for disrespecting my girl.

Connor shoves my shoulder in response. "Relax man, you know I'm teasing. I'm happy for you."

Kallum snickers. "Wow, look at you Mason. Finally wearing a leash like a good boy."

I clench my jaw so hard I can feel the tension in my temples. *He gets one. One low blow for losing his spot to me.* "I do love a little choking, Kallum. Plus, Violet and I grew up together. It's been a long time coming."

"Now that's interesting. So, what, the girl next door tied you down? Are you sure you're up for that?" Kallum's smirk is starting to piss me off.

"I don't really see it as being tied down. Just starting a new chapter of my life with a person who's really special to me and has been for a while now."

"Alright, alright. I hear you. Young love. Very precious." Kallum chuckles to himself sardonically.

I open my mouth but Connor gives me a look and shakes his head. Ignoring that Connor was the one who brought up Violet, I let it go.

We enter the conference room and head toward the back, taking a seat next to our goalies who are currently in a heated discussion about whether a Hawaiian deep-dish pizza includes a layer of just pineapple or pineapple dispersed throughout the pizza. A few minutes later our coaches stroll in. Coach Patrick quickly rattles off the highlights of our game before spending the majority of the meeting discussing areas of improvement. Win or lose, there's always room to grow. The Rangers haven't gotten remotely close to the Stanley Cup in years, and I plan to be the one to change that. Although I've been on a hot streak lately, which has helped my team secure the #1 spot in our division, I know I need to keep my head on straight. It's one thing to have a solid start to my rookie year and win a bunch of games during the regular season. It's a completely different beast to be a stand-out player during the playoffs when you're up against some of the best hockey players in the league.

Toward the end of the meeting, Rowan names me player of the game. The room breaks out into a sea of cheers and chirps as he reaches into his gym bag, pulls out a tattered old cowboy hat, and places it on my head the way an archbishop would crown a king. Rowan's first year on the team, about ten years ago, the Rangers were one win away from making it to the playoffs. Rowan scored the final goal, securing their playoff spot. That's his last memory of the night as the team immediately went out to celebrate. He woke up the next morning with a hangover from hell and completely naked sans the cowboy hat on his head. From that night on the cowboy hat was gifted to the MVP of the game, along with the cautionary advice to never mix tequila, beer, and whiskey.

The meeting concluded with a reminder that we'd be playing the Canadiens and Bruins next week. The latter had a near-perfect season and would be one of our biggest challenges yet. A few of the boys discuss grabbing brunch at the hotel restaurant but I politely pass, wanting to get back to Violet as soon as possible. Before I can slide out of the room, Coach asks if I can hang back for a minute.

A wave of nerves hit me as we wait for the room to empty. The world of professional hockey could get very political, and while I knew I was doing well, I wouldn't be the first rookie who was having a killer year but got sent back down to the farm team because they needed to open up salary space.

"Is everything alright Coach?"

Coach Patrick is one of the warmest people I've ever worked with. So I'm not sure if he looks happy because he has good news, or if that's just his permanent state.

"We've been really impressed by your game lately Mason. The way you've gelled with the rest of the team, and created so many openings for us hasn't gone unnoticed."

"Thanks Coach. I'm very excited to be here." *Please, please don't send me back to Connecticut.*

"While we initially moved you up to the first line on a temporary basis, the rest of the coaching staff and I have been talking about keeping you with Rowan and Connor."

Holy shit. "Are you serious?"

"Very."

"I won't let you down, Coach. I promise."

"I know you won't." The flicker of emotion in his eyes conveys what we've all been thinking — this is going to be our year.

"Go catch up with the boys. We'll talk more about this when we're back in New York."

I rush out of the room and catch Connor waiting outside the hall for me. I pull out my phone and send Violet a quick text before giving Connor the news.

Need to talk to you.

Connor slaps a hand on my shoulder. "What was that about?"

"Coach says I'll be staying on the first line going forward, as long as I keep playing like I have been." I thought saying it out loud would make it feel more real, but it still feels like a dream I'll wake up from any minute.

"Ho-ly shit! That's amazing, let's fucking go!" Connor's yelling draws the attention of a couple other teammates, and suddenly, I'm getting showered with congratulations. We stand around talking for a bit about ways to improve for next week's game. It'd been about 3 hours since I left Violet this morning, and I am now itching to see her again. I tell the guys I'll see them later and head for the elevator. Tapping my foot impatiently, I watch the numbers on the elevator pane increase. Back on our floor, I scan my key and open the hotel room door. I glance in the bedroom and see an empty, unmade bed. A quick peak in the bathroom proves no sign of Vi.

I was gone for much longer than I had originally told her, and she was probably famished given we never made it out to dinner after the game last night. I smile to myself thinking about how delicious *my* dinner had been. Maybe if I was a good boy, I could have Violet for lunch too. I check my phone and see a text from Violet that I had missed a few minutes ago, letting me know she was in the hotel cafe getting food and would be back soon.

> Good. No need to bring me anything, I'll be having you as my snack.

twenty

· · ·

Violet

three years ago

chicago

I'M in line at the cafe, contemplating if a breakfast sandwich will hold me over when a group of Mason's teammates shuffled in behind me.

"Mason's at it again? I swear if the NHL had a record for how many girls you can sleep with in a season he'd already be in the Hall of Fame."

The comment draws a laugh from a handful of other players and my stomach sinks a little. I know Mason's history, but it doesn't feel great to be grouped in with his past playthings.

"Seriously." A different voice speaks up. "I thought I was a menace when I joined the team a few years ago, but Mason. He's next level. Dude's a legend no matter what he manages to do on this team."

"Should we take bets on how long until Hayes sends this new girl packing? I say no longer than a week."

Wow, this guy is such an asshole.

"Don't be a dick, Kall."

"All I'm saying is, I feel for the poor girl. She seems nice enough. It's a shame she doesn't realize she's being played."

"Perhaps he is a changed man." More laughs.

"C'mon, we've all been there. All-star rookie year, flying girls out to games so we can have some extra fun…celebrating after a win. Whisper a few sweet nothings so they feel grateful to be sucking your dick."

My jaw is on the floor. I know Mason wouldn't treat me like that but damn…these guys just play-by-played our evening. Maybe I didn't know the new Mason.

"I don't know, man. Sure, he has a past, but he seems pretty serious about this one."

Thank you, kind sir.

"And the hot little blonde I saw sneaking out of his hotel room yesterday morning? Is he serious about her too?"

What.the.actual.fuck. Mason told me last night he hadn't been with anyone since we last kissed. If that wasn't true, why would he feel the need to say it?

"Yeah man, she was freaking gorgeous. Had to be a lawyer or something with the fancy suit she was wearing."

I was no longer interested in the sandwich. My chest is twinging with pain, and my heart is racing so fast I feel like I'm suffocating. Even if he did sleep with someone yesterday, that was before we had gotten together. And it didn't change anything now. But why would he lie about not being with anyone?

Instead of standing there in the cafe and driving myself crazy with all the questions, I decide to go to the one person who could give me some answers. As I watched the numbers of the elevator tick up one by one, all I can think about is how an hour ago, my head was filled with Mason saying, "You. I want you." And now the only voice in my head is my father's. "No one ever wanted you."

twenty-one

. . .

Mason

three years ago

chicago

I JUMP up at the sound of the lock clicking. "Finally, I almost had to eat this $15 bag of— Vi? What's wrong? What happened?" She looks crushed. I move to bring her into my arms, but she gently pushes me away, putting distance between us. I already hate this feeling that's building in my stomach.

Violet's looking at me curiously, like she's trying to see me through a new lens. She stands up straight and looks me dead in the eye. "Did you sleep with someone yesterday morning? Before you came to pick me up."

Out of all the things that could've come out of her mouth, I never in a million years would've guessed it would've been that. "What?" I laugh a little because I am relieved. My laugh only hardens her face.

"I overheard some of the guys on the team talking downstairs. They kept making jokes about how I was another girl on your long list of hook-ups and had no idea what I was getting myself into. They mentioned a blonde sneaking out of your room yesterday. But you told me last night that you hadn't been with anyone since we kissed."

I can see the hope in her eyes, hope that this is all some big misunderstanding. Seeing her so upset and knowing that it was because of my actions (real or not) makes my heart feel like it's being slowly ripped out of my chest. I hate how she's looking at me right now, like she's waiting for me to tell her something that will give her permission to hate me. She's on the edge, waiting for me to push her. What would I even say? How could I prove to her that there wasn't anyone —oh fuck. Monroe. Monroe left yesterday morning.

"It's not what it looks like." I wince at how the words sound coming from my mouth. Like someone who knows they messed up and are trying to cover their tracks. "Let me explain—"

"Honestly you don't even need to. It's unfair of me to expect more from you. It's not like we were together at the time." Violet wraps her arms around her torso like she's physically trying to hold herself together and I want nothing more than to comfort her. But, honestly someone should be holding me at this point. Whether she realizes it or not, every time she mentions my inability to commit, it feels like a swift kick in the ribs. Is this what heartbreak feels like? Despite my own hurt I move to get closer to her, and she takes a step back, as if just being next to me causes her pain.

"Listen, I know my past doesn't inspire a lot of confidence in my ability to commit to one person and settle down. It's not something I can exactly deny." I wasn't helping my own case, but in this specific instance, I hadn't done anything wrong. Violet was going to have to stop using my past against me. How many times would I have to try and get closer before she would fully let me in? I could clear the air at this moment, but my reputation wasn't going away. I made my choices and now we would both have to live with them. Or at least I hoped she would. "But babe, the blonde that was sneaking out of my room was Monroe."

Violet's eyebrows knit together. "Monroe?"

"I invited her to come out this weekend as a surprise for you. I know how long it's been since you've seen each other. She ended up having to leave early for a work emergency." I shove my hands in my pockets unsure of what to do with them, since she won't let me touch her. Won't let me hold her and tell her things will be alright.

"Monroe. I see." She lets out a breath as she takes a seat on the couch. She isn't looking all that relieved. Was she hoping I had someone else in here?

"Why do you still seem skeptical about this?" *About me.* I would never intentionally hurt Violet, the very thought of it makes me feel sick. But in truth, I didn't know the first thing about being in a relationship. Not to mention the fact that hockey kept me away from home most days. Is that what Violet deserved? A partner who couldn't be there for her when she needed them most? How long would it be before I let her down or worse, broke her heart?

Through all my stupid and reckless moments, Violet had always been there for me, and here I was asking her to give me parts of herself when I had nothing to offer her. I know nothing about adult relationships and Violet wasn't going to be the girl I practiced on. Talking with Monroe had me in my feelings with no thoughts about how this would actually play out. And in this moment, I regret putting everything on the line. I couldn't risk losing her completely. I *wouldn't* risk it. I condemn myself to never knowing true happiness again as I say, "Maybe we should put a pause on the whole relationship thing." The oxygen turns thick and it's hard to breathe as my words settle over us.

She looks up at me from the couch. "What?"

"I would never intentionally hurt you, and there really wasn't anyone else here yesterday, but I just don't know if I'm ready for this. Ready to be in a committed relationship yet." *I don't know if I'm worthy of you yet. Or if I ever will be.*

"Are you serious?" For someone who, moments ago, wasn't surprised I would sleep with two different girls in the same 24 hours, she sounds incredulous at my stupidity. "You hadn't thought about that before you asked to fuck me?"

Another kick in the ribs. "I'm sorry. I wish I could take it all back, but I can't. I can't give you more."

"I don't even know what to say to that. I don't know what to say to you right now." Her eyes close and I lose track of how much time we spend in silence. When she finally looks up at me, her face is void of all emotion. No sadness, no anger, just indifference. That's my least favorite look thus far. "Well Mase, I think it's best I cut this trip short and head back home today."

"You don't have to leave. We can still explore the city and—" I abandon my attempt to salvage this trip as she brushes past me and starts throwing her belongings back inside her suitcase. She finishes packing in a matter of minutes and calls an Uber to the airport. I insist on helping her carry her bag to the lobby, which leaves us standing in the elevator together; the silence between us is so thick you could cut it with a knife. Violet bolts out of the elevator, with me jogging to keep up behind her. At this moment, scrambling to keep up with her, I wished she had a leash on me. I wished we were tethered, and she couldn't go without me. I wasn't strong enough to hold on, I was weak. As I watched her march through the hotel doors, I was overcome with a sense of intense dread. "Violet, wait."

She turns around to face me, her eyes still emotionless. "What is it, Mason?"

Honest to god, I feel like crying. "Promise me we're okay. Because I really can't let you leave without knowing we're okay. Or that we will be." Maybe it's an unfair ask, but Violet and I have had our fair share of fights, most of which were sibling-like squabbles, but this felt different. It felt permanent.

She stares at me for what feels like an eternity. Her car approaches as she gives me a tight-lipped smile and mutters, "We'll be okay, Mason" before turning her back to me, entering the car, and leaving me wondering whether things would ever be the same again.

twenty-two

. . .

Violet

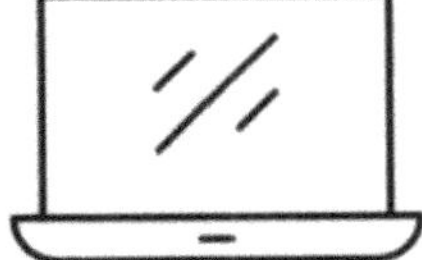

present day

THE PROS of staying in an apartment with Mason are that it's significantly nicer and also significantly warmer than my place. The con is being alone with the man who broke my heart. I'm currently failing not to stare at him as he strips off his winter coat and red flannel, to reveal a t-shirt that did very little to hide the tattoo which now covers the entirety of his left arm.

Mason decided to get his first tattoo to celebrate moving to New York and playing his first game with the Rangers. He was adamant he didn't want something super recognizable, like a city skyline. He opted for an outline of the Catskills mountains in upstate New York, in shades of black and gray that cover his shoulder. The mountain ranges on his bicep have been extended, leading into a series of forest trails and pine trees that cover his entire forearm. The artwork is absolutely stunning.

"The bottom piece is inspired by our trip to Mount Greylock, do you remember it?" Damn, he caught me staring.

"Do you mean the trip where you and your dad convinced the moms, me, and Monroe that the top of the mountain was only a two-mile walk when it was actually *five*? In the dead of winter, no less." Monroe and I had clawed our way to the top. The only thing motivating us forward was plotting how we would shove Mason off the mountain as soon as we caught up to him.

"It was 2.5 miles."

"Yeah one way."

"Alright fine, we may have overexaggerated how quick of a hike it would be. But it was worth it in the end."

My final hundred steps to the top were fueled by nothing but rage and spite, but as soon as I stepped onto the peak of the mountain, I felt time stop. From the top, we could see miles and miles of valleys covered in the most beautiful sheet of white snow. The pine trees surrounding us looked straight out of a movie, and it had been one of the most magical things I had ever seen. I was so enamored by the view I couldn't bring myself to leave, even after the parents and Monroe headed back down to our cabin. I just sat there looking at the horizon. Mason had stayed with me. By the time we headed back down, my anger was forgotten and we filled the hike with our normal banter and jokes. Everything was so much easier back then.

"I got the forearm tattoo a few months after I was forced to retire." His voice is so raw and vulnerable I can't help but lock eyes with him. "It was hard for me to really remember a lot of happy memories at the time. Especially since so many of my happy memories were tied to hockey and well..." He lets out a self-deprecating laugh. "Our time sitting on top of that mountain was one happy moment I kept thinking of. So, I decided to get it tattooed as a reminder of better days."

I didn't know what to say to that. I also could use a reminder of better days, but I couldn't say that out loud without unraveling in front of him.

"What is it Vi?" He walks over to where I'm sitting in the living room and leans against the loveseat across from me.

I'm picturing a tattoo of my own, scrawled across the sleeve of my arm so I never would forget it — You are good enough, Violet. You are.

"Nothing."

"Vi, I know that look. You're holding something in." He sits in the chair across from me and leans in, now at eye level with me. He didn't say it, but the expression on his face was clear. *No more avoiding this.*

"I don't know if I can talk about this Mason. I only managed to keep myself together after spending all last year building myself back up — piece by piece. I don't have it in me to do that again." I bring my knees to my chest and wrap my arms around them as if to stop my heart from being ripped out.

A pained look covers his face. "Violet, I never meant to hurt you this badly. I thought I was doing the right thing. The guys were teasing me all weekend about how I wasn't a relationship guy, and it's not like I could deny it. Right before Monroe left, she warned me not to hurt you. Warned me to protect your heart with everything because that's what you deserved. And that's what I thought I was doing. I was in my head and scared that I wouldn't be what you deserved. Scared that I would hurt the most important person in my life. When you came into the room, tears in your eyes, thinking I had lied to you, I couldn't handle it. I couldn't handle knowing I had caused those tears. So I decided to end things before they ever really started. I thought I was protecting you."

"And I wasn't adult enough to take that risk myself? You just decided it was best to walk away rather than letting me choose to trust you?"

"I can't say with certainty that it was the right thing, but it felt like it at the time. And even now, I think I still feel that way. I have always cared about you. I have always loved you; there will never be a moment where I don't. But I hurt a lot of people that I loved while I was injured, and a part of me is glad you weren't a casualty in that disaster." He takes a breath, and it looks like the first real breath he's taken since we ran into each other.

"Violet, I feel like an entire piece of my heart has been ripped out these last three years. Being shut out killed me. I never thought that it would come so easy for you."

"You think it was easy for me?"

"Wasn't it?" His eyes lock with mine, glassy as if holding back tears.

"Letting you go was one of the hardest things I'd ever done," I confess.

"Then why did you do it?"

I suck in a deep breath. If he was able to bare himself to me like this, despite how much it was hurting him, couldn't I do the same? "I was in a rough headspace when I came to Chicago. I had just seen my dad, and he said some awful things. How he never wanted me, how I ruined his life, how no one would ever love me. As much as I wanted to shrug off his words…they kept playing in my head. Especially the ones about how no one would ever love me."

Mason surges forward a bit and then sits back down like he was about to walk out the door and annihilate the man and then thought better of it.

"We had that amazing night together, and I thought, 'This is it. I've finally found someone who wants me'. But then you pushed me away and I, well, I meant it when I said I would come back. Please know that I did. I was healing and focusing on myself, and then suddenly, a week of not talking to you went by, then a month. And it hurt like hell to ignore you, more than I can put into words. But I thought I was protecting myself. So, I shut you out, and eventually, getting out of bed wasn't so painful.

You thought losing me would hurt too much, so you didn't even try. I thought being your friend while mourning what we could have been would end me, so I just didn't."

"I really thought I was doing the right thing Violet. I'm so sorry."

I move my head up to meet his eyes. "I'm sorry too. For cutting you out of my life. You didn't deserve that."

He hesitates for a moment. "So uhm— how are you? How is school?" Mason laughs at his own attempt to lighten the mood. His attempt to bring us back to normalcy is sweet, though heavier than he could have known.

"I'm…still healing. I had a particularly rough first year. I almost dropped out actually." I've never said those words out loud to anyone. Not even my mom or Monroe knew the full extent of how bad things had been. How close I had come to giving up on my dreams.

Concern covers Mason's face. "Are you serious? What happened?"

I rehash the entire tragedy that was my first year of grad school. I've only scratched the surface when I see the anger start to build in Mason's eyes. When I tell him about the time my old mentor essentially alluded I was a diversity hire, rage fills his eyes and I watch his hands open and close into fists.

When I finish recounting how she took credit for my whole project and published it without me, Mason just stares at me in disbelief. "Jesus Violet. I can't believe all the shit you had to go through."

"As the saying goes 'Don't meet your heroes.'" I roll my eyes.

"You're not still working with her, are you?"

"No. No. After I found out about her publishing my work, I finally snapped. I set up a meeting with the chair of our department and disclosed all the events that went down. The good news was I had already shared multiple drafts of that same paper with other professors for their feedback, so they were able to vouch for me. The department asked her to reach out to the journal and have me added to the article as an author, which she did. Reluctantly. I joined Bethany's lab after that. And things started to finally turn around for me."

Mason rubs his thumb in soothing circles on the back of my hand. "I wish I could've been there for you."

"It wasn't just you I shut out that year. My mom, Monroe. I couldn't face anyone. I just felt like I was being so…ungrateful. Like so many people would give anything at a chance to chase their dreams and here I was, living mine and miserable about it. I spent my whole first year being ripped apart day by day and not even realizing it until I couldn't recognize myself anymore. It took me a whole year to regroup and feel grateful again. That was the only thing I could focus on. And if I'm being honest there are still some days where I find myself unable to let go of all the hurt."

"I can't imagine how hard that must have been."

I shrug, ready to take my heart off my sleeve and put it back in my chest. I gesture to him, hoping to redirect the conversation. "I'm not the only one with shit worth moping over. I was so sorry to see that you had to medically retire."

"Yeah, thanks. I went through a similar thing, deep down wanting to reach out to people but not being able to bring myself to do it. At the time it felt easier to shut them out than to have to deal with their pity."

We sit in silence for a while, just holding hands and reflecting. I had always defaulted to putting up walls when I got hurt, but I never considered that my own defense mechanism could also hurt me. In an effort to protect ourselves from pain, here sat two very damaged, lonely, people.

I break the silence ready to bury the hatchet and bury myself in a Mason-hug. "Do you think you can forgive me? For putting up a wall between us. For letting my insecurities get the best of me, and for not being there for you when you needed me?" The thoughtful look on Mason's face is replaced with a smile. "Yes. If you can forgive me for doing the same."

"Done." I stick my hand out to shake on it.

Mason grabs my hand and gives it one firm shake.

I was thinking about where to take our conversation next, when I let out a huge yawn.

"You can take the guest room." Mason points to the door to the right of the kitchen.

"Are you sure? You're already doing me a favor by letting me stay here, and I don't want to impose."

"I'm sure. I already set your bags in there earlier."

"Oh, great thanks for doing that…um I guess I'll go get ready for bed then." I head toward the door and enter the room, calling out, "Goodnight." Shutting the door behind me I try my best not to think about the fact that Mason is only two hundred feet away, and even that feels like too much distance.

twenty-three

. . .

Mason

I WAKE up and decide to get a head start on making breakfast. Clearing the air with Violet opened my eyes to some changes I desperately needed to make. I didn't want to be the Mason who never made an effort to check in on his friends or call his parents back. Or the Mason who took things, or people, for granted. I didn't want to be the Mason who never took any of his relationships seriously to give himself an out. I wanted to be better. For myself, for those I loved. I couldn't change the past, but I could try to move forward.

Violet was making changes too, it seemed. One of the hardest parts about seeing her again was realizing that the person I had once known better than I knew myself was a complete stranger to me. She'd always had difficulty letting people in, trusting them. And I hated that she was more guarded around everyone now— the walls she had up were now covered in barbed wire. I wanted to be the guy she once trusted but without all the commitment phobias. The one person she let past all her defenses. Maybe one day she would share her lunch with me again.

Penny makes an excited noise, cueing me that Violet has entered the dining room.

"I ran into your mom recently. She says 'Hi.'"

I couldn't help but feel a twinge of guilt. Another relationship I needed to fix. *Add it to the list.* "You went back home?"

"Yup. Just a little day trip to Castle Harbor, though both of our moms acted like it had been *years* since I'd last seen them."

"Dramatic as always, those two."

"And meddlesome." She grumbles to herself.

"Oh?"

"They staged a whole intervention. About how we weren't talking to each other anymore. They'll be glad to take full responsibility for our makeup."

I'd like to say I was surprised but, "That tracks. I kinda got my own version of an intervention a few years ago."

"Oh? Do tell."

"I'm sure it was the same as yours. Ya know the usual, 'You need to fix things…apologize…' all that good stuff."

"And?"

"What makes you think there's an 'and'?"

She gets up from the table and leans her hip against the counter, now only a few inches from me. Penny saunters off, probably late for some demon cat seance. "C'mon just tell me."

My attention goes back to the eggs in my pan. "Part of the intervention may or may not have included pictures of how happy I was before our fight and how miserable and tired I looked at the time."

Violet closes her eyes and covers her mouth, a suppressed laugh escaping. "I'm sorry. I shouldn't laugh." She breaks again, bursting into a fit of giggles. "Interventions are a serious matter."

"Yes, it was very serious when they pointed out the growth of the bags under my eyes and how I wasn't filling out my shirts like I used to. Your mother poked at my gut for emphasis Violet."

She's in tears now. "I'm not...I promise...I'm laughing at them. And how extra they are."

"Mhmm sure, Vi."

"Well, if it makes you feel better, I'm like 90% flattered."

"And the other 10%?"

"I feel bad that they were picking on you. I know I was equally a mess at the time."

"Shut up there's not a single moment where you didn't look beautiful."

My words make her blush, but she pivots from the compliment. "Well since we're sharing embarrassing stories, I had a pretty awful date like...a year ago. Some random guy I matched with on Bumble. We agreed to meet at some nice-ish restaurant in the North End." She pulls out a water bottle from the fridge before sitting on the countertop next to me.

She eyes me, looking for confirmation that it's okay to continue her story. I wasn't thrilled to hear a story about her on a date, but friends talked about this sort of thing. I give her a smile, encouraging her. "Nothing super fancy, but you can still imagine my surprise when he showed up in a New York Rangers jersey."

Ha. I liked this guy. "No way. Near Bruins territory too? That's ballsy."

"Oh, it gets better. You wanna take a guess whose jersey he was wearing?"

"Hmm, maybe Connor's?" I try my best to hide the smile.

"Yours." She rolls her eyes. "I did my best to ignore this, but then he asked where I was from and I was stupid enough to say Castle Harbor."

I have a shit-eating grin.

"Listen, I know. Rookie mistake. Trust me you have no idea how much I wished I could take it back. But anyway, he spent the rest of the night asking if I knew you, if I ever saw you around town, and whether I could get him an autographed photo for his man cave. I debated climbing out of the bathroom window to escape."

"Sounds like a solid plan to me. Did you?"

"No, I just slid out of the backdoor like any self-respecting person would."

"You ditched my number one fan? That's cold."

"I can probably find his number if you want to meet him. I'm sure he'd be much happier to hear from you than me."

I turn off the stove and Violet goes back to sitting at the dining room table as I place the tomato, sausage, and basil frittata on some plates and bring them over. "Careful, the bottom's hot," I caution as she reaches over to help me.

"Is this your mom's recipe?" She blows on her fork before taking a bite, answering her own question.

"You know it."

"So how exactly did this whole coaching thing happen?" Violet asks.

"I needed a job, and the one thing I knew like the back of my hand was the game. The position is technically provisional pending how much I'm able to help the team. Lots of people would be better for this job, so I gotta prove my worth in these next few games. "

Violet shakes her head "That, my friend, sounds like a classic case of imposter syndrome. Trust me I would know. I'm a grad student, it's basically a requirement for us to have it."

"What are you talking about you're insanely qualified." Frankly, I couldn't imagine anyone who deserved success more than Violet. The moment she set her mind on something she would give it her all, often give her whole self, to achieving that goal.

"Yeah, but that doesn't stop someone from feeling like an imposter. It's actually pretty common among people who *are* really qualified. You feel like you got lucky, and you don't really deserve your success or that you've somehow tricked other people into believing you're super smart and capable." She looks down nervously and fidgets with the hair ties on her wrist for a moment before continuing, "I've definitely had a lot of moments where I've struggled with it, especially during my first year with all that...drama that went down, but I think you just have to remind yourself that you have worked really hard and to not listen to the negative voice in your head."

I was in complete awe of the woman in front of me. This wasn't the first time, and I knew it wouldn't be the last. The way she managed to fully encapsulate what I was going through while also making me feel less alone meant everything to me. "You're pretty incredible do you know that?"

"I mean obviously." She winked, brushing off my words.

"I'm serious Vi. In case no one has told you how amazing you are recently. I want you to know it."

A small blush creeps up her neck as she gazes down at her soup, "Thanks, Mason."

The sound of a series of texts pulls us out of the moment abruptly. Violet takes a moment to check her phone. "Speaking of being a grad student, my research assistant got locked out of the lab. I gotta go help her. Oh, and my landlord says my heat is back on. Mind giving me a ride back to my place? I'll owe you one."

I'm bummed she's leaving so soon, but I'll happily take a Violet favor to use down the line. A favor I had a feeling I'd be cashing in on soon.

twenty-four

. . .

Violet

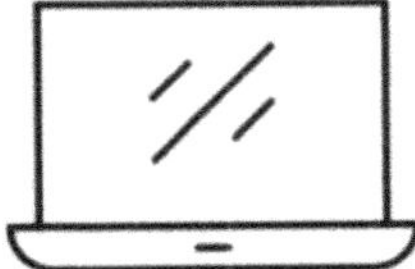

I START to unpack my overnight bag when my mom calls me. She doesn't bother with pleasantries and gets right to asking whether I've spoken to Mason. Evidently, her and Melissa had already started prepping for our annual Christmas dinner and need to know whether we had made up so they could plan accordingly. I could practically see her jump up and down with excitement as I relay the news that Mason and I had indeed talked.

"So, you two fixed everything then?" My mom screams into the phone over the sound of customers and espresso machines in the background.

"Yeah, we're friends again." *Just friends* I reiterate to myself. It was a necessary reminder given I had a not-so-PG-13 dream about Mason last night. One that featured him laying me out on the dining room table while he…enjoyed his meal. And I'm not talking about the frittata he made for us this morning. I woke up covered in sweat from the words dream Mason had whispered in my ear, dazed and confused about what the hell had just happened. I had no explanation as to why my brain chose to plague me with such dreams. I blamed it on the fact that he was sleeping a couple hundred feet away. And that I was touch deprived.

"Friends?" The disappointment in my mom's voice leaks through the phone. "You're really telling me you don't feel anything else?"

"Well, I wouldn't say that…" A part of my heart has always belonged to Mason even in the years we were apart. "We just don't want to rush into things, so we're testing the waters as friends."

"So should I tell Mel to expect you both for Christmas?"

"I wouldn't go that far. I wasn't the only reason he was avoiding Castle Harbor." Monroe had hinted that Mason's reluctance to go back home was spurred over a bad fight between him and his dad, at the time I figured she was exaggerating. Mason and his dad were practically inseparable and always had been…or at least that's what I had thought. But when Mason chose to move to Boston instead of Castle Harbor following his retirement…I realized another thing we now have in common next to our shunning skills —strained relationships with our fathers.

"You can put me down for sure though."

"Sounds good. Everything else going okay?"

"Yeah same-old same-old. Busy with teaching. Trying to keep my head above water in my stats class. Scrambling to find time to analyze the data I've spent hours collecting."

"You sure you're doing okay?"

"I'm being pulled in a million different directions, but that's the standard grad student experience." I shrug though she can't see it. "Nothing, I can't handle."

"And Bethany…she's good to you?" There's a protective

edge in my mom's voice. I'll never forget how enraged she was when I told her some of the things I had endured my first year.

"Yeah, she's great. She supported me in applying for this big fellowship. Hopefully I'll hear back about it soon."

"Well, I'm crossing all my fingers and toes for you…I gotta run, but I love you loads, *aziz*."

"Love you too, Mom."

I feel the sudden urge to call Mason and debrief my day. In addition to it being way too soon to resume bff behavior, I also realize I had lost his contact when I changed my number a while back. Apparently, Mason had also realized this.

Today, 4:13 p.m.
To: Violet Amin (<u>aminv@westchesteru.edu</u>)
From: Mason Hayes (<u>mhayes@westchesteru.edu</u>)
Subject: Phone Number

I figured friends should have each other's phone numbers 617-993-1670 (or you can just unblock me).

p.s., Penny has spent the last hour rotating between staring at the door waiting for you to come back and glaring at me as if *I'm* the problem.

-M
--
Men's Ice Hockey Assistant Coach
Westchester University

I skip the email response and text him instead.

> Hey it's Violet. Relax, I would never block you. I just changed my number.

MASON

Well damn

Some poor stranger's out there reading SOS
messages about me being mauled by a cat

Followed by images of said mauling

You two seemed fine when I left this morning

Yes, but now the little menace realizes
you're gone

So, she's decided to take it out on me

Wow you went from demon cat to little menace.
Maybe Penny will turn you into a cat person

Unlikely

Btw are you free Friday night?

I should be, why?

We have a game against Boston College. Any
interest in cheering me on?

Can you cheer for coaches? Is that a thing?

You can totally make it a thing

Sounds fun. I'm down

Great I'll drop the tickets off at your office

twenty-five

. . .

Violet

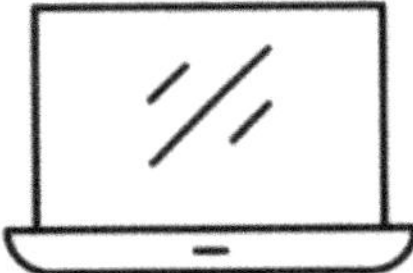

I **ENTER** Westchester's Ice Arena and walk to my seat, taking in the massive crowd in front of me. Nearly the entire student body is here tonight, which is unsurprising given Westchester is a hockey school through and through. Maybe that was a byproduct of the university being in one of the biggest hockey-loving cities in the nation, or maybe it was just due to the fact that our football team had one good season in the last 20 years, and we were all desperate to root for something worth our pride. I sit right as both teams come out onto the ice for warmup.

It was always exhilarating seeing Mason in his uniform, but nothing could prepare me for Mason in a suit. From the looks of it, Mason had already stress-removed his tie and unbuttoned his collar before his players hit the ice. After filing into the coaches' section, he shrugs off his jacket to reveal a button-down gray dress shirt that clings to his muscles like a second skin. It was probably 55 degrees here, and the man was stripping down like it was the middle of summer. A stranger settles in the seat next to mine and I do my best to pretend that I wasn't just ogling the coach. "Vi, is that you?"

I turn to see a face I almost didn't recognize due to the new beard and the man bun on top of his head. "Mikey?"

A wild smile comes over his face, likely realizing I'm not here for my interest in collegiate sports. "It's good to see you Vi. Hayesy told me you two made up."

I never understood why the default for hockey player nicknames was to take a part of their last name and attach a 'y' at the end. "Yup. We're back to being friends again."

"Ah. *Friends*. Right."

"You sound like my mother. Seriously. Just friends."

"Riiight. Friends wake up extra early every morning to buy their friend's chai lattes."

"I didn't realize buying someone tea was such a big deal."

"For you it is." He winks. "I ran into your mom and Melissa yesterday. The two seem really excited about the possibility of future developments."

"Future developments are for the future. For now, just friends."

"Oh, c'mon Vi. You're telling me after nearly two decades of pining you two are just going to…stay friends?"

"I forgot how annoying and meddlesome you are." I roll my eyes, taking a large swig of my iced Coke.

"I think you mean 'charming' and 'caring.'" He snickers.

"Whatever helps you sleep at night."

"Usually a good book and a rub-n-tug. But let's say I had a bet going with Bradon on whether you two would get together before or after the New Year. Who do you think would have better odds of winning?"

Bradon was the final member of Mason and Mickey's trio. He had grown up in Rockport, a town just north of Castle Harbor, and had been one of Mason's biggest rivals. The two absolutely hated each other growing up but playing on the same team in college seemed to squash the feud. The three of them were practically inseparable after Mason's freshman year.

"Dalton Michaelson—"

"Uh-oh, not my government name."

"There will be no bets about my relationship status. On second thought, I'll wager $50 for after New Year's and happily take your money."

"Alright then. Keep your secrets. Just remember when it comes time for the wedding, I'm gonna be the best man."

"Oh please, you—" I'm cut off by the arena lights dimming and a highlight reel coming on the jumbotron.

The game starts off slow. Both teams look sluggish on the ice and the crowd's only bragging right is that Westchester is leading with attempted shots. Mason leads the team back up the hallway, and as they settle into the bench, I can faintly make out his lips moving. Whatever he says lights a fire under their asses because five minutes into the second period, Jake scores a goal, and the arena erupts. My first impression of Jake wasn't great, and he still complains about how his tutor is a 'literal drill sergeant' but he's been making progress, and it makes me happy to see him get to play.

Boston College tries their best to retaliate against Jake's goal, but they mishandle the puck and a few seconds later, Westchester scores again. My eyes are locked on Mason as he screams with excitement from the bench, Coach Jameson patting him on the back in celebration.

We are up 4-0 at the start of the third period, and the BC players are getting agitated. While I've spent almost my entire life watching these brutes annihilate each other, I'm still a little shocked at the body checks being dished out. Two of our players are limping for god's sake. I'm thankful I wasn't there when Mason was seriously hurt.

A BC player illegally rushes one of our players, knocking him into the boards head-first.

"C'mon ref open your fucking eyes! That was a dirty hit!" The crowd follows my jeer with a round of 'boos' as the ref refuses to call a penalty. I can see Mason is equally as upset and Coach Jameson makes a move to talk to the ref. I turn to Mikey to voice my frustrations. "What a rat."

He's nodding his head and grinning. "I forgot how fun it was sitting next to you during games. All that anger at such a young age. It was as impressive as it was terrifying."

"It has been a while so I'm a little rusty."

"Remember when our parents saved up to get tickets to the Bruins Canadiens game and you nearly got us kicked out?"

"Just because *one* security guard gave us a dirty look doesn't mean we were about to get kicked out."

"And the drink that was spilled on the Canadiens' fan?"

"An accident. Obviously. A Coke at TD Garden costs like 20 bucks, why would I intentionally spill it?"

He shakes his head as we turn our attention back to the ice. Westchester answers the hit with a few of their own, and by the end of the game, the players look exhausted as they celebrate their shut-out win.

"Are you coming out for drinks with us?" Mikey asks as we wait for the group in front of us to move out of the aisle.

Mason hadn't mentioned anything to me. "I don't want to crash your guys' night."

"You're not crashing, I'm inviting you."

"Sure, why not."

———

Cornwhall's is packed to the brim with undergrads, so we decide to head to O'Malley's instead. The local dive bar is a hot spot for grad students due to its close proximity to campus and discounts for Westchester staff. They are also one of the few bars around that carded, which meant no awkward run-ins with any of my students. Mikey and I secured a table near the bar and pool tables. So far, he was two Bud Lights and a tequila shot in.

"What happened to the days where all it took was a single beer to get you buzzed?"

"I'm older now Vi. And no longer conditioning for hockey season. You keep buying me beers and you'll have to apply for another grant to pay the tab."

"I already told the waitress you'd clean the toilets to cover your bill."

"I've done worse for less, Vi." He winks while chugging the remains of his second beer.

I roll my eyes before scanning the bar. I am surprised Mason isn't here yet. I see a group of guys walking in the front door, Carlos following closely behind.

"Hey Carlos!" I wave my hand in his direction.

Carlos scans the crowd at the sound of his name and a smile breaks out when he spots me. He heads to our table.

"Violet! I feel like I haven't seen you in forever." Carlos gives me a small hug and his hand lingers on my waist before he settles in the chair next to mine. "I didn't know you drank anything other than my chai lattes."

"Ugh I miss your chai lattes. I've been busy running participants this week and haven't had time to drop by, but I'll definitely be around next week. Carlos, this is my friend Mikey. Mikey, this is Carlos, my favorite barista and manager of the Beanery."

Mikey sticks out one hand while flagging the waitress over with the other. "Nice to meet you, man."

"So how do you two know each other?" Carlos gestures between us.

"We grew up together in Castle Harbor. Just outside of Boston." I clarify.

"I still can't believe I haven't made it up there after living so close. How do I book the official Violet Amin tour?"

Mikey gives me a knowing look. "Yeah there's a lot to love

about Castle Harbor. Including the people. Right, Vi? Remember the love?"

"Don't start," I warn him before turning to Carlos. Carlos has always been a flirt, but he doesn't mean anything by it. The charm is good for business. "Castle Harbor's a super small town. Everyone knows everyone. We're all one big, dysfunctional family."

"I grew up in Phoenix and think I had a neighbor named Ray? Oscar? Our community wasn't all that close. So, what brings you two here tonight?"

"Celebrating the Westchester win against BC. Cornwhall's was undergrad central, so we decided to come here."

"Since when are you into hockey?" The surprise in Carlos' voice pains me a little. Grad school Vi is not as vibrant as she used to be. The idea of me engaging in any social activities would probably surprise the man who only sees me huddled in a coffee shop every day.

"Uh, since always. I grew up watching it. I think most kids in the greater Boston area do. I stopped following it for a little while...but now I'm getting back into it. Mikey actually used to play for Westchester a couple years back." I wait for Mikey to contribute something, but he seems content just sitting there, almost done with his new beer.

Carlos tries to keep the conversation alive. "Oh that's cool. So that's why you went to the game tonight? Reliving the old glory days?"

Mikey perks up, presumably at the opening to bring up Mason again, and offers, "Something like that."

Carlos makes to slide off the chair. "Looks like you've both made your way through your drinks. Why don't I grab us some more, Mikey another beer? What about you Violet?"

"Hmm. I'd love—"

I'm cut off by the sound of a pint glass gently being set on the table in front of me, my eyes catching the tattooed arm attached.

"Downeast Cider. Right, Vi?"

Mikey looks pleased like he'd hoped this would happen. I turn around slowly and see Mason standing behind me. He still has on the gray dress shirt from earlier, with the sleeves rolled up to his elbows. I have the sudden urge to run my fingers over the exposed tattoo.

"Um yes. That's what I wanted. Thanks."

"Carlos, good to see you again." Mason's tone suggests otherwise. "Sorry I couldn't grab you a drink. My hands were full." He gestures to the beer in his hand and the cider on the table for me.

"Don't worry about it. I was just heading over to the bar—" Someone shouts Carlos' name and I look up and see the group of guys he came in with playing pool. "I should probably get back to my friends. I'll see you later Violet."

Mason slides into Carlos's seat taking a big sip of his drink. "So, what did I miss?"

twenty-six

. . .

Violet

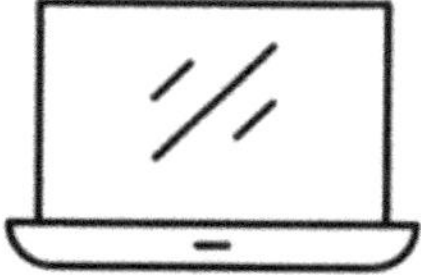

FOR A MOMENT it feels like we're all teenagers again. The only thing missing is Monroe. A big part of me wishes she could be here right now, if only just to help balance out the testosterone.

"Dude, I can't lie. It felt kinda weird being back in that arena. Like I was walking into a time capsule." Mikey takes a swig of his beer before continuing. "Does it feel weird coaching in the same place you used to play for?"

"It was definitely an out-of-body experience at first. And honestly, I don't know if I'll ever fully get used to it. There are moments when I still feel like I should be the one on the ice, and not even because I want to play, but because that's all I've known."

"I'm sure you want to go out there and show 'em how it's

really done. You say the word and I can call up Bradon and see if he's down for some 3 on 3," Mikey jokes.

Mason rolls his eyes. "Between my busted head and the fact that neither you nor Bradon have played in years, I don't like our odds."

"What are you talking about? We can take these Westchester kids. Bradon and I are in a beer league now so we're ready whenever you are."

"No way. Since when are you two playing hockey again?"

"Mmm, I think we started the team maybe like six months ago? We're looking for a coach if you want to pull double duty."

"You guys would be a bigger pain in the ass to coach than my current players."

Mikey smirks, taking another swig from his beer.

"I think you're selling yourself short," I interject. "Your players seem to respond to your coaching. I feel like every time you stepped up, their game got better."

Mason looks sheepishly at his beer. "Thanks Vi." Genuine compliments have always made Mason uncomfortable. And he's so cute when he's uncomfortable.

"That hit from #23 was dirty, though. I guess I can't be too surprised given we were playing Boston College."

Mason's eyes widen as he sips his drink, nodding vehemently. "Yeah. It was super dangerous. If it wasn't for Coach Jameson holding me back, I probably would've gone off on the refs."

One of the things I've always loved about talking hockey with Mason that he never makes me feel inferior or like I didn't know what I'm talking about. Some guys have such a complex when it comes to a woman sharing her opinion on the sport. But Mason always listens, even when we have different opinions.

"Whatever you couldn't say to the refs, Violet certainly did." Mikey winks at me.

Mason turns to me. "I thought I heard a ladylike, 'Open your fucking eyes ref.'"

"No, you didn't."

"So, it was someone else who called the BC player a rat?"

I blink. Okay fine. Maybe those were my exact words. "How do you even know that was me?"

"Vi, even in a sea of people, I'll always recognize your voice." Dammit, I hate when he casually says something romantic. Fate also did seem to bring us together. That and Mason's persistence. We could've spent the next however many years at Westchester ignoring each other's existence, but Mason refused to have that.

"Eesh man, that was a little too cheesy for my taste. But comments like that bode well for my wallet." Mikey throws a teasing wink in my direction. He either has a death wish or there is something in his eye.

Mason scrunches his eyebrows together. "Huh?"

"I was telling Vi—" I swiftly kick Mikey in the shin while innocently sipping my cider.

"Fuck wh—," Mike catches my challenging gaze, "—would ya look at the time? I have a sex appointment with that blonde over there. See ya love birds." Mikey jumps off the stool before I can shatter his other shin.

"I don't know how you didn't strangle him all the time when we were kids." I huff.

Mason is clearly curious about Mikey's abrupt departure but chooses to leave it alone. "His persistence and tendency to be a jackass is part of his charm."

Mason leans in closer to whisper something about Mikey striking out across the bar, and I'm immediately hit by *him*— the smell of pine needles and soap. My eyes trail down his neck and exposed collarbone, and my body feels warm. It's been a while since I had a man in my bed and man would I— *Whoa there Vi. We are not going there. Get a grip woman.*

As I recover from my momentary blip, I realize Mason has caught me staring. He takes this as permission to return the favor and takes me in fully; I feel my heart racing as his eyes trail down my multicolored blue sweater. I feel frozen in time and space as he tucks away one of my loose curls.

Mason's green eyes are nowhere near my eyes when he says, "Don't tell Coach Jameson, but I was entirely too distracted by the fact that I could hear you out there tonight."

"Sorry for all the heckling. I know I can get carried away during games." I'm not sorry. I hope that ref lays in bed thinking about what a turd he is.

"That's not what I meant." His hand trails down my arm as he entwines our fingers together.

He presses his lips to my ear. "Knowing you were in the crowd always lit a fire under my ass when I was playing. I felt the same energy today when I was coaching."

Objectively what he is saying isn't sexual, but in a whisper, it feels explicit. Time to throw some water on this fire he's stroking. "Well, I'm glad you invited me. It felt like old times again."

He straightens, "I hope that's a good thing. Although I did subject you to Mikey for a few hours so maybe I should be apologizing instead."

"Yeah, on your knees Hayes." *Fuck that was definitely sexual.* I take two large gulps of my cider and let the alcohol wash over me. It's funny how drinking calms you down enough to not say something stupid, only to fuel you to say the next stupid thing with abandon. The cider rushes straight to my heart as I say, "Mikey and Bradon have a bet about how long we remain platonic."

Mason raises an eyebrow. "Oh yeah?"

"Yeah. The wager is pre- or post-New Year's. I'm thinking about throwing $50 in. I happen to have some insider info."

A flicker of heat flashes in Mason's eyes as he leans closer, his face inches away from mine. "Huh. I'd thrown in $100 to tip the scales p—"

"Did you two see that!?" Mikey's voice is the firefighter hose we needed, extinguishing that dangerous flame we were stoking. "I've never struck out at O'Malley's before."

"I told you the mullet wasn't doing you any favors," Mason quips. He's cool and collected as ever. Like we hadn't been moments away from kissing.

"The mullet has been a big hit for the past six months thank you very much. This is not a me problem." Mikey steals Mason's beer and finishes it off. "I'm 0-2 in being appreciated tonight. It's a shame really."

I snort. "I can't believe she didn't want to sleep with you, considering how humble you are."

"I know. Guess I'll just have to stick to being an arrogant jackass. Now if only I had a best friend or two that could buy me a drink and help me lick my wounds."

"Yeah, if only." I laugh but still make a move to slide out of my chair when I feel a warm hand on the small of my back.

"I'll grab it." Mason stops me before heading to the bar, empty glasses in hand. The heat from his palm still burns as he walks away.

"You know in another life I really think I could've been a solid matchmaker." Mikey points his eyes at Mason.

I roll my eyes. "I wouldn't quit your day job."

Mikey would be a good matchmaker if the goal was for couples with intense chemistry to fuck each other senselessly, break up painfully, and forever pine for one another pitifully. *Meet Mason and Violet. They are your token best friend's brother, friends to lovers to enemies, workplace romance. And they lived happily never after.* Jesus. Maybe I also needed another drink.

twenty-seven

. . .

Violet

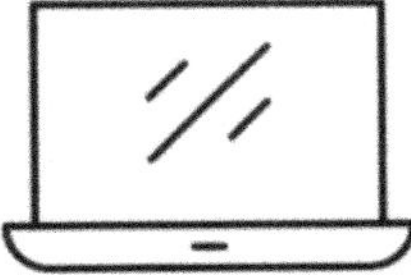

"ARE we sure it's not too late to quit academia?" Maya groans, shoving her laptop across the desk after spending the last three hours trying unsuccessfully to fix her coding script.

"Well, given that you've already received your PhD, are about to finish your postdoc, and are actively interviewing for faculty positions…I'd say that ship has sailed for you."

"I don't know. I feel like we could still throw caution to the wind and set up a bookstore-café together. Or maybe even move to Scotland and set up a little Bed 'n Breakfast while we charm the townies with our American ways." She sighs hopefully.

"Are you watching Outlander again?"

"Sam Heughan's just so dreamy. I could drown in him and his accent." Maya stands up and stretches, digging through her bag for a charger. "Instead, I'm drowning in scripts that refuse to run."

"Don't forget reviewer comments that make me question everything about myself and my abilities as a researcher," I add, thinking about another item that was added to my to-do list this week.

Nothing builds character and fuels imposter syndrome more than the process of sending your research papers to be published in academic journals. If you're lucky enough to get it past the editor, it's then sent off to a few leading experts in your field for them to tear it apart. The funniest part is that we celebrate getting ripped apart because at the very least it means we weren't outright rejected. Sure, you may have to respond to dozens of comments and restructure your whole paper just to appease the reviewers, but at least you'll get your work published. Woo.

"You know, I bet if we put our brains together, we could start our own romance-only bookstore in my hometown." I only semi-joke.

"You say the words Violet and I'll drop everything now. Nothing sounds more perfect than being in a small town, curled up next to books with happy endings, and sipping on a vanilla latte. Instead, here we are, basing the success of our careers on validation from anonymous Reviewer 2's. Speaking of which, any news on your fellowship application yet?"

After endless late nights, at least ten rounds of edits from Bethany, one and a half mental breakdowns, and an ungodly amount of tea, I was finally able to submit my fellowship application two weeks ago.

"Things have been quiet and probably will be for a while. Bethany told me that at some point in the next few months, a panel of faculty will review applications and vote on who gets the award."

"Well, I'm crossing all my fingers for you, though I doubt you even need it. Your materials are so strong."

"You have to say that as my friend." I let out a self-deprecating laugh.

"No, I'm serious Violet. You are literally one of the most hardworking and dedicated people I know. Your resume is more impressive than most postdocs and you just started your third year. And that's even accounting for all the bullshit you went through your first year with she-who-will-not-be-named." Maya is teasing, but I still feel a twinge in my chest.

Aside from Bethany, and now I guess Mason, Maya's the only person who knows the full extent of what I endured. The first time she and I met followed a particularly brutal meeting with Dr. Atkins.

"You know I had my initial hesitations about accepting you as my student Violet. I wasn't sure if someone coming from a state school could handle the rigor of our program."

"I understand." I didn't. University of Vermont may have been a public school, but it still had an excellent research program.

"The department encouraged me to look past that due to your... diverse background, but now I'm wondering if that was a mistake."

"It's not. I'll work harder, I promise." I wouldn't cry in front of her. As much as I wanted too I wouldn't. This is what I wanted. I wanted to work under the best, so naturally, she was going to be super hard on me. This would all be worth it in the end.

"You better. No more excuses, no more leniency, and no more hand-outs. I expect more. A lot more."

"Violet?" Maya's voice brings me back.

"Yeah, sorry. Thinking back to my first year just brought back some memories..." As much as I loved researching brains and learning about how they develop and function, sometimes I wished I could just turn mine off.

A wave of understanding and sympathy comes over her face. "Shit, that's my bad. I didn't mean to—"

"You're totally fine. It happens sometimes. I really thought after a year of working with Bethany I'd be able to magically erase all the bad memories, but..." But somehow, I still found myself feeling haunted by the past. Some days were better than others, but I still wasn't able to fully let go. I don't know if I can, no matter how much I want to.

Maya shakes her head vehemently. "No, do not erase them. You were in an extremely toxic environment where she verbally harassed you and emotionally manipulated you every day for a year straight. Use that to fight back and make her regret ever doubting you."

"I think I just feel guilty sometimes," I confess.

"About what?"

"I don't know. About the fact that I can't let go, I guess? Like yes, I went through something awful, but I'm in a better place now, and I have been for a while. Our lab is so supportive, and I couldn't ask for a kinder and more thoughtful mentor than Bethany. But I still have moments where I feel upset and hurt by what happened to me. And I feel like that makes me ungrateful. Like I'm not appreciating the good things that I have in my life now, because I'm still holding on to the past."

Maya walks over and gives me a hug. "You're not ungrateful, you're just human. And you're allowed to feel happy and safe here while still being pissed about the ways you were mistreated."

I had repeated those same words to myself, but something about someone else saying them helped. "Thanks Maya. I really needed to hear that."

"Of course, that's what I'm here for." She reached down for her backpack and slung it on her shoulders. "Any chance you want to come over and work at my place instead? I can't promise that there's any food in my fridge, but I can promise that KoKo will give you lots of affection." KoKo was Maya's rescue dog. The small Jindo doubled as our lab mascot and the best emotional support animal a stressed academic could ask for. When you're as lonely as I am, the prospect of a dog snuggle sounds like a pretty good Friday night.

"It's a date."

twenty-eight

· · ·

Mason

MY CURRENT SHITTY mood was brought to me by the sterile scent of chlorine burning my nose, paired with the fluorescent lighting that always managed to give me a headache, and the fact that I had been waiting over an hour for my doctor to show up. Like most people, I had never loved going to the doctor's office. My disdain only grew after my injury; coming in day after day to have tests run on me like a lab rat, only to be told that I would never play hockey again, didn't exactly make me feel any better. Still, I force myself to go to my check-up appointments because, at the end of the day, you only have one head. I may not have taken care of it before, but at least I can try now.

"Sorry to keep you waiting so long Mason. Somehow I got

double booked." My neurologist, Tabitha, gives me a sheepish smile as she enters the room.

"S'all good."

"So how have you been since the last time I saw you?"

"About the same. Every now and then, I'll get a migraine or wake up feeling super dizzy which lingers the whole day." Those are the moments where I feel the most resentment about my retirement. Some days, I can convince myself that I just need some more time to recover, and eventually, I'll play again. Then symptoms return, and I'm reminded of how unlikely that pipe dream is.

"And how long do those last?"

"Migraines usually go away in like an hour or so. Dizziness goes away the next day. I take my pain meds when I need them."

"And that seems to help?" I give her a nod. "Good, good. Any recent accidents?"

"Nope."

"And you're avoiding any sports with physical contact?" she presses.

"Yup. I'm coaching hockey now, but I'm never involved in the drills. Just demonstrate what to do and let my players handle it."

"Be sure to keep it that way. Well, it sounds like things are going well. Unfortunately, in some cases of post-concussion syndrome, migraines and dizziness persist for a while. We'll continue to keep an eye on it, and if anything gets worse, call the front desk to get you scheduled earlier."

"Will do Doc."

I leave the doctor's office feeling even shittier than when I entered. I knew I was injured, and so did everyone (including millions of strangers I'd never met before), but it never got easier hearing how broken beyond repair you were. A distraction right now would be great. Luckily for me, my phone starts ringing.

"You would think after living in New York for nearly eight years I'd be used to the cold, but I swear every year this shit catches me off guard." Connor had just gotten back from playing a series of away games on the West Coast where the weather was much warmer. It seems the first thing he wanted to do when he got home was call me and complain. "I don't know how or why people decide to move to the Northeast and stay here. Do they hate the sun? And happiness? Is that it?"

"Yes, that's it."

"I went to pick up a coffee yesterday after a shower, and by the time I got back to my apartment, my hair was frozen — like icicle frozen."

"Next time wear a beanie." I quip.

"Your answer to preventing my frostbitten scalp is a beanie? You're as bad as the rest of them." I can practically hear his eyes roll through the phone. "I also got hit with a gust of wind so cold I swore my balls tucked into my stomach. I don't know how many more winters I have in me."

"Well, you are coming up on the end of your contract soon. You could always see if you could go back home. Or at least somewhere warmer." Though I'd be really surprised if the Rangers didn't re-sign him. Beyond them not having the salary space to give him a contract that he deserves, I don't see a reason why Connor would leave.

"Yeah, I just don't know if I want to go through all of that. Adjusting to a new team is hard enough when it's just players coming in and out, add moving across the country to a place I've never lived before. It's a hassle."

"Sounds like we just need to get you a better winter coat then. And maybe some beanies."

"Fuck off."

"Hey, you were the one who called me, remember?"

"Yeah, yeah. Don't pretend like you don't miss me too."

"Who are you again?…Cody, was it?"

"Is that any way to speak to the guy receiving a philanthropy award?"

"Depends. Is the philanthropy for scalp frostbite awareness?"

"Yes. Second Chance cares very much about scalps."

Most NHL teams pair with a charity organization to help give back to the community. The Second Chance Foundation is geared toward supporting families who are either at risk or are currently facing housing insecurity and helping them get back on their feet. The organization is particularly important to Connor, who has always been very transparent about the struggles he endured when he was growing up and how Second Chance helped save his family.

"Congrats man. Well deserved."

"Thanks, Mase. They called last week and let me know they picked me to receive their philanthropic leadership award this year."

Knowing him, this award probably meant more than the Stanley Cup. For as much as Connor loved hockey, he loved helping people even more. A real bleeding heart on this guy.

"Well duh. Look at all the work you've done for scalps all across New York! Now, when do you receive this award? I'll get my suit pressed."

"They're planning on giving me the award during the annual Rangers gala in two months. They want to highlight the work I've done to develop a mentorship program between them and the Rangers, so it'll be when we have a bye-week. Uhm...I'm allowed to pick someone to give an opening speech and present the award to me, and I was hoping that person could be you?"

"Seriously?" Damn, I'm feelin' misty.

"You're my best friend Mason. And a lot of the work I've been able to do has been because of you. You're the one who encouraged me to talk to our PR team about working with Second Chance."

My throat tightens. "Of course I'll do it. I'm really honored that you asked me."

"And you'll still say yes when I tell you the whole team will be there?"

"Ah." Can I handle being in the same room with guys who

are getting to live the dream while mine was taken away from me? I haven't really kept up with this season, mainly because every time I turn on a game all I can think of is what could've been, but the Rangers have always been a solid team and my players still talk about how they are current favorites for winning the Eastern Conference. It didn't matter; I could do this for Connor. He is one of the only friends from my time with the Rangers that stuck with me after my retirement. One of the few people who kept pushing through all my attempts to shut out everyone I cared about because I was too afraid to face them. I could do this for Connor.

"That means Kallum will definitely be there..." Connor hedges. "I understand if that changes your decision."

Kallum and I had a rocky start to our relationship when I joined the team and promptly took his starting line spot. Over the years the resentment he had toward me continued to build until it came to a head. The worst incident featured a small fight in the locker room after I missed a game-tying goal and he continued to rip into me. Rowan pulled us apart after a few punches were thrown. It was one of my lowest moments as a Ranger. "I'm not gonna let him get to me, or stop me from doing this for you."

"I appreciate it, man. Really."

"I can't promise I won't punch Kallum in the face if he says something stupid. But I will promise to do it after the event. And not in public."

Connor lets out a small chuckle. "Fair enough. You do also get a plus one." He leaves it there, waiting for me to reply.

I decide to take the bait, "A plus one?"

"Yeah, maybe someone who's short, cute, has curly hair. Someone you've been pining over for the past couple of years?"

I can't deny that Violet's face immediately flashed into my head when he mentioned a plus one. Though it's only been a few weeks since we started rekindling our friendship, every lunch date or latte run instilled my hope that we could be something more one day. It helped that every interaction Violet and I had recently always included some level of flirty banter. "We're just friends."

"So, I take it you haven't told her that you want more?"

"I don't want to scare her away. Especially now that I have her back in my life. Being friends is the safer option."

"Okay, and maybe as your friend she'd be willing to come as moral support as you face parts of your past?"

"Maybe..." Having Violet there with me would make the night much easier. She could always tell when I was on the verge of panicking, and her presence grounded me.

He clears his throat. "Alright, well, I should probably get going. I'll send you more details soon."

"Sounds good, congrats again."

"Thanks, although I guess I should also say congrats to you too."

"What for?"

"For finally working things out with Violet. I'm happy for you, man. You deserve this. You deserve some happiness in your life."

And for the first time in a long time, I agreed.

twenty-nine

. . .

Violet

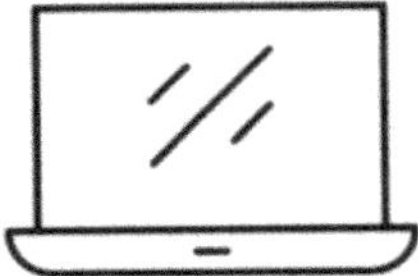

AS AN INCREDIBLY TYPE-A, lives-and-breathes-by-their-calendar person, I am a bit nervous about letting Mason take the reins on planning our evening. It's not that I don't trust him or think he will pick something I won't want to do, I just hate things out of my control. But learning to trust people again is the key to my healing (or so my therapist says), so here I am, Stephanie, trusting people.

Mason and I have hung out several days in the last few weeks. While our "hangs" usually take place at the Beanery or eating lunch together in his office, I always leave wanting more time with him.

Despite my initial hesitance to ever look in his direction, I had managed to fall for him. Again. However, in my defense, I probably never stopped loving him. I just shoved those feelings down and tucked them away. In hindsight, I should have

shredded the feelings. Because they have now untucked themselves and are residing in the pit of my stomach, threatening to
climb up my sternum and squeeze my heart like a vice. But this
isn't entirely my fault. Between that longing look in his eyes and
the several flirty comments that found their way into our conversations, I knew Mason was fighting his own pesky feelings.

Tonight is the first time we are hanging out outside of
campus. I was an absolute mess of nerves; resisting the urge to
text Mason and demand he tell me everything he has planned
for us tonight. I know he would immediately tell me too, especially if he knew how anxious this was making me.

I rummage through my closet, throwing a few different
sweaters on the bed. The one detail Mason did share was that I
should bundle up. I decide on my trusty winter coat that's
managed to keep me warm through several Nor'easters. I finish
lacing up my boots when my mom calls.

"Hey honey, I just wanted to check in and see how things are
going. I feel like we haven't talked in forever."

I almost remind her that we spoke less than a week ago, but I
knew she just misses me. Maybe I should get her a cat for
Christmas.

"Hey Mom. Things are going. I'm heading out with Mason
soon so I can't talk for too long."

"Oh, is tonight the night you'll finally tell him how you've
been feeling?" The question is innocent enough, but judging
from the giddiness in her voice I can tell she's really hoping I
finally bite the bullet.

I instantly regret spilling the beans to her last week. Such was
the struggle of your mom being one of your best friends. "I'm
not sure. I don't want to rush things." I mumble.

"Rush things? You've known the man since you were 6! Life's
too short for you to second-guess every move you make. Sometimes you just have to trust your gut and take a leap."

"That's never been easy for me."

"I know *aziz*, but if you're going to take a leap of faith for anyone, I'd be willing to bet Mason would be there to catch you."

"Yeah, I think he would too. Thanks, Mom."

"Anytime…I do have a favor to ask you."

"What's up?"

"Melissa really wants Mason home for Christmas."

Oof. "Mason's views on going back to Castle Harbor really haven't changed."

"I know, but maybe he'd reconsider if he knew you'd be there too?"

"Mom, I don't know…"

"Just for Christmas dinner. Melissa's already talked to Joe about being on his best behavior."

"I really think you're underestimating how much Mason doesn't want to be in a room with his dad."

"Can you just ask him? The worst thing he can do is say no."

I really would love to have Mason back home, but I won't betray his trust by manipulating him into going back to Castle Harbor. Daddy issues run deep, and if he isn't ready then he isn't ready. "I will tell him I'm going, and if that entices him then so be it. But if he doesn't want to see his dad, I'm not going to ask him to do that. It's not fair to him."

"Honey, I didn't mean to imply —" Her response is cut off by a knock on my door.

"Alright Mom, Mason's here so I gotta go. Love you, bye." I hang up the phone, spritz my curls with hairspray one final time, and grab my purse.

I slide on my coat as I open the door. Mason is leaning against the wall, a black beanie covering his locks, and the sleeves of his wool-lined jacket rolled up to reveal a sliver of his tattoo. Under this puffer jacket I look like the Michelin Man, while GQ over here is rocking the hell out of a beanie. So unfair.

The power of the beanie possesses me and I extend my arms out for a hug. Just like how the old Mason and Violet would greet each other. He responds as such, scooping me into his arms as he rests his cheek on my head.

"Hey." I can hear the smile.

"Hi." I'm sure he can hear mine as well. "Sorry, I was on the phone with my mom." We break apart, and he steps back to allow me to the close the door.

"'S'all good. How's Elaine doing?"

"She's fine. Meddlesome as always. It is her, not me, that is insanely out of their mind curious about what we are doing tonight."

His face breaks out into a smile as we walk away from my building. "I'm finally teaching you how to ice skate."

———

The Boston Common is one of my favorite places in December. In addition to the annual Christmas Tree lighting that attracts all the locals, the normal trees in the park are also decorated with festive string lights. Even in below-freezing temperature, everything about this place felt cozy. Growing up, I would always beg my mom to bring me into the Common so I could pretend I was the main character in my own Christmas movie, but there was always one part of the park I was too scared to go. During the summer, the Frog Pond was the perfect place for little kids to splash around and cool off, but during the winter was when it came to life. With the pond frozen over, everyone from kids to grandparents brought out their ice skates and flooded into the small outdoor rink. I was always too scared to go. Too scared of getting hurt. The Hayeses would bring me, and I would watch Mason and Monroe skate around for hours. Never moving from the bench. Mason always swore he'd get me out there.

"I can't believe I'm finally doing this." I'm unbelievably nervous about falling, busting my tailbone, and spending my days sitting on a donut, but I'm also excited. I'm buzzing with energy as we stand in line at the skate rental booth. Mason brought his own obviously. A gust of wind blows through, and while my energy is keeping me warm, the wind cuts down to my bones, causing me to wince and I rub my gloved hands up and down my arms. Perhaps it was time for a new winter coat…

Mason wraps an arm around my waist and tucks me into his side, his warmth surrounding me. "You're gonna love it. It's always such a rush every time I get on the ice."

"How many times do you think I'm going to fall on my ass?"

With my head pressed against him, I can feel his chest vibrate as he laughs. "Honestly, it's a rite of passage. I still eat shit sometimes too."

"Okay I'll ignore the obvious joke about the pro hockey player who can't skate and jump to…that seems dangerous considering your history. Should you be doing this?"

"I'll be fine. My doctors cleared me for skating a while ago. It's just the contact aspect of hockey, ya know, the fact that pucks and 200-pound men are flying around the ice, that made them nervous."

"But falling on your ass on a hard surface rattles your brain too. I would know; I tried rollerblading once."

"I'll hold on to you the whole time if you want."

"Says the guy who just admitted to eating shit sometimes. But sure, at least you'll break my fall when we both go down."

"Making sure you're comfortable is my top priority." He winks, and I feel it in my frozen bones.

After we collect my skates, we head to the bench to put them on. Unsurprisingly, Mason has both of them laced and ready to go before I can even take off one of my boots. He kneels to start helping, and I hear the petulant child in me start an argument about how I can do it myself. Before I can open my mouth, he grabs my foot and lightly squeezes, almost as if reassuring me that it is okay to accept his help. I continue to watch as he slides on the skate and adjusts it into place, tugging on the laces and tying them nice and snug. He repeats the same actions with my other skate, and by the time we're both set to go my third sweater no longer feels necessary. Was that some sort of hockey player foreplay I just discovered? Or am I so touch-deprived that even a small gesture like helping me get my shoes on feels intimate?

He stands up and extends a hand to me, which I gladly take to hoist myself up. I walk— well, really waddle— over to the rink clutching his hand. Mason takes the first step onto the ice and my legs refuse to move. "You coming, Vi?"

I nod my head but can't make my feet move an inch. So much for not letting my fears get in the way of trying new things.

Mason steps back over the border and puts his hand out to me. "Hey it's okay to be scared, but I promise I won't let you get hurt. Do you trust me?"

That is usually what parents say to their kids before they let go of the back of the bicycle. And the kid falls anyway. I will probably fall too. But Mason will be there to catch me, and that's enough to get me to take his hand and step over the border.

"Yes. Let's do this."

thirty

Violet

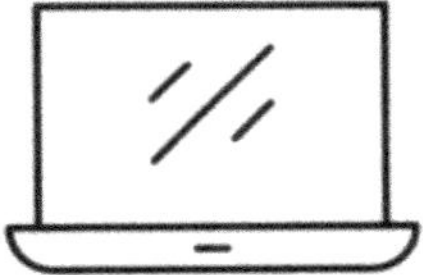

I **LOOK** like Bambi on ice the first thirty minutes, but Mason stays with me the whole time. I keep insisting he leave me behind and go do some twirls or whatever he likes to do out here, but he insists he's having fun right where he is. I eventually manage to glide on the ice without feeling like I'm going to tip over face first, and the next thing I know we're doing laps around the pond. Very slow, very small laps but still. Childhood Violet is rejoicing. I look to my right and see Mason beaming.

"You're doing great, Vi."

"This is so fun! I can't believe I'm doing this." I loosen my grip on Mason's hand and pick up some speed. "Do you think I could try skating on my own?" I'm not entirely sure where this burst of confidence came from, but I wasn't going to question it.

"Absolutely." He gives my hand a final squeeze before letting go. I stumble a little but manage to stay upright.

"If coaching for Westchester doesn't work out, you could definitely make a killing with ice skating."

"Oh yeah?"

"Definitely. Look at how fast you managed to teach me. Next stop, Olympics!" My enthusiasm sets me off balance a little, and I wave my arms like I'm treading water.

"Mmm…" He presses his lips together, suppressing a smile.

"Aren't coaches supposed to encourage their players? Don't laugh."

"You look like …someone looking for the light switch in the dark. It's cute."

"Don't be rude." I gently smack his arm. "Maybe we can do pair skating in the Olympics! I'll dazzle the crowd with my beauty and grace, and you can do all the fancy tricks."

"Eh, the uniform isn't my style. I could never pull off sequins."

"C'mon. Just imagine how great your ass would look in those tights."

"Thinking about my ass now, are we?"

I open my mouth to respond when I see a kid barreling toward me. He notices me at the last second but rams into my side, and my legs slide out from under me. I stick out my hand to try and stop myself from falling on my face and jam my wrist on the ice. A second before I can process that horrendous pain the back of my head knocks the ice.

Fuck. First fall of the night is not a pretty one. The kid looks at me sheepishly and apologizes before skating back across the rink. I'm lying here like roadkill as his friends skate around me. Mason squeezes past and scoops me up bridal style, skating off the ice. He sets me down on a nearby bench.

"Oh god, Violet. I'm so sorry I didn't see that kid coming." His eyes are filled with panic as they scan my face. "Can you tell me the date?"

"What?"

"What is today's date?" He repeats himself.

"Ice skating."

"Violet, it's December 8th. Fuck, you're concussed."

"Oh, no I thought you meant what did we do for today's date. I know it's the 8th." I realize I just called this a date. "But this isn't even a date so—"

"Can you track this for me?" He asks, moving his finger around. He speaks like he can't hear my ramblings about this date-not-date. I follow his finger until he appears satisfied. He looks off into the distance, working his jaw. He looks kind of mad.

"What's wrong, Doc? I can handle it I promise."

He doesn't laugh. Not even a smile. Tough crowd. He drags his hands over his face.

"I can't believe I let you fall."

"We both knew I was going to fall at some point."

"Yeah but I didn't think you'd fall on your *head*."

"My wrist broke my fall. My head barely touched the ice."

"What if you have a concuss—"

"I promise you, I'm fine. Hell, I could probably race you right now if you want to get back on the ice."

He ignores my attempt at humor. "Maybe we should take you to the ER just to be safe?"

"Mason." I take his shaking hand into mine. "I don't feel dizzy or confused. My wrist hurts, but I can move it. I don't think I need to go to the ER."

He glances back to the ice and then looks down at his feet. Maybe *he* was the one who wasn't ready to face his fears today.

"My Olympic career ended as quickly as it started. Why don't we call it a night for the skating? I am 100% fine, but also very much in need of a warm blanket and some hot chocolate."

"I was planning on inviting you over to my place for dinner after. If that sounds alright with you."

I really was fine, but my wrist was hurting like a mother-fucker, and the fall gave me a pounding headache, which is making me feel cranky. I want to be in my bed, nursing my wounds alone. But I can't leave Mason. Not when he looks like he hates himself right now.

"That sounds perfect."

———

Mason continues to watch over me like a hawk, and I try not to be annoyed. I know concussions are a sensitive topic for him. Plus, I can't remember the last time someone dotted over me like this and honestly, it was pretty nice.

The moment we entered his apartment he guided me over to the couch like an elderly person with a fall risk and insisted I relax while he made dinner. He came back about five minutes later to hand me a hot chocolate. A girl could get used to this.

While he's in the kitchen, I take in my surroundings. From what I can see, his apartment gives off your classic bachelor pad vibes: a massive couch pressed up against a wall of exposed brick, a large TV to the left with his Xbox close by, and to my right I see his autographed Patrice Bergeron jersey hanging on the wall. I still remember when he got it as a Christmas gift over a decade ago. Mason shed a few tears (he denied it afterward), and his dad looked so happy knowing how much the gift pleased his son. I miss seeing them like that. I wonder if I ever will again.

"I'll be done in a sec." I hear the clinking of bowls, and a moment later he heads out of the kitchen, two steaming bowls in hand and a towel thrown over his shoulder. He places his bowl on the coffee table before placing the towel under my bowl and handing it to me. I look down to see what's for dinner and my heart clenches.

"Is this my mom's beef stew?"

"Same recipe. Elaine shared it with me when I headed off to college."

"This takes hours to make."

"I made it before I came to pick you up. It's no big deal." He shrugs.

"You can't even get some of these ingredients in local grocery stores."

"There's an Iranian grocery store that just opened up, like an hour drive outside of the city." He nods his head toward my bowl. "Why don't you try it before you give me too much credit, alright?"

I take a bite and I'm brought back to the first time we met in our old elementary school cafeteria. The first time he defended me, and the first time he left a mark on my heart. One that's never gone away. One that I wanted to hold onto for as long as I could. We scarf down our dinner in silence, leaving our empty bowls on the coffee table.

"So…how was it?"

"Don't tell my mom, but you make a better Amin than I do. That was amazing."

"That's incredibly high praise." He makes a motion of zipping his lips shut. "Now I know you must be ill." He lets out a small laugh before scanning my face. "You sure you're okay? Head's not hurting at all?"

"My head is perfectly fine." My heart, however, was filled with cracks and sharp edges, and for the longest time, I thought it would always be that way. I was used to it being broken, but I wanted something different now. I wanted something more. Something better. "Can I ask you something?"

"Anything."

"What are we doing?"

His eyebrows come together, "What do you mean?"

"I mean…" I toy with the hair tie around my wrist. "Are we just hanging out as friends? Are we dating? You planned this whole thing where you helped me achieve a childhood dream, overcome my fear, and made me my favorite dish and that *feels* like a date, but I just…I don't know what we're doing."

"Do you want it to be a date?"

"Depends. Did you plan this as a date? Or is this how friends hang out now?" I can feel the cracks and sharp edges of my heart warm smooth over with hope. For the longest time I thought it would never be hopeful again, always expecting the worst. But at this moment, I am hopeful. Hopeful that this is a date.

"I asked you on a date tonight. Whether or not it ends as one is up to you."

My words barely come out as a whisper, yet somehow, it feels like they echo against the walls. "It's a date then."

"Good."

I wait for him to continue as he leans back against the cushions and throws an arm over the coach. The epitome of calm to my current state of 'freaking-the-fuck-out.' Is this really happening?

"I've spent the last few weeks trying to keep things platonic because I thought that's what *you* wanted." He laughs, looking anything but amused. He looks sort of tortured actually. Like keeping things platonic has pained him, and he's now realizing it was unnecessary.

"So, you want this." I gesture between us. "You want…me?"

He scoots over on the couch so we're only a few inches apart.

"Violet, I want you. I know I've said this before and fucked it all up, but it's always been true. I am only now mature enough to actually act on it."

I feel simultaneously elated and miserable because I know that's true. I've always known, deep down, that Chicago was just a blimp in our eternal timeline. That Mason was growing, though perhaps more slowly than I was, and if I waited, he would catch up. But it felt good to be mad, to harden myself against yet another person making me feel like I wasn't good enough. But it was years of anger wasted. And I want to be happy. I deserve it dammit.

Mason continues, "I've wanted you for a very long time. And if you want me, I'm yours. I've always been yours, even when you didn't want me to be, even when you tried to forget me."

With his words, I swear I feel my heart slowly piece itself back together. It wasn't perfectly healed, and maybe it never would be, but it would be safe in his hands. That I knew for certain. I take his hand and place it on my chest. "You have my heart. Always."

"Always." The words from his mouth are a promise.

"Then act on it already."

Mason grabs my face and kisses me so hard I see stars.

thirty-one

. . .

Violet

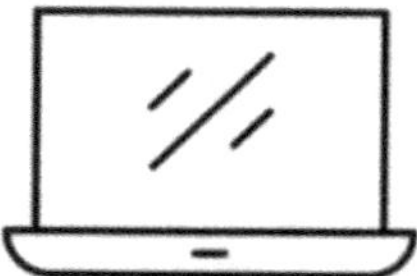

THE TEMPERATURE of the room shifts immediately as our lips connect. I run my fingers through Mason's hair tugging him even closer to me as we slide down the couch. He's on top of me, clawing at my sweater trying to find an opening at the hem. My heart flutters at his needy touch, a man deprived for far too long and finally able to satiate the hunger. This isn't general hunger either. Mason is hungry for me, and only me and my heart knows it. It's the hottest thing ever.

I let out a small whimper as Mason breaks the kiss and moves to leave a trail of kisses down my neck, nipping against my skin as he makes his descent.

"Fuck Violet." He runs out of skin at the neckline of my sweater. He moves to take it off, and I flinch a little when the material catches at my wrist.

"Shit your wrist. Your head! Are you okay? Maybe—"

I put my finger to his mouth to stop any suggestion we stop. "I'm fine. Here." I shift out from under him and move to straddle his hips. I carefully strip my sweater off. "Better. Now, I've had enough of the tiptoeing. Take that hoodie off so I can finally see that tattoo that's been tempting me for weeks."

The hoodie is flung across the room, and I can't stop myself from soaking him in. I start by pressing a soft kiss to the shoulder covered in beautiful shades of gray and black ink. I trace over the artwork with my fingers, sending a shiver down his body. A satisfied hum fills me, as does the desire to draw that out from him again. I move my hand toward his waistband.

My eyes trail down his body to where my hands are teasing the skin over his jeans. As I start to unbutton his jeans Mason reaches around and unhooks my bra. He trails his hand up and down my back as the straps fall off my shoulders. I'm covered in goosebumps from his soft touches and my nipples are painfully hard.

"Are you cold?" he asks, eyes fixating on my breasts.

I shake my head, holding my breath, as he licks his lips and looks up at me. He maintains eye contact while breathing on my sensitive nipples. "You're so fucking beautiful, Angel." My entire body goes limp as he calls me the same nickname he did so many years ago.

Mason brings one of his large hands up my stomach and grips my right breast tightly into his palm, the rough calluses of his hand feeling heavenly. He pinches my nipples gently and I can't stop myself from arching my back and grinding on top of him.

"That's right, Angel. Move those hips against me like you're taking my cock." I oblige and that seems to be his undoing as he finally moves his mouth on top of my neglected breast.

A groan leaves his mouth, and I grip his hair forcing his face even closer to me as his tongue darts out to draw light, teasing circles around my nipple. The slight scruffiness of his beard scratches me, and the light teasing followed by hard scratching is euphoric. I was never really into guys with beards, but the moment I saw Mason with one, everything shifted.

"Have I told you how much I love this beard?" I move my finger to trace his chin, followed by his lips, before placing another scorching kiss on them.

Mason responds by teasing my slit with the tip of his finger, which I immediately slide down on. With his finger inside me fully, I set my own pace and ride his hand. Mason matches my pace, and the mix of hunger and pride in his eyes tells me how much he appreciates my new-found confidence, in stark contrast to the insecure Violet he had back in Chicago.

"That feels...so good." I can't believe how close I am to coming fully undone and we have barely even started.

My eyes shut, and I hear him tsk. "Eyes on me, Angel." He waits until I lock my eyes, and when I do, he rewards me by adding in another finger. "So fucking responsive."

"Mason." His name comes out of my lips a mixture of a command and a plea.

He lets out a moan, slowly pulling his hand out of my wet core and sliding me completely off him, much to my dismay. I watch him slowly slide his jeans off to reveal his boxer briefs. My mouth waters at the faint outline of his cock.

Mason cups my chin into one of his hands so I'm staring into his beautiful green eyes and traces my lips with his thumb. "I'm yours." He places a gentle kiss on my forehead followed by a much rougher one on my lips. "Do you hear me, Violet? I'm yours. All of me, it's all yours." The words carry more than just hunger in them, and with my eyes locked onto his I see a hint of vulnerability.

"You're mine Mason. Always have been, always will be." I turn my head and place a kiss on the palm of his hand that's cradling my face.

His eyes shut as a shudder runs through his body. When they open, a wicked smile forms on his face. He grabs my waist with his hands and adjusts us so he's laid flat on the couch, and I'm sitting on his chest. I make a move to lower myself onto him, but he stops me. "I want you to ride my face, Angel."

My entire body lights up like it's on fire. Mason's tongue was a dangerous thing. One I had missed dearly. "I've never done that before."

"We don't have to do anything you don't want to." He confirms, drawing circles on my thighs with his fingers in a comforting caress.

"Oh I want to, trust me." Now that the offer was up in the air, there was no way I was turning it down. I take a breath before adjusting myself so my thighs are on either side of his face, my core hovering over his mouth.

"Vi, I'm trying to be a gentleman about this, but if you don't sit on my tongue already, I might lose my shit."

"You really have a mouth on you, don't you?"

"Sure do. Now shut me up." My eyes stay locked on Mason as I do exactly what he says, lowering myself down until I feel his lips connect with my clit, "Such a good girl letting me lick this pussy."

I let out a loud moan as he sucks on it gently. In a matter of seconds I'm writhing on top of him as he slides his tongue into me. I get confirmation that Mason's enjoying this as much as I am a moment later when he lets out his own moan. God he was so damn good. Our eyes lock as he gives all his attention to my swollen clit. A shiver runs down my spine and he pulls away for a moment probably sensing how close I am.

"Look at what a mess you're making, Angel." He tsks and I look down to see some of my wetness on his beard. "Such a perfect fucking pussy." Mason groans, placing a wet kiss along my thigh, "I've been dying to taste you again, Vi. Dying to bury my tongue inside."

He makes no move to continue though, leaving me frustrated. "I don't remember you being such a tease before," I mutter in frustration.

A small laugh leaves his lips, "I like seeing you squirm a lot more than I thought I would." He brings his thumb to my clit matching the same pattern his tongue used earlier, "Love knowing I'm the one that's driving you this crazy...the one that's making you this wet." He drags his tongue up my slit teasing my clit on the way. "Plus dragging it out will only make you come harder in the end. So really it's a win-win."

I take matters into my own hands, gripping his shoulder tightly and using my other hand to toy with myself. From that moment on Mason loses all his self-control. He drags his tongue back against my slit and *finally*, buries his tongue inside me again.

His groan vibrates throughout my core as he continues to lap me up, slow at first and then hurried as I buck my hips in response. My nails dig into his shoulder, hard enough to leave a mark, but he's undeterred. If anything, it only motivates him more. He moves to slide a finger inside of me, "Oh god, that's it Mason. Baby I'm so, so close."

"You wanna come, Angel?" His voice is so soft, a stark contrast to the way he's playing with me. I can't bring myself to say anything, so I just nod instead. "You just need me to tell you it's okay, don't you? That's what's going to send you over, isn't it? My permission?" Oh god is that it? It might be, given I suddenly felt the pressure build even more. "Come then. Come all over my face Angel, so I can make you come all over my cock next."

His words are all I need to fall into an orgasm that shakes through my entire body. I lean my head against the arm of the couch catching my breath as I come down. Eventually I move so I can bury my face into his neck as he holds me, "You're so damn beautiful Violet." Mason whispers against my temple. "I have no idea what I ever did to deserve you."

"You were right. That was amazing." I sigh, extremely content.

"Can you say that first part again?" he teases, absently stroking his hands down my back and through my curly, frizzy mane. "It's not every day I hear those words come from your mouth."

"Don't be annoying." I laugh.

"Me? Never." He opens his mouth to make another quip when I slide my hand down his chest, tugging down his boxers before I grip his cock, stroking it. I watch as Mason's eyes roll to the back of his head as I squeeze him, "Violet. I'm not gonna last much longer if you keep doing that."

"That's the idea." I taunt pressing a kiss to his lips leaning down until I'm nearly eye level with his cock.

Mason's hand comes up to cup my face, stroking small circles on my cheek with his thumb, "You don't have to, you know. I don't expect that from you just because I ate you out."

"I know. I want to."

He lets go of my face and I go to work. His cock is already rock hard and standing at attention and lick my lips when I notice the precum on his tip. I use my thumb to spread it over the rest of him causing more to leak out, "You'll be the death of me Violet." Mason's words fill me with confidence "Fuck Vi—" He sucks in a breath and bucks his hips into my hand.

"Good?" I ask already knowing the answer.

"It's incredible. You're incredible."

A smile comes over my face and I move my mouth closer, tracing the tip of his cock with my tongue. "Oh *god*, Violet." His hands immediately come to my hair, moving my curls out of the way as I bring him as deep into my mouth as I can. The rest I cover with my hand as I continue to drag my tongue up and down his length while maintaining my pace. Mason continues to move himself inside of my mouth, but always gently, never pushing me beyond what I was already allowing. When I feel his fingers slightly tighten in my hair, I know he's close and I start to stroke him faster when he pulls out abruptly. "Not happening, Angel. When I come, I'm gonna be buried inside of you."

He reaches down and throws me over his shoulder before I have time to think, walking me over to his room. A few seconds later he gently places me on top of his king-sized bed, and I moan at how comfortable it is compared to my cheap yard sale mattress. "I could stay here forever." I drawl stretching out like a starfish.

"You won't hear any complaints from me." Mason pulls out a strip of condoms ripping one off and leaving the rest on top of his nightstand. "If you don't think I have plans for the entire night, you are sadly mistaken." He teased sliding a condom on his still hard cock before climbing onto the bed.

"You've worn me out quite a bit already." I tease, placing a soft kiss on his cheek.

A flash of worry crosses his face. "We can stop now if you're not feeling okay."

"I feel fine. Great even, although I know one way I could feel even better." I smile making room for him to settle between my legs.

Mason adjusts us slightly, placing a few pillows underneath my head. He moves us closer to the edge of the bed before turning me on my side. I notice his closet doors are made up entirely of mirrors and I'm on complete display as he throws my right leg over his. His wild eyes take me in and I don't think I've ever felt more beautiful. I watch through the mirror as he leans down to press a tender kiss on my temple and lingers for a moment before pulling back and adjusting himself, so the tip of his cock is at my entrance. He presses his lips to my ear as I continue to watch him sink inside of me through the mirror. "That's it Violet. That's it. God look at you. Look at what a mess you're making taking my cock."

His eyes are locked on where we're joined, and he starts off slow. Teasing me relentlessly making sure to drag his cock against my clit as he enters me again, but I grab his hands in mine bringing one to my breast and the other down to my clit, both of which he immediately tends too. All while we both watch the mirror as he thrusts into me mercilessly. "You. Are. So. Fucking. Perfect Violet." His thrusts become fast and deeper as he places another rough kiss on my cheek, "I'm yours, Vi. All yours." His thumb starts drawing figure eights on my clit and moves his head to rest it on my temple, eyes never leaving the mirror, as he continued to whisper words of encouragement into my ear - how good I feel around him, how tight I grip him, how he can't wait to bury his tongue in me again.

His words were my undoing, "Mason, baby, I'm so close-"

"Come. Come Violet, I'm right there with you." And with one final thrust we both go off, panting and gripping at each other. All I can see are stars as Mason leaves dozens of small kisses on my forehead while I stroke his arms as they wrap around me. "You're perfect Vi. So perfect." He gently pulls out of me, and then brings me fully back into his chest placing another kiss on my lips. A few minutes later he sighs, letting go of me, "I'm going to grab us some water, do you want anything else?" I shake my head but manage to sneak off into the bathroom and make it back before he does. When Mason returns, he's holding two water bottles and a steaming mug. "Is that tea?" He hands over the warm mug and the familiar scent fills my nose.

"Honeycomb Black Tea to be specific. I told you I bought a bunch once they discontinued it. I figured you'd want something more substantial after all we just did." He sat up next to me, the both of us propped against the headboard as I sipped on my tea.

I rest my head on his bare chest as he toys with my hair and eventually, I feel the mug being taken from me as my eyes start to shut. The next thing I know I'm being tucked under the covers as he whispers a small 'goodnight' into my temple.

thirty-two

. . .

Violet

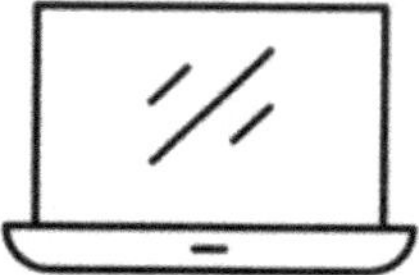

THE SOUND of the wind rattling the windows wakes me up the next morning. While the outside world is in the trenches of winter, in this bed with Mason's arms wrapped around me and my head tucked under his, all I feel is summer. I look down and see my hand entwined in his and I press a tender kiss to his fingers. His head moves a few seconds later and he nuzzles my neck with his bearded chin.

"Morning." Mason's rough voice, along with the soft kiss he leaves on my neck, sends sparkling heat through my body.

"Sorry, I didn't mean to wake you." I yawn. My body feels a little sore from last night and I debate getting up and stretching.

"You didn't, I was already up." Mason moves one of his legs over mine, trapping me in place. "You looked so content. I didn't want to move and mess that up."

His hands trail up and down my legs while I trace the intricate design of his tattoo. "I'm going to need to bring over some silk pillowcases if this becomes a regular thing. I can't have my curls suffer while the rest of my body is sated," I tease.

"*If* this becomes a regular thing? I thought I made it clear you're stuck with me."

"Yes, stuck with you, not your pillowcases." We lay tangled in each other for so long I lose track of time. It feels like the whole world around us has stopped. My phone vibrating against the nightstand is a cruel reminder that the world is, in fact, still moving. Sometime after I had fallen asleep Mason brought all of my things back into his room, and while I loved his thoughtfulness, I wish he had left my phone in the living room so we could've stayed in our bubble for a little bit longer.

He loosens his grip on me slightly so I can reach over and send whoever it is to voicemail. None of my research assistants were scheduled to run participants today, so I don't have to worry about any work-related emergencies. The call was likely spam. I make to nuzzle my way back into Mason's cocoon. We get about 30 seconds more of peace before my phone goes off again. I let out an irritated groan, this time flipping over my phone to see who was this determined to ruin my morning.

Nice. My mother is cockblocking me. "It's the matchmaker. She's probably calling to get an update on how things went last night."

He tucks one of my stray curls behind my head before wrapping an arm around my shoulders and grinning wide. "I'm sure she'll be thrilled to know you're in my bed."

"Pervert."

"Well, you don't want to leave her hanging." He nods his head toward my cell. "You know she won't give up until you answer and every call that goes to voicemail is only going to increase her determination."

Ugh. I make a move to slide off the bed so I can make this call as quick as possible, but Mason refuses to let go of me and instead reaches over to accept the call and puts it on speaker.

"I promise I'll be quiet." He whispers in my ear as my mom's voice fills the room.

"Violet Amin, did you send me to voicemail?"

"Who is this?"

"That's funny. So, tell me all about last night. How's Mason? What did you two get up too?"

Mason's eyes widen as he hears my mom's question, my face flushing a bright red remembering all the things he did to me last night that no mother should ever hear about.

"Mason's good. He took me out skating at the Frog Pond which was a lot of fun."

"Oh honey, you finally went skating. I'm so proud of you." My mom had spent her fair share of time sitting next to me on the bench when I was a kid. "Anything else?" she pries.

"We had dinner."

"That sounds nice, where did you go?"

"Um. We went over to Mason's apartment, and he made me dinner." *And we ate your beef stew Mom, and it was incredible, and I've definitely fallen for him again.*

My mom's voice notches up several octaves. "Ah so you went over to his place to *hang out* did you?" Mason, being the actual 14-year-old he is, can't control his laughter and hides under the covers. I make to clamp my hand over his mouth, and he responds by grabbing my hand and nibbling on my fingertips. He will be punished for this.

"Was that Mason in the background?" My mom gasps.

"Hi Elaine, how are you?" Mason gives his best I-am-a-polite-young-man voice.

"A lot better now, knowing you're with Violet," She beams. "You are *with her* now right? Because I don't know how much longer I can take with the whole 'will they, won't they' you two put us through."

"She's so dramatic," I whisper under my breath.

"I heard that, Violet Amin. Don't sass your mother." She turns her attention back to Mason. "So...?"

"We're together, Elaine. And I have no intention of letting her go." His words are so matter-of-fact that they feel less like a reply to her and more like a promise to me.

"Well, it seems like I have some important news to share with Melissa."

"Great. First Melissa, then the town," I grumble.

"Oh, it's not my fault word travels fast here. I'm sure everyone will be delighted though."

"You're impossible. Do you know that?"

"I bet Castle Harbor's going to be in complete chaos once you finally spread the news, Elaine," Mason smirks.

I elbow him in the ribs. "Don't encourage her."

"You know what else would send Castle Harbor into disarray? If you were to come back home for Christmas, Mason."

I cringe at her request. This is what I get for answering a call from my mom while still in a post-sex haze. Bubble = burst.

"Elaine." His lighthearted tone has turned more serious. "I really don't know if I feel comfortable doing that."

My mom's not having it. "Well, Melissa has already talked to Joe about being on his best behavior for Christmas Eve dinner."

"I don't know…"

"You can stay at our place when you come visit." It's more of a statement that a question.

"I don't want to inconvenience you, Elaine."

"Never. Melissa and I have been talking about doing a little stay-cation girls' weekend for a while now. This will be the perfect excuse. You and Violet can spend some time together and you can be reminded how Castle Harbor used to be home." She pauses, ready to lay down the final blow. "Plus, you know how much our girl loves spending her favorite holiday in Castle Harbor."

"Mom. Enough. He already told you no. You promised you would let me ask him and accept whatever decision he made." I may have to put up with my mom's pushiness, but Mason sure didn't.

Mason lets out a deep breath and looks over at me. He's uncomfortable, I can tell. But he's biting his lower lip which means—

"I'll be there Elaine. Vi and I will work out the details and keep you posted."

She is satisfied with herself; the sigh on the other line tells us as much. "Okay, now I really need to run and tell Melissa. I love you two. Bye."

"Mason I'm so sorry. She's literally the pushiest person on the planet." I place my hand on his bare chest while taking his face in my other hand. "You don't have to go just because she asked."

He turns his face so he can kiss the palm of my hand. "I know, but I probably should."

"I just hate feeling like you're being forced into this."

"I am, but honestly I need a kick in the ass or else I'm never going to do it." He shifts us slightly so he can wrap his arms around me again as he buries his head into my neck.

His voice is muffled by my curls when he says, "Plus I will finally get to make out with you in your childhood bedroom. Been wanting to do that for years. Maybe for foreplay I'll climb in through the window." He looks up at me and finds I'm shaking my head and smiling. "I'll have you by my side the entire time, Vi. I can face anything as long as I have you."

There's nothing more I can say so I wrap my arms around his neck and hold him tight against me hoping he can feel how my heart beats for him. I'll always be on his side whenever he needs me the most.

thirty-three

. . .

Mason

"ALRIGHT BOYS, that's it for today. Let's bring it in." I wait for everyone to skate off the ice and head to the locker room. The past few practices I've taken the lead on coaching and while at first, it felt like I was pushed into the deep end of a bottomless pool, over time I've felt more comfortable. While this job had initially fallen into my lap, the more I coached the more it felt like this had been my calling all along. I thought nothing would ever match the rush of playing, until I got to guide my freshmen into scoring their first goals and helped our senior players set new personal records. Those moments filled my heart with the same amount of joy I felt when it was me scoring goals.

Whether Coach Jameson had noticed my impact on the team thus far was another story. He stops me before I head down the tunnel into the locker rooms. "Any thoughts about the lines for the game against Bolton?"

We are just over a month out from our big rivalry game, and the pressure to win is palpable. Bolton was slowly climbing up the ranks in the Hockey East division, and a win against us would put them right behind UCONN.

"I think we stay with what we've been doing the last few games."

"The lines you picked." There's no judgement in his statement. Very matter of fact.

"The boys are getting increasingly comfortable playing in these new pairs, and it's only benefitted us so far. Also, none of our opposing teams have figured us out yet which is always a good advantage to have." I shrug as if to say, 'But if we don't do that it's totally fine and don't blame me if it doesn't work because you agreed.' Coach turns me into such a chickenshit sometimes.

All I get is a nod. "Any news on whether Jake will be in the mix? I can't let him on the ice if his grades have gotten worse."

"I have a meeting with him and his teaching assistant this afternoon to check in about how things are going with his tutor. I should have an update soon."

"Well, if he's been trying half as hard in class as he has been learning these new passing drills, he should be in fine shape." With the ice cleared we both head to our offices. "Keep me posted on how the meeting goes. Better we start planning now if we need to replace Jake, instead of a week before the Bolton game."

"Trust me Coach no one wants to beat Bolton as much as I do."

"I guess that's the perk of having a Coach who was once a player. No need to fake interest in the rivalry."

"Is Bolton's coaching staff still the same?"

"Sure is."

"Good. It'll be nice to remind them who's in charge on this side of the city."

He turns away from me as he enters his office. As I head further down the hall, I see a short figure with curly hair leaning against the door frame of my office, deeply immersed in her phone. "You're here early."

Violet glances up, jumping at the sound of my voice. "On time or naked, that's what I always say."

"I'll be sure to show up late to our next date then." I unlock my door and hold it open for her as she walks in. "Practice wrapped up about twenty minutes ago so Jake should be here soon."

"Sounds good. I told Jake's tutor, Eliana, to be here at 4 p.m." Violet settles in one of the chairs across from my desk and I fight the urge to drag her chair around to my side so she's right next to me.

I lick my lips as I watch her shrug off her winter coat and drape it over the back of the chair. She's wearing a tight-knit cream sweater that covers more skin than it shows, yet I can't help but imagine what a late Violet would look like naked in my office. The way she would tug on my hair while I trailed kisses along her neck—

"Mason?" My name brings me back to reality and the smirk on her face lets me know she caught me daydreaming.

"Sorry, what?"

"Do you have any extra chairs? For our meeting?"

"Right."

I return to my office, extra chairs in hand, and see Jake standing alongside a brunette who has a stack of assignments in one hand and coffee in another. I set the two chairs down and settle back into my seat. Eliana walks over without a word, taking the chair closest to Violet. From the scowl on Jake's face, I can assume he's going to make this meeting as painful as possible. Before I can ask Jake to sit down so we can get this over with, Eliana turns and gives him a menacing look, eyeing the empty chair. He rolls his eyes and takes a seat next to her, a scowl still permanently etched onto his face. I am going to take a wild guess and assume tutoring has not been going well.

"Alright, so why don't we get started," Violet offers. "I'd like to first hear from you both about how tutoring has been going, and whether any changes need to be made. Then we can discuss Jake's eligibility for the rest of the semester."

Violet hands me Jake's reports. This fucker's grade was in the toilet a few months ago. Coach Jameson will be happy to hear it has much improved, but we were still not fully in the clear yet. One missing assignment and he'd be out for the rest of the season. Westchester took their GPA cutoffs very seriously and if his GPA dipped any lower, he'd have to spend the next semester bringing it up from the sidelines.

Eliana is the first to speak. "We had a bit of a rocky start—" Jake snorts, "—but over time, we came up with a mutual agreement on what it would take for us to stay on track. And things have been better since then."

"*'Mutual agreement'* is a very nice way of saying she threatened me several times saying she'd let me flunk if I didn't do all these assignments on her hellish timeline."

"Part of my responsibility as your tutor is to make sure that you complete all your assignments in a timely manner. It's not my fault you have issues with planning and prioritizing your responsibilities."

"And it's not my fault they gave me a *drill sergeant* for a tutor. Seriously, could you *be* any more uptight? I don't respond well to authoritarianism."

"You can get snippy with me all you want Jake, but that doesn't change the fact that my methods have been working." She looks smug as she turns her head away from him. "You're welcome by the way."

"You are so full of yourself," He seethes.

"Just giving my student a dose of his own medicine."

"You know what?" He leans over his chair to bring himself

closer to Eliana, who doesn't cower away. If anything, she looks just as ready to go off as he does. And either I'm completely misreading this situation or there is some…heat behind all this anger.

"Okay," Violet interjects. "I hear that some things have been effective. Jake, from looking at your assignment grades before you started tutoring to now, you've really turned things around." Eliana beams from her chair while Jake rolls his eyes. "But maybe we can work on being a bit more flexible when it comes to scheduling?" Jake perks up, watching Eliana's disgruntled face as she gives Violet a small nod. I don't know how, but Violet has managed to find a tutor whose even more stubborn and hot-headed than Jake is. Maybe that's why she picked her in the first place.

"So, he can keep playing?" My question seems to frustrate Eliana. I know his education is important and all that shit, but we are here for one specific reason.

Violet looks at the grade book on her laptop for a few seconds before turning her attention back to me. "He can keep playing."

"Thank *fuck*," Jake exhales.

"But I do recommend he keeps up with his tutoring. At least until the end of the semester. And maybe for next semester too if he plans on taking more psych classes. Pending Eliana being available. She's our best psychology tutor and tends to be in high demand." The latter comment is not-so-subtly aimed at Jake, who seems to get the message.

He flashes Eliana an apologetic look. "You are a really good tutor, that acts like a drill sergeant."

She rolls her eyes before saying, "Thanks." She turns her attention to Violet. "I have to head over to lab if that's okay? I'm helping Maya run a scan soon." Ah, that explains Violet's protectiveness. I didn't realize Eliana was also one of her research assistants.

"Yes definitely. We'll talk more later." Violet gives her a wave as she heads out of my office.

Once Eliana exits, Jake turns his attention to Violet. "Have you considered giving her a day off or something? She practically lives in that lab."

Violet looks as caught off guard as I am. "I'm sorry?"

"It wouldn't kill her to have some fun. All she does is school, tutoring, and research."

"Research can be fun," Violet challenges.

"God, no wonder you hired her. You're like, the same person." He shakes his head and turns to me. "So, am I good to go?"

"Yeah, you're all set. I do want to finalize some things with Violet, so just shut the door on your way out."

I wait until I can no longer hear Jake's footsteps before I stand up from my desk and lean over to Violet's chair, pressing a kiss to her temples and then a longer one to her lips.

"What was that for?" She smiles.

"I just missed you from all the way over here." I kiss her again.

She rolls her eyes before opening her mouth for me, and I groan at the sound of someone knocking on my door.

"Mason," Coach's voice rings through. "Are you still in your meeting? Any news on Jake?"

I press one last kiss to Violet's lips, nipping hard on her bottom lip as a promise of what's to come later, before opening my door and getting Coach up to speed.

thirty-four

· · ·

Violet

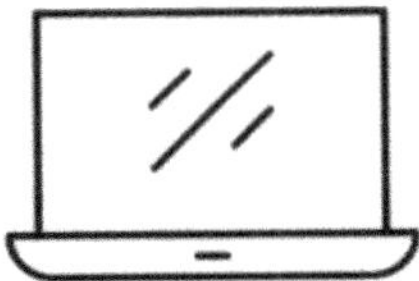

"OKAY, I THINK THAT'S EVERYTHING." I watch as Mason places my bags in the back of his car. Admittedly, I don't need to bring two large duffle bags and a suitcase worth of clothing for a three-day trip home, but in my defense one of the bags was primarily filled with Christmas gifts. Mason shuts his trunk before walking over to the passenger seat and holding the door open for me.

"Was there enough room for your stuff?" I ask, sliding into the car.

"Yeah, I just strapped my bag to the roof." He smiles before the closing my door, re-rounds the car, and hops in the driver seat.

"I like to think my tendency to overpack and overprepare are all part of my charm."

"I've traveled with you before, so I knew what to expect." He reaches over the console to rest his hand on my thigh.

"Fair enough." I wait until we pull off on US-1 to address the elephant in the car. "So, how do you feel about seeing your dad tonight?"

His grip on my thigh tightens for a second, followed by his thumb drawing idle circles. "Honestly, I'm really nervous about it...I know how much our moms have put into making Christmas dinner perfect and I don't want to ruin it by losing my cool."

"You won't ruin anything." I place my hand over his, kissing the side of his arm. "Plus, I'll be by your side the entire time, and I have no issues keeping him in line. Just like I do his son."

That manages to bring a huge smile to his face. "Look who's all tough now."

"It's the least I could do after all you did for me growing up."

He shoots me a confused look before turning his attention back to the road.

"Oh c'mon. I think everyone we went to school with in Castle Harbor was convinced I had a secret Mason-Bat-Signal. You always managed to show up whenever someone was picking on me. Sometimes I was a little embarrassed thinking about how defenseless you thought I was."

"Violet, let me make one thing clear. I have never once thought you were defenseless. I just liked defending you." He brings my hand to his mouth and places a kiss on the back. "I probably did it an excessive amount back then because I didn't know how else I could show you how much I loved you."

"Oh." I really had to find a better response every time Mason decided to drop a sweet and romantic confession out of nowhere. I knew he understood how difficult it was for me to talk about my feelings, even with those closest to me. He hadn't pushed me to change that about myself since we'd gotten together, but that didn't mean *I* didn't want to change that part of myself. No matter how hard it was. "Well, it really meant a lot to me. Still does."

The rest of the drive is spent in comfortable silence, with the occasional sing-along to whatever Christmas song was playing on the radio. We're lucky enough to avoid traffic and before I know it, I'm met with the familiar 'Welcome to Castle Harbor, America's First Seaport' sign that stands next to a statue of a fisherman. This time of year, the fisherman is decked out in an array of Christmas lights.

"Glad to know some things never change." Mason drives us down a series of winding roads toward the back shore, which gives a perfect view of the rocky coastline of our beaches. Even in the dead of winter nothing beats seeing the never-ending coastline and the array of rocks and hills that surrounded the harbor and overlooked the entirety of Cape Ann. The left of the road is lined with mansions so massive they are more like castles. Monroe and I pretended they were when we were kids.

"Did Monroe get in already?" I ask as Mason heads toward the street we both grew up on.

"Yeah, she took the train in last night and my mom picked her up from the stop. Have you told her about us yet?"

Shit. "It totally slipped my mind. How mad do you'll think she'll be?"

"About the fact that at minimum 90% percent of the town found out before she did? I'd say she's gonna be pretty pissed."

"Maybe she hasn't even heard yet? You did say she just got in, right?"

"Monroe's been in Castle Harbor for over twelve hours now. She probably knows more details about our relationship than we do. I bet Giana Silvera has already sent her a three-page report on how compatible our astrological signs are."

"Oo I would like to get my hands on that report."

Mason is parking in my mom's driveway when the front door of the house flies open and Monroe comes rushing out.

"VIOLET AMIN. YOUR ASS IS DEAD."

"Okay so in my defense…actually I have none. Other than the fact that it was the end of the semester, and I was running on pure autopilot and completely spaced." I step out of the car and extend my arms out for a hug. "Forgive me."

She raises an eyebrow at me. "I had to find out from Marge Preesley that you were shacking up with my brother. *Marge Preesley*. Who, by the way, could barely get out Mason's name before sobbing over the cat-sitting incident of 2012."

A load groan comes from Mason as he steps out of the car. "How many times do I have to say it. I did *not* kill Mr. Noodles. That cat was just old."

Monroe rolls her eyes before turning her attention back to me, my arms still extended. She glares for a few seconds before breaking and giving in to my hug. "I can't believe you two are finally together." She squeezes me tightly for a moment, and then leads me into the house. "How did it happen? When did it happen? You have to tell me *all* the details…pause. Maybe not all the details because there are some things a sister really doesn't ever need to know about her brother."

"Should we maybe help Mason—" I turn around to see him carrying in all our bags with ease.

Monroe drags me into the house where I spot my mom in the kitchen, already having made substantial progress on a bottle of Prosecco. Monroe slides me a glass before taking a seat on one of the bar stools. "Details. Now."

thirty-five

. . .

Violet

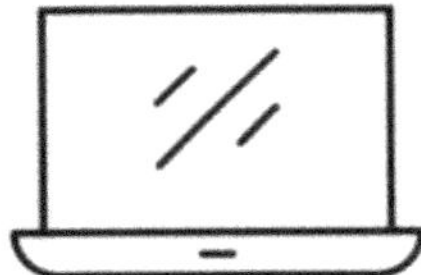

"ARE you sure we can't just order some takeout tonight and hide away in your room?" Mason buries his head into my neck and wraps his arms around me from behind, as I take one final look at my outfit in the mirror. Christmas Eve dinner was always followed by an extensive photo-op, driven largely by my mother, who always fussed about how we never had enough family photos. The frames covering the walls begged to differ, but who was I to get in her way?

"I'm pretty sure my mom made her signature shortbread cookies just for you, so no. You don't want to face her wrath if we skip dinner." I lean into his embrace, taking his hand into mine. "Are you having second thoughts about coming back?"

He hugs me even tighter and presses a kiss to the side of my head. "No. I forgot how much I loved it here. How magical this place feels during the holidays…"

"But?"

"I just don't know what to say to him."

"We'll figure it out together," I promise. "Worst case scenario we can just pretend he's not even here, okay?"

He presses a kiss on my shoulder. "Okay."

That proves to be much easier said than done, as Melissa practically forces Mason into the chair closest to his father. Joe decides to make me the center of the conversation, ignoring his son who is seated right next to him. "So, Violet your mom tells me you're applying for this big fellowship?"

"Yeah, I've submitted all my app materials and am crossing all my fingers and toes right now. I could really use the money to help free up my schedule."

"I thought the school already paid you?" Joe takes a sip of his wine.

"Yeah, but the payment is tied directly to my work as a teaching assistant. Which means the time I'd be spending on research gets sacrificed to other responsibilities like grading papers, leading discussion sections, and holding office hours."

"And this fellowship would help with that?"

"Exactly. I would basically be getting paid to do my research which means I wouldn't have to teach anymore."

"I see. Well, good luck. They'd be stupid not to give it to you."

"Thanks Joe." I glance over to Mason who is looking at me lovingly. "Although one downside of not teaching is I won't see Mason as much anymore. One of his players is in my class this semester."

Joe finally turns his attention to Mason. "I heard you were coaching for Westchester."

Mason straightens up. "Yeah. For a few months now."

"Would've been nice if you had told us. Or even mentioned that you were back in Boston. You know, your mom and I had to find out from someone else."

"I meant to reach out to you two."

"I'm sure you did." Joe rolls his eyes. "Just like you meant to return all our calls when you were playing with the Rangers."

Mason's good posture deflates at his dad's criticism. "I'm not proud of how I acted when I was still in the NHL."

"You just packed your bags and disappeared. Never even once thought about the people you had left behind."

"Joe." Melissa's warning goes unacknowledged as he continues.

"Even after you got injured, and all your fancy New York friends abandoned you, you *still* didn't come home. Instead, you acted like you were so much better than this town and the people in it." Oh no.

"Cut the shit, Dad. You know exactly why I didn't come home after I got hurt. Or do you not remember our conversation?"

A flash of guilt comes over Joe's face, but he remains silent.

"Do you need me to jog your memory? Because no matter how hard I try to forget it I can't." Underneath the table, Mason reaches for my hand, which I immediately offer, before he continues. "I remember calling you an *hour* after I was told I had to retire, hoping the man who I had always looked up to would be there for me, and all you had to say was, 'I don't know why you're so upset. This is honestly great news, Mason.'"

"I didn't mean it like that." Joe's voice is pleading, first to Mason and then to anyone else at the table who was willing to hear him out. None of us meet his gaze. If it wasn't for Mason's grip on my hand, I probably would've stormed out already. How Mason hadn't already done so or has managed to stay calm for as long as he has, is beyond me.

"What *did* you mean?" Mason's voice is void of any emotion as he turns to his dad.

"Just that you retiring meant you would finally come home. Finally go back to being the Mason that I raised and was proud to call my son. You became a whole different person when you moved to New York. At least Monroe would come home every now and then. You, on the other hand, practically abandoned us."

"That's not true!" I cut in, slamming my hand on the table in frustration. "Just because Mason wanted to build his own life in New York doesn't mean that he changed or that he abandoned his family."

"Then what do you call him never picking up the phone or coming back to Castle Harbor to visit?"

"Maybe him just being busy? It's not like he wasn't traveling around playing for the NHL or anything. I can't believe you're trying to turn this whole thing around and blame it on Mason, when you're the one who drove the wedge between you two in the first place." Joe is being ridiculous, and I'm determined to let him know it. "It's not like New York is super far from here. You could have easily driven down to see him if you wanted to. You're his father, it's your responsibility to be there for him."

I watch Mason's dad carefully, ready to counter every bull-shit argument he throws at me. Instead, he runs a hand down his face and lets out a heavy sigh before conceding. "You're right Violet. I could've done more."

"Don't say that to me, say that to him." I point my thumb in Mason's direction.

"I'm sorry Mason. I never should have said what I did back then, and I should've tried harder to be there for you. I know it's not an excuse, but I missed not having you here, and I went about it wrong. Really wrong."

Underneath the table, Mason squeezes my hand three times, letting me know he was okay. "I appreciate it Dad. I've missed you too, and I hope one day we can go back to how things were before."

The initial silence after is painfully awkward, until my mom shifts her attention to Monroe. "So, 'Roe are you still with that… *artist?*" My mom does her best not to crinkle her nose in disgust.

"Yes, Jacque sends his regards. He really wanted to be here."

Mason snorts in response. Yeah, I'm not sure if anyone is

buying that. The one time Jacque did come up to Castle Harbor he threw a fit when he realized it was during the Summer Festival. He emphasized how much he hated carnivals, small town traditions, and basically anything fun. I had tried my hardest to stay neutral about him, but the second he insulted my favorite Castle Harbor holiday he made it to the top of my shit list. We've all been crossing our fingers, hoping Monroe will come to her senses and dump the pretentious wannabe socialite.

"Maybe we can go on a double date when you two come to New York in a few weeks?" She looks so excited as she turns to me. I don't know if I have it in me to tell her that I'd rather walk around the entire city in nothing but a t-shirt and jeans in the dead of winter than succumb myself to two hours of Jacque mansplaining the New Age movement. All while he speaks over Monroe and downplays her accomplishments.

"We'll keep you posted. We're not sure how long we'll be there." Mason comes in with an incredible save. I nearly kiss him then and there for managing to spare her feelings and get us out of a nightmare dinner.

"Why are you two heading into the city Mason?" It's the first civil question Joe has asked today.

Mason takes the olive branch. "Connor got this big award for all the work he's been doing with The Second Chance Foundation, and he asked if I'd be willing to give a speech."

"That's amazing. What an honor. For the both of you."

Mason shrugs. "I'm just the guy who gets to hand him the award."

I chime in. "And the guy who is one of the organization's biggest donors. Also, weren't you and Connor the ones to pitch having the Rangers officially work with Second Chance? Don't sell yourself short."

Did I choose to emphasize all Mason has done as further evidence to Joe about how *incredible* his son is? Maybe. But I also want Mason to know that I see everything he does. See how big his heart is. And I love him for it.

"You know, I've been wanting to do a bit of pro-bono marketing with my firm," Monroe interjects. "Do you think Connor would be willing to put me in contact with someone at Second Chance?"

"Definitely. He'd do anything to help grow the cause. Why don't I give you his contact info and you two can figure out a time to talk more?" While Mason shares Connor's phone number, I catch my mom and Melissa exchanging glances. Those two need to be separated.

thirty-six

· · ·

Violet

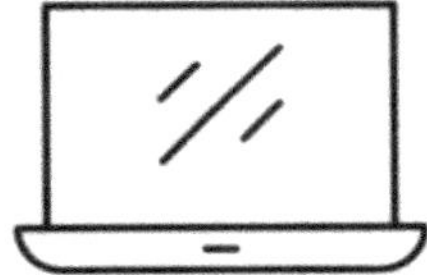

THE IMMEDIATE WEEKS following the holidays are a whirlwind for Mason and I. Between the hockey season picking up, and all the homework assignments, papers, and exams I have to grade, I feel like the last time Mason and I really got to spend time with each other was well…Christmas. While I was staying at his apartment most nights, we haven't had time to grab lunch or even dinner and his weekends are spent traveling with the team.

In the few moments of calm, I can't help but think about how much I want Mason. Being with him feels like waking up to the first snow of the year — a type of magic you never thought you could feel but once you experience it, you never want to let it go. While I am still getting used to speaking from my heart, Mason is vocal, texting me daily about how much he misses me and wants to see me outside of his dreams. But all that changes tonight. The first Friday night when neither of us have any responsibilities or prior obligations.

"Angel, we should probably get going soon," Mason calls from the living room.

I do a quick double take in the mirror and grab my winter coat from his closet before joining him. His eyes light up the moment they meet mine and I walk over to him, wrapping my arms around his neck. "Hi."

"Hey." He takes his bottom lip between his teeth, as he slowly trails his eyes down my body. "God, you look beautiful." He leans down to press a soft kiss to my temple before burying his face into my neck. We hold onto each other a bit longer than we should have before rushing out the door. Mason walks out behind me and moves to open the car door for me. As I climb in, he smacks my ass.

"Mason."

"My love." He beams, dipping his head in so I can see how satisfied he is with himself.

My heart leaps and I try to school the smile that's creeping up on my face. "Watch those hands. Now, can we go have some pasta?"

"Absolutely. Just stay on your best behavior and you won't be needing any more spankings."

"So, what was that one for?"

"For making me wait 28 years to see you in that little dress."

I prepare my sarcastic reply when my phone rings. When I see it's Eliana, I press accept. "Hey, what's up?"

"Please don't hate me." Her voice sounds groggy like she's come down with something.

"I could never hate you. Are you okay?"

She takes a deep breath. "I was supposed to help Maya with a scan in like 30 minutes, but I came down with something and I really hoped it was just allergies but it's not."

Ah fuck. There goes my date night. "No worries, I can totally cover for you. Just focus on getting some rest."

"I feel so bad, I know it's your date night. Maybe if I wear a mask and take some more ibuprofen—" She breaks into a coughing fit.

"Do you need me to come over? I can help drive you to an urgent care." I shoot Mason a concerned look and point him in the direction of student housing.

"No, I'm fine. I have a uh…friend taking care of me."

"Okay I'll head to campus to help Maya. Let me know if I can drop off some medicine or soup."

"Thanks Violet. And sorry again."

"No need to apologize. Feel better, Ellie." I hang up the phone and turn to Mason with a remorseful look on my face. "Looks like I'm going to need some more spankings."

"You're right about that. But honestly, all I care about is spending time with you. Whether that's at a fancy restaurant or curled up on the coach back home eating takeout after you're done working, doesn't matter to me."

"You're the best. Do you know that?"

"Promise to scream that later?" Mason smirks at me as he pulls up to the campus MRI center, and I realize I'm incredibly overdressed.

"Would you hate me if I asked you to bring me a change of clothes? And maybe my laptop?" If I was going to be on campus, I may as well make the most of it and get some extra work done.

"Of course. I'll text you when I'm outside."

———

"Are you sure there's no one else we can call so you can go on your date?" Maya asks as we sit in the MRI control room.

"I don't think any of the new research assistants have been certified yet to work with the scanner. It looks like you're stuck with me," I tease.

"You know I love having you around. I just feel bad that you canceled your date night."

I shrug. "I still get to spend the night with him which is really all that matters."

"Well, I appreciate you jumping in to help me. Soon you'll have all the data you need."

I only had a few more babies to scan before I was done. Hopefully I'd only be a *little* late in meeting Bethany's deadline. Have I had time to analyze any of the data I collected or write up my results? Of course not. But that was a problem for future Violet.

My phone vibrates with a text from Mason, indicating he's here. I head outside to let him in, pausing when I see him carrying a picnic basket. "What's this?"

"Well, I figured since we couldn't go to the restaurant, I would bring the restaurant to you. I canceled our reservation and put in a takeout order instead. I even ordered extra for Maya."

This man had to be the most thoughtful person I'd ever met. I couldn't believe he was all mine. "I—I don't even know what to say."

"How about you let me in before we both freeze out here?"

"Shit. Yes. Absolutely." I unlock the door and pull him into a room next to the lobby before all of the 'WARNING. MRI SAFETY ZONE AHEAD' signs. "Let me just give Maya her dinner really quick."

I peak my head back into the control room and slide over the Tupperware of ravioli.

"Mason got us food from Ristorante Florentine."

"Violet if you don't marry the man I will." She begins diving into her dinner.

"Noted."

"I think the family just arrived. I can go get them prepped if you want to bring Mason in here as you get the scanner ready.

Also tell him he's officially my second favorite person. Behind you of course."

While Maya talks to the family, I make Mason go through our metal detector a few times. "I feel like I'm going through airport security." He laughs.

"I've been to one too many MRI safety trainings. Perhaps I'm a bit paranoid." When I'm sure he's fine, I bring Mason into the control room. "You can set the food down over there. Once I start the scan it's pretty straight forward."

"I can't believe you do this with babies. I could barely lay still the last time I got an MRI."

"You just hope and pray that they stay asleep. Sometimes it works...sometimes it doesn't." I log onto the computer as Maya instructs the mom on how to place her baby inside the MRI scanner. When she comes back, I start the machine and let Maya take the reigns as I turn my attention to Mason.

He pulls out several different takeout containers, laying out an array of entrees and desserts. "I can't believe you did all of this for me."

"I'd do anything for you." He scooches over to create enough space for me to sit next to him. "Now are we feeling Carbonara or Ravioli?"

"Honestly both."

"That's the correct answer." He flashes me a smile while handing me a fork as we both dive in.

"Any news from Coach Jameson about this job becoming a bit more permanent?" We had one somewhat tense conversation about alternatives if he did have to find work elsewhere. In an ideal world he would find another local university to work for, but if that didn't pan out we may have to consider long distance. After so many years apart from each other, we hated the idea of being separated again.

"Coach has made comments about how far the team has come because of the changes I've made, but beyond that..." He shrugs, momentarily pinching his eyebrows together in concern.

"Jake managed to bring his grade back up before the end of the semester. Seems like excellent coaching to me."

He shakes his head. "I can't take credit for that; it was all you."

"Actually, it was all Eliana. She was the one who was willing to tutor him." How she managed to make it to the end of the semester without strangling Jake, I'll never know. "Your guys absolutely destroyed Bolton before winter break, which in my opinion should count as *at least* four separate wins."

"Excuse me. Violet Amin. Are you saying you're officially a Westchester hockey fan?"

"Well, I may or may not have a slight crush on Westchester's Assistant Coach so that's certainly played a role…"

Even in the dim office lighting I see a faint hint of red on his cheeks. "What about you, any news on this fellowship?"

"Bethany hinted that the review committee would be meeting soon, probably in the next few weeks."

"Well, there's no way you're not going to get it. And once you do think of all the free time you'll have to watch me coach." Mason winks.

"Hopefully. I really need to get to work on writing this paper I've owed Bethany for months." Which meant I had to analyze the data first…and before I could even do that I needed to clean and organize said data. The list of things I had to accomplish felt endless.

"Don't forget our project either," Maya interjects, "I finished processing most of the data this week, so hopefully we can start drafting the paper soon. Ideally, I'd like to get it submitted in the next few months before I go on job interviews."

Fuck. Okay. I had completely forgotten to account for this project we'd been working on together. This completely threw off all my plans, but I guess I could make that work. I pull out my phone to look at my calendar and grimace. Each week looked worse than the one before it.

"I'm sorry, I know how stretched thin you are right now," Mason whispers, rubbing a soothing hand up and down my back as I lean into his embrace.

"I just feel like I'm constantly falling behind. My cohort mates who don't have to teach are so much further along in their projects and publishing papers already. I know I shouldn't compare myself to anyone, but it's so hard not to. Especially when there's so few academic jobs and everything is so competitive." *And maybe I wouldn't be in this position if I hadn't lost an entire year trying to prove my worth to someone who never saw it and instead tore away at every piece of me.*

Thinking about all the impending deadlines I have, and how incredibly far behind I am, is enough to make my heart race so fast it feels like it's about to rip out of my chest. I feel sweat start to roll down my back, and suddenly getting air into my lungs feels like work. I didn't even realize my hands had started to shake until Mason takes them into his.

"Hey, hey it's going to be okay Vi." He presses a small kiss over the pulse point on my wrist.

It takes me a few minutes of deep breathing, five seconds in seven seconds out, to come back down. My head still feels a bit dizzy, but I've been through many panic attacks in my lifetime I know it will fade. "Sorry. I guess I'm a bit more stressed about all the things I'm juggling right now than I realized."

"Panic attack?" He guesses.

I nod. He always could read me better than anyone else.

"Do you still get them often?"

"Uhm, not really. The last one happened a few months ago. I think I've been more stressed about my thesis and waiting to hear back about the fellowship than I've been letting on. You know me, I always push down my emotions until they erupt like a volcano." I let out a self-deprecating laugh in a failed attempt to make light of the situation.

"If there's anything I can do to help—"

"You do. You did. Just by being here for me. That's all I need."

"Always. You don't even have to ask."

And while I have a tendency of second guessing nearly every good thing in my life, I know with all of my heart that he means it.

thirty-seven

. . .

Violet

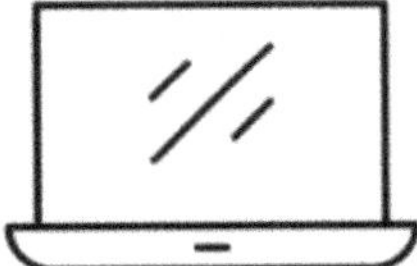

"ALRIGHT VI, I think it's time that you call it." Mason gives my knee a small squeeze before moving his hand to rest higher up on my thigh.

"Probably for the best, I was getting a little motion sick trying to grade assignments in a car." I slam my laptop shut and place it back into my bag. "I did manage to get through most of them though. How much time do we have left?"

"I'd say another two-ish hours depending on traffic."

I scrunch my nose, "Gross. Has New York always been this far?"

"Yup. Is Eliana feeling better by the way?"

It had been about week since our makeshift date at the MRI center. "Mhmm. She was back in the lab on Wednesday and apologized to me like ten times even though I told her she didn't need to."

"That sounds familiar."

"We are a Type A dream team."

He pauses and shoots me a quick look. "Did you know Jake is taking another psych class next semester?"

"That's surprising." While he had managed to bring his grade up in PSYCH101 I never got the impression that he enjoyed the material.

"I thought so too."

"So, we will be co-parenting our problem child again next semester?"

"I don't think so. He already has a tutor lined up."

"Oh? Anyone I know?"

"Eliana. I guess he hasn't scared her off yet."

"Or, she likes the fear. She was definitely getting some pleasure out of torturing him."

There had to be an explanation as to why she didn't tell me. Maybe she was worried I would scold her about spreading herself too thin. Probably because she was. As a chronic people-pleaser I could spot another one from a mile away.

"Well just so you know, when the semester ends and I'm no longer Jake's TA, I don't have to be impartial anymore. If he steps one toe out of line with my girl, I will break his kneecaps."

"Could you at least wait until the end of my coaching season to do that?"

I deliberate for a few seconds. "Sorry but, no. Girl code is not bounded by hockey seasons. I act immediately. Your coaching season be damned."

"Noted. If it makes you feel any better, I don't think you need to worry too much."

"Why? Because you'll keep him in line?"

"No, because I know she will." He lets out a small laugh. "Plus, I have a feeling he's a lot more like his coach than he likes to lead on."

"I'm not entirely sure I'm following."

Mason gives my thigh a small squeeze before leaning over to

give me a kiss on my cheek. "I'm sure you'll find out soon enough."

———

Two hours later, we arrive at our hotel in the center of the upper east side. It's not until we are standing in line to check in that I realize the last time we spent a night together in a hotel ended with us...ending. I'm staring at nothing, recalling the feeling of my heart breaking— completely oblivious to the line of guests moving until Mason gently pulls me forward.

"You okay?" He whispers into my ear and wraps an arm around my waist.

"Yeah." I say this knowing he can tell I'm lying.

"What's wrong?"

"Nothing, I'm just having a moment and being dramatic."

"Vi." His eyebrows knit together as he rubs a soothing hand up and down my back.

"Really. Please ignore me."

"I know you're really stressed right now. You can totally stay in the hotel room and work while I go to Connor's award ceremony. I'm sure he would understand."

I shake my head. "No, I want to go." He waits patiently as I decide if my melodrama is worth speaking aloud.

"Violet, you don't have to tell me if you don't want to. But I am here for you if you need me."

"I just don't want to hurt your feelings," I mumble.

"You won't. And even if you do that's for me to worry about."

I shake my head. "That's not true. We're in a relationship so of course if you're upset that impacts me."

"Fair enough. So how about you share your feelings and then I'll share mine, and we can figure it out together?"

I blink once, then twice as I realize how smart that suggestion is. "Wow. You're good. Are you sure you're not the psychologist in the relationship?"

"Violet."

"Okay fine. It's just now occurring to me that hotels make me sad. Because of, ya know, Chicago."

His face falls, and I can tell I've brought his mood down with mine. I should have just kept my thoughts to myself.

"I'm sorry, Vi. I hate that you have that memory of us. Hopefully we can replace some of those bad memories with good ones with weekend." He winks in an attempt to lighten the mood.

"I feel like it's so hard for me to move on from things. I just want to live in the moment but there's a part of my brain I can't turn off that always brings me back to times I'd like to leave buried."

Mason wipes away a stray tear from my cheek that managed to fall without me noticing. "It's okay if you can't fully let go of the past Violet. All of what we went through brought us here. I just hope you know that I wouldn't trade a single bad day of mine if it meant I had to give up a good day with you."

I lean my head up to place a soft kiss on his lips. I want us both to shake off our hotel history and kissing his lips usually does a good job of wiping my mind's slate clean. "Sorry, I didn't mean to bring the vibes down."

His face softens and he rests his forehead on mine.

"We're here together now Violet, which is all that matters to me. Having you by my side is all that matters to me."

thirty-eight

. . .

Mason

AFTER DROPPING our bags off in the room, we grab a quick lunch and head straight to Central Park to see whether Wollman Rink lives up to the hype (Violet claimed the Frog Pond in Boston was better, I agreed to disagree). Violet skates laps around me like a pro the entire time. Meanwhile I tried my best not to have a heart attack every time I think she is going to fall.

Afterward we mercifully dodge a double date with Monroe and her heinous boyfriend. Instead, we meet Monroe at her fancy office, where she catches Violet up on the drama surrounding one of her clients.

"Wait. Wait. So, you're telling me her husband cheats on her on national television, and the network threatens to fire *her* instead of him?" Violet exasperates.

"She was deemed a liability for not being able to 'handle her emotions' while working." Monroe rolls her eyes.

"Welp, we can check the box that reads 'sexism.' Also didn't this happen like years ago? Why are people still bringing it up?"

"Because she's finally coming back into the limelight to host another reality TV dating show. After her divorce, she wanted to lay low for a while and shifted to producing. Now that she's decided to show her face again, the claws have come out." Monroe bites her lip. "I'm really worried the press is going to scare her away from this job. For her sake, she really needs to take it. You can only hide from your problems for so long until they come back to bite you in the ass." Monroe's office phone rings seconds later drawing a groan. "Speaking of avoiding your problems...it's my boss."

I tuck the crumpled piece of paper into the pocket of my coat after giving it one last read through. I never get anxious with public speaking, mainly because post-game interviews were low stakes. But this was different. Connor deserved so much for all he'd done, and the least I could do was deliver a speech that spoke to his character and had minimal fuckups. This is ultimately what led me to re-read my speech for the hundredth time this week while Violet finished getting ready. Maybe I should have a beer before I get up on stage. Only one. Enough to dampen some of the nerves, without turning me into a complete mess.

"You're going to do great, Mason. Connor wouldn't have asked you to do this if he didn't think you could handle it." Violet's voice comes from the bathroom.

I'm cracking open a beer from the fridge as Violet steps out of the bathroom. The strapless, silk floor-length red dress clings to her body like a second skin, with a slit on the side that exposes her leg.

"Maybe you'll give me a heart attack before I even make it downstairs."

"I guess I don't have to ask you what you think about my dress."

"I think it's an absolute crime that I'm not going to be able to touch you the way that I want to for the next three hours, Angel." I walk over to her, bringing her into my arms. I trail a faint line of kisses down her neck and onto her shoulder and marvel at the goosebumps that form on her skin.

"I'm not opposed to leaving early." Violet's eyes show a sly glint. "But only *after* you're done with your speech, and we get to congratulate Connor."

"You drive a hard bargain, but I accept your terms. Let's get going." I take her hand into mine as we head toward the elevator.

I booked our room at the same hotel the Rangers' gala was being held (just in case we needed to make an emergency exit). We make it halfway up to the conference hall when the elevator dings and in enters Rowan with his wife. A smile lights up on the face of my former captain as he clamps a hand down on my shoulder. "Well look what the cat dragged in. It's good to see you, Mason."

Of all my former teammates I could've run into first, I'm glad it's him. Rowan was always the rock for the younger members of the team, and he took his leadership role very seriously on and off the ice.

"You too, man. You look good. A little old though. Is that gray I see?" I tease, pointing at a few streaks in his hair.

Rowan rolls his eyes, my comment bringing a small laugh from his wife, Tanya.

"I aged 10 years after being your captain," He deadpans.

"I missed you too, big guy." I really had. The nerves I felt about running into my former teammates had dissipated just by seeing Rowan. That and the woman who hadn't let go of my hand since we walked out of our room. We step out of the elevator into the area outside of the conference hall.

"So, are you going to introduce this lovely lady at your side, or do you plan on just keeping her hidden away from us for the rest of the night?" Rowan asks.

"I'm Violet. Mason's girlfriend."

Pride fills my chest at Violet's words. I'm not sure I would ever get over the feeling of her saying she's mine.

Recognition flashes over Tanya's eyes. "We met a few years ago, didn't we? In Chicago?" I feel Violet tense at my side as she nods. Tanya lets out a small squeal before turning her attention to her husband. "I told you. I told you they were endgame, didn't I? I'm never wrong."

"It seems like everyone else in our lives knew it was coming before we did." Violet shakes her head.

"Nah, we knew too. We were just too stubborn to admit it. At least we got there eventually." I place a kiss on her temple before directing my attention back to Rowan. "I heard you guys are killing it this season."

"Hopefully it continues that way into the playoffs. Gotta make my last season count." Rowan pauses waiting for my reaction.

"You're retiring?"

"You can't be surprised. You were the one chirping at me a few minutes ago about how old I was looking."

"You're actually serious?" Sure, thirty-four was on the older end of NHL players, but Rowan's never had a major injury.

"Tanya and I had a long conversation about it, and I realized it's my time. Plus, I don't want to miss a second of my daughter's life, so it all made sense." Rowan rests his hand on Tanya's stomach, and I finally notice the small bump.

"Holy shit, you're gonna be a dad? That's amazing." I give Tanya a small hug and pat Rowan on the back. He'd always talked to us about how much he wanted to be a dad and now he finally got his wish.

Rowan is beaming at his wife. "Thanks man. We're both really excited about it. I'm sure retirement will be an adjustment though. Got any pointers for me?"

"I never thought that anything would compare to the thrill of being out there on the ice, but I've been coaching at my alma mater recently and it's been really re—" I'm cut off by the one person I had dreaded seeing the most.

"That's incredibly noble of you Mason." Kallum's voice is dripping in sarcasm.

What a fucking dick. You would think after years of not playing on the same team he would've finally gotten over our one-sided rivalry. I guess not everyone changes with time. "Kallum. Nice seeing you again."

"You too. Though I can't lie, I am a bit surprised to see you here at the Rangers gala..." He trails off, meaning to imply something like, '*Wild seeing you here since you're not on the team anymore.*'

"Connor asked if I could make a speech for his philanthropy award." I shrug.

"Speaking of which, we should probably head in and see if we can try to track him down," Violet speaks up, likely feeling as repulsed by this man as I am. "Nice seeing you again Tanya. Rowan."

thirty-nine

. . .

Mason

I SEE Connor seated with his family. He greets me with a warm smile before throwing his arms around me.

"It's good to see you again, man. I'm glad you decided to take up my offer and bring a plus one." Connor takes Violet's hand into his and brings her in for a hug as she introduces herself. "Oh, trust me, I know exactly who you are. Mason couldn't shut up about you when he was on the team. Or after. I'm just glad to see you guys finally together."

"She definitely made me work for it." I tease receiving an elbow to the ribs as she rolls her eyes. "It was worth it though. She'll always be worth it." Violet's cheeks turn pink. I take it that I'm forgiven.

"So, you run into any of the boys yet?" Connor asks, gesturing for us to follow him toward the podium.

"We caught up with Rowan and Tanya. I still can't believe he's going to be a dad. And that he's retiring."

"Dude, I know. The whole locker room has changed so much these past couple of years. Well maybe not the whole locker room." Connor watches Kallum saunter in like he owns the place and rolls his eyes. "Some people are still assholes."

"Yeah, we had the unfortunate experience of running into Kallum as well," Violet speaks up. "In an ideal world that will be the first and last time I talk to him." Ditto.

"I did request that you two be sat at our table with my family and Rowan. So hopefully we can make it through the night without any jabs being thrown. Verbal or otherwise." Connor winks at me.

"I make no promises," Violet grumbles.

"Well, if you do start any fights can you give me a warning first? I wanna make sure I get to see it."

The conference hall is now packed with my former teammates, coaches, and other Rangers staff. I feel my heart start to race as I take in all the familiar faces. Scanning the room, I lock eyes with my former agent who lifts his drink and gives me a sheepish smile. The last time we talked was to discuss contract termination. Violet squeezes my hand as she notices me. "Say the word and we can head back up to our room."

An event coordinator interrupts us before I can take Violet up on the offer. In a blink I'm being handed a microphone and shuffled on stage. *You can do this Mason. This is for Connor.* I toggle my attention between one of my best friends and the woman who has given me the confidence to be here today. I lean into the mic and launch into my opener.

Everyone laughs at my stories of when we first joined the Rangers. As rookies we went through our fair share of hazing including someone covering our gear in itching powder right before practice and falling asleep on the bus and waking up sans an eyebrow. The emotional moments hit too. How Connor had always been there for me when I needed him. How much work he had put in over the years to help his family and so many others get out of poverty. No one deserved this award more than him, and I was just grateful that he wanted to include me in this moment.

Walking off the stage, I see Violet and Connor's mom wipe tears from their eyes, and I'm able to finally let out a breath. I wanted to make sure that tonight was special for Connor, and I was hopeful that I had done that. I keep my arm wrapped around Violet's shoulder as Connor gives his own speech and then joins us back at the table for dinner. After a three-course meal, Tanya insists on taking Violet around to meet the other WAGs and I decide to bite the bullet and follow Connor as he goes to catch up with Coach Patrick.

Coach's face lights up when he sees me, and I feel my heart tug as I remember how much I missed playing for him. "Mason, my boy. It's good to see you again." He clamps a giant hand on my shoulder. "I'm glad you decided to come tonight."

"I wouldn't miss this." No matter how much I felt like a third wheel now.

"Well, I'm glad to see you back on your feet again. What are you up to these days?"

"Oh, haven't you heard Coach?" Kallum's condescending voice rings over the crowd. "Our boy Mason here has decided to follow in your footsteps."

Coach looks at me confused. "I'm working as an assistant coach at Westchester."

Coach's lips curve up to a faint smile. "You always had a special eye for hockey. I'm glad you're not letting your talents go to waste. Those kids are lucky to have you."

I swallow the lump forming in my throat. "Thanks Coach."

"Well don't be a stranger Mason. Especially if you need any advice on how to control a bunch of hot heads with egos the size of Canada. I'm always here if you need me." Coach leaves with a pat on my shoulder, and Kallum breezes away from our group as quickly as he joined.

I head straight for the bar needing a bit of social relief. In many ways, I think tonight has helped me take another step forward. I had convinced myself that no one really cared about me after I got injured. And while it was true that some of my friendships were fleeting, tonight showed me that others, like Rowan and Coach, would always be there when I needed it. I just needed the courage to reach out. I tip the bartender for my beer when another familiar face approaches me. Marty Williams was my agent from when I signed my first NHL contract all the way until the end.

"Mason Hayes as I live and breathe."

"You're looking good Marty." I nod.

"I could say the same to you. I heard you still have an itch for the game." He stands next to me, a mischievous look in his eyes.

"I guess word spreads fast. Yeah, I'm a coach now. At my alma mater."

He crosses his arms as he scans my face. "And would you say that's enough for you?"

"Enough?"

"Do you feel as alive as you did when you were on the ice? When you were scoring goals? And the crowd was cheering *your* name?" he pries.

"Sometimes. Maybe. I don't know. I don't know if anything will ever feel that way." Thank you so much for reminding me, Marty.

"Hmmm…interesting." Marty keeps eyeing me. "I may have something for you if you're interested."

"Oh yeah and what's that?" I snort.

"A spot in a professional league. In Europe."

"C'mon, Marty. That's not funny."

"Whose joking?"

"I don't know if you forgot. I was forced to retire."

"Per the NHL's rules. Lord knows they've been coming down

extra hard on concussion cases. Some may say harder than they need to. Didn't one of your doctors say the results were inconclusive about whether you should return?"

"Yeah, in the beginning. And then my symptoms wouldn't go away. The team doctor said it was best for me to call it." I can barely get the words out of my mouth without flinching.

"So, different doctors gave you different opinions then? When was the last time you had any concussion symptoms?"

Marty takes my silence as a response.

"Listen. All I'm saying is, the team I'm thinking of will run some tests on you, and I have a strong feeling you'll pass them. I'm no doctor, but it sounds like you've healed. Just asking you to think about it and keep me posted."

"I can't believe you're actually asking me to make a comeback." Except I could. Marty saw the world in one color — green. And I was positive he would get a large cut of whatever deal I signed abroad. *If* I were to sign a deal abroad.

He holds his hands up in defeat. "I'm sure you're a good coach Mason, but you're still so young. Your legacy doesn't need to end with the NHL. With you on a European team, maybe we could even see you in the Olympics in a few years. Think it over and give me a call. How many times do you get a second chance at your dream?"

His words linger in my head, and from across the room, Violet sends me a bright smile. *How many times do you get a second chance at your dream?*

forty

• • •

Violet

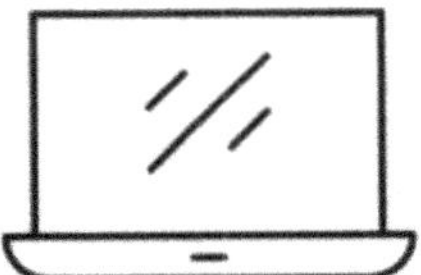

WE MAKE it through the entire gala without needing to make any flash exits. The night was a smashing success, though I could tell that something was weighing down on Mason.

"What's going on in your pretty head, Angel?" Mason burrows his face into the crook of my neck, his beard drawing out goosebumps on my skin, as we ride the elevator down to our room.

I lean into his embrace. "Just wondering how you're doing. Tonight couldn't have been easy for you."

"Some moments were easier than others. The good outweighed the bad. I missed a lot of the guys on the team, it was nice catching up with them again."

"I'm glad."

"Me too. Although there was one aspect that felt like

torture." He trails his hand to my exposed thigh while nipping at my neck.

"It was seeing Kallum again, wasn't it? I honestly have no idea how you managed to play alongside him for so many years —" I let out a small gasp as Mason slams the 'STOP' button on the elevator and pushes me against the wall.

"Violet." His voice has sunk two octaves and hell if it doesn't light my entire body on fire. "Where are your panties?"

The only word I can manage to get out is a soft "Oh" as his fingers dip under the slit of my dress and grab my hip, moving me so I'm pressed against him.

"My dress is really tight, and I didn't want any underwear lines so I decided—"

"So, you decided you didn't need them. Without telling me?" he tsks.

I stick my chin out in defiance. "Last time I checked, I don't need your permission when it comes to what I choose to wear… or not wear for that matter."

"My permission? No. But a man does need to know that he's spinning his wheels talking to a bunch of dudes when he could be taking advantage of this easy access. I wouldn't have kept us there as long as I did."

"Well, I guess we'll just have to make up for lost time."

"And how should we do that?" He lifts me up slightly, hooking one of my legs around his waist, causing my dress to fall open. A wicked glint flashes in his eyes before they trail down my body.

"You're pretty creative, I'm sure you'll think of something."

He presses his lips onto mine gently, pulling back when I try to deepen the kiss. He moves his tongue down my neck and nips at the one spot that always draws out a moan from me. I need him. All of him. Uninhibited and wild. I'm panting and desperate in a matter of minutes.

"Mason, stop teasing me. Please."

"You mean how you teased me all night wearing this dress?

Or how you forgot to mention the fact that you were bare underneath it?"

"That's not fair. You needed a distraction. I was helping you."

"Is that so?" His hand releases the leg hooked around his waist and moves to my stomach. So close to where I need him desperately, but not close enough. He presses his lips to my ear.

"You were just helping me out?" I nod. "Hmm. Then I guess I should thank you for being such a good girl huh? How does that sound?" He trails his finger down to my core no doubt feeling how wet I am already.

"Please Mason." I grind my hips against his finger.

"Oh Angel, I fucking love hearing you beg."

He leans his forehead against mine, finally sliding a finger inside of me as my entire back arches off the wall in ecstasy. His thumb meets my clit and draws circles on it as he adds another finger inside of me, pumping them in and out relentlessly.

"Always so wet for me. You feel so good."

My hands claw into his hair, locking our mouths together as I ride his hand. I would never have enough of him. All I wanted was more. More. "More, Mason. I need you," I pant. He quickens his movements on my clit and I know I can't hold on much longer.

Mason brings his lips to my ear. "Let go, Violet. Let go." With his words I fall over the edge. He releases my arms and buries his face into my neck, leaving a bunch of soft kisses on my shoulder. I love how quickly Mason can go from domineering to soft in a matter of seconds. He knows exactly what I need and when I need it. Mason moves away for a second, taking off his jacket and throwing it over the security camera. "Only I get to see you like this Angel."

I respond by reaching for Mason's zipper, undoing it in seconds, and pulling his throbbing length from his boxers. The tip of his cock is leaking precum, and I can't help but trace it with my thumb.

"You'll be the death of me Vi." Mason pants, tucking one of

my wild curls behind my ear as he watches me stroke his cock. I move to sink to my knees so I can take him in my mouth when he shakes his head and stops me. "Can I taste you first, Angel? I've been dying to bury my tongue in your tight little pussy since you put on this dress. And I don't know how much longer I can hold out."

Mason sinks to his knees and tosses one of my legs over his shoulders exposing me to him. He nuzzles his face against my thighs, the feeling of his facial hair against me causes goose-bumps to form on my skin.

"Does my beard bother you?" He peers up at me and I realize my fingers have moved to his chin, toying with his beard.

"No. No. It feels good. Really good." I attempt to bring his mouth closer to my core.

"You sure? Because I can shave it off if you—"

"Don't you dare." *Okay maybe I was more attached to his beard than I realized.* "The only thing you should be doing right now is taking care of me." I'm desperate for his touch, spreading my legs further open for him.

He smiles devilishly as he locks his eyes with mine and takes my swollen clit into his mouth. If not for Mason's firm hand on my stomach, I would've lost my balance. He moves his tongue lower, lapping me up slowly. Mason lets out a moan that rocks through my entire body. Fuck he was good at this.

"So damn good." I gasp as his thumb finds my clit while he continues to lick me like a man starved. My eyes shut as my next high approaches. When I finally have the strength to look at him again, I see him stroking his cock, getting off to the sight of me riding his face. I'm so close to coming again that all it takes is a few quick strokes of his tongue on my clit to have me turning into a mess again.

Mason stands up and brings me into his arms stroking my hair, his cock still hard against my stomach. "You're doing such a good job, Violet. Coming all over my fingers and tongue like a good girl." He locks our mouths together, and I moan at the taste of myself.

"I want more Mason. I need you buried inside of me." I'd never been this vocal in my previous relationships. I honestly didn't know I even had it in me. But I trust Mason more than anyone.

"Fuck Violet. God I love you. Turn around and place your hands on the railing."

He moves me so I'm bent over. I feel his hands on the back of my dress as he tugs the zipper down enough to release my aching breasts, tugging gently at my nipples. He presses a small kiss in the center of my exposed back before hiking up the bottom of my dress so that my ass is bare to him. I look over my shoulder and watch as he sheaths himself with a condom. Leaning over me, he places a kiss on my temple before sinking into me inch by inch until I'm full of him.

His hand reaches over to my front and starts toying with my clit as he moves in and out of me. From this angle, I can feel every glorious inch of him, and a part of me wonders how long we can stay in the elevator without anyone noticing.

"Mason that feels *so* incredible." I moan.

"You feel so damn tight Violet. You're gripping me so well. Look at you." He lifts my chin so that I am face-to-face with my reflection. My hair is a complete mess on top of my head and Mason's entire body is flushed – desire all over his face. He moves his hips at an angle that has me moaning so loud I feel the elevator shake. Before I can even warn him, I come.

"That's it Violet, that's it. You feel perfect wrapped around me. Come right on my cock, I'm right behind you. I'm right fucking there." Mason turns my head so he can kiss me as he comes down.

We hold onto each other until our breathing comes down. Mason takes his time zipping up my dress, wiping off the smeared makeup on my face, and trying his best to tame my frizzy curls before turning the elevator back on. When we reach our floor, he scoops me up into his arms bridal style, carrying me to our room. "My legs work perfectly fine you know," I tease.

"I know. But I like taking care of you." He opens the door to our room. "Especially after we just—"

"Screwed each other's brains out?" I offer.

He rolls his eyes. "Ever the romantic, Violet Amin."

"Sorry," I whisper sheepishly. "I love you."

"I love you too, Angel. I love you too."

forty-one

. . .

Mason

"JAKE AND CRAIG, swap out for Dylan and Tristan. Adam, run the same drill again," I yell across the ice. My eyes are glued on the puck as I watch it go from Tristan, to Dylan, back to Tristan, and finally over to Adam. He goes for the shot — a one-timer that has the puck flying into the top right corner of the net. *Beautiful.* The two freshmen have certainly managed to improve their game ever since I gave them their shot against UCONN a few months ago.

"Good. Now run the next play. Adam, start behind the net. Pass to Tristan and then to Dylan. Dylan, take your shot whenever you see an opening. Keep running the drill until that puck hits the net. Ollie—" I call out to our goalie who looks right at me. "Don't go easy on them," I warn.

Jake, standing next to me, smirks as our goalie stops Dylan's first shot attempt with ease. "Damn Coach, taking it out on the freshmen I see."

"Every player has to be ready if we want to go to the Frozen Four this year."

"We will be. Adam and I have been watching tapes every night for the past two weeks. UCONN has only gotten better since we last played them. But so have we. No other team has worked harder than we have this season. It's going to pay off. It has to, right?" Jake looks hopeful.

I don't have the heart to tell him sometimes hard work doesn't pay off. "It will. If Dylan manages to get his slap shot in order." My voice reverberates across the arena.

"Loosen up on your grip a bit, Dyl. Don't be afraid to let your stick do most of the work." Jake advises his teammate, catching me by surprise. A few seconds later, I watch as Dylan gets one past our goalie, a small celebration breaking out on the ice.

"Damn that was nice boys." Jake cheers, tapping his stick on the boards in encouragement.

"Not upset it's not you out there?" I ask, raising my eyebrow. Jake from a few months ago would have been foaming at the mouth to upstage his teammates.

"Every player has to be ready. And every player deserves their moment." He shrugs, amending the words I had spoken earlier.

"I like this side of you, Keeley. I'm sure the boys appreciate it too."

"Yeah, yeah. Don't get too emotional on me Coach. I can always go back to being a menace." He winks before skating back on the ice to give Dylan some more pointers.

I let out a laugh that doesn't quite match the way I feel inside. Any day now Coach Jameson will tell me whether I made the cut as assistant coach or if I should start dusting off my LinkedIn profile. While I feel more comfortable coaching now, I still have moments where I feel like I'm *pretending* to be a coach. I go through the motions: contribute my opinions during staff meetings, shout plays from the sidelines, and give heartfelt pep talks during games. From the outside, I appear to be a seamless fit. But on the inside, I'm scared shitless.

Coaching had started off as a job that I needed to pay my bills post retirement, but it's quickly turned into something I love. Something that's made me feel things I haven't felt since I was in the NHL. And with that love came this overwhelming sense of fear. Fear that one of my calls will cost us the game. That my line changes will ruin the rest of our season. That I will let my players down. Fear that I would have another thing that I love taken from me again. I'd like to believe that my fear hasn't impacted some of my recent decisions, but I knew that was wishful thinking.

Two weeks ago Coach offered to let me serve as Head Coach for the Hockey East Championship tournament. I told him I would think about it. From the disappointment on his face, I knew he was hoping I would immediately jump at the opportunity, but I couldn't silence the thoughts in my head about whether I was ready. Whether I *could* lead this team on my own. Winning the Hockey East Championships was crucial as it would secure our spot in the Frozen Four. It felt too important to use the tournament as a test of whether I was cut out for the job. Really, I was doing the responsible thing by letting Coach Jameson continue his lead. Or at least that's what I kept telling myself. If I felt the weight of the world on my shoulders when I was a captain at Westchester, as their coach it felt like I was carrying the whole universe.

"Mason."

I startle at the sound of Coach Jameson's voice. "Yes, Coach?"

"Send the boys to the locker room and meet me in my office." His voice gives no indication of whether I'm receiving good or bad news.

"Let's pack it in, gentleman." I wave everyone toward the

benches and highlight the strengths and weaknesses of our practice today before sending everyone home.

I walk into Coach's office and take a seat across from him. For five minutes he shuffles around the paperwork on his desk before making eye contact with me. He hadn't explicitly said anything, but I had a feeling in my gut this wasn't good.

"I'm afraid I have some bad news, son."

"You're retiring?" I joke, trying to lighten the mood.

"I spoke with Don Neeley last week. He heads the athletics department and manages the budget."

"I'm sure that was a riveting meeting."

"They're trying to hire a new football coach to revamp the team, which means our budget is taking a hit." Coach shakes his head.

"I see." My chest feels both deflated and tight at the same time.

"But Don said he could probably figure something out if we wanted to hire someone else."

My chest reinflates. "That's good."

He pinches the bridge of his nose. "I told him we wouldn't need the extra money."

"Oh." My mouth goes dry, and I feel my heart sink to my stomach. He doesn't need the extra money because he won't be extending my contract. *Fuck.* Coach Jameson was one of the last people who still believed in me after I got injured. One of the last people to give me another chance. And I blew it. "Can I ask why?"

"You tried very hard Mason. I could see that." His words are meant to comfort me, but they fall flat.

Coach hesitates like he doesn't want to hurt me.

"Go ahead and say it, Coach. I can handle it."

"You have an eye for the game, there's no denying it. I'm just not sure if I can trust your judgment as a coach. You've had a few good suggestions, ones that have helped make a difference, but every time I give you the opportunity to take the lead and *really* be a coach you deflect the responsibility back to me. You rely on me too much to make decisions, and I need a partner who is independent. I already know that I can do this job, but the question is can *you*?"

Honestly, I wasn't sure. I wanted to believe that I could be just as good of a coach as I was a player, but everything he said was true. I don't even think I can look him in the eye. I thought I felt passionate about coaching, like it had replaced the emptiness my retirement left me with, but maybe I was just lying to myself. Maybe I didn't want it bad enough and that's what Coach was seeing. Or maybe it was all the moments I second guessed myself. Despite all my accomplishments with this team I haven't been able to silence the voice in the back of my head that said, *'Who are you trying to fool into thinking you could be a coach? Everyone knows you're a fraud. Nothing but a washed-up ex-hockey player.'*

I had thought I'd been able to keep my insecurities hidden. Had hoped Coach didn't catch all the moments where my hands started to shake after I called out a play, terrified that my decision was wrong. All the moments I held back from speaking my mind because I didn't want to mess things up. But he had. Coach caught all my moments of self-doubt. And it made him realize I wasn't cut out for this job.

I look down at my hands. "I'm sorry, Coach."

"I know you are, Mason."

"I should probably get going." My whole body feels numb as I stand up and head toward the door.

"Your contract doesn't expire until the end of the season. I better see your ass at practice next week."

"You got it." I give him a small nod before leaving his office. I bolt straight to my car, needing to put as much distance between myself and this arena as possible. The drive home gives me time to replay Coach Jameson's words in my head.

When I arrive home, I dial a number I haven't used in years.

forty-two

. . .

Violet

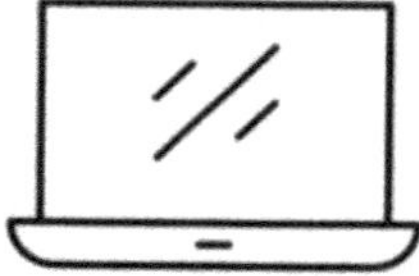

IN MY TWENTY-SIX years I've learned one thing — the universe is all about balance. The low points in life are not permanent, and neither are the highs. Recently my life has been filled with highs. My heart felt whole anytime I was with Mason, which was often. We'd reached a lull in the semester, so I could redirect my attention to finishing one of the many outstanding manuscripts I'd been putting off. Life as a grad student didn't get much better than this, which is why I knew my laptop was going to burst into flames or my kidney was going to stop working any minute now. My good luck had to run out.

And it did. This afternoon in my inbox. I'm staring blankly at a rejection from the fellowship I had poured my whole heart into.

Not my first rejection, and not my last, but this one stung a bit more. Maybe because I had felt stretched thin this year and was hoping — really *dying* — for a break. Or maybe because everyone had so much confidence in me, and for once I felt confidence in myself.

Even worse was getting the email rejection as I was headed to my weekly meeting with Bethany. Though she always managed to find a way to cheer me up, I felt like I had let her down after all she had done for me. Bethany gives me a tense smile as soon as I enter her office and gestures for me to shut the door. The only time we have closed-door meetings is when I have to vent or cry about something.

"So, I take it you heard about the rejection?"

"I did. I'm so sorry, Violet." Her sorrowful expression likely matched the one on my face.

"It's fine." My tone doesn't quite meet my attempt at trying to lighten the mood. While being an academic often means experiencing rejection, everyone knew the main way to success in our field was to get funding. It was more than just receiving money. Getting a fellowship was an indication that your research ideas were innovative enough to warrant support. As a grad student it meant that you were on the path of success to being a professor one day. Which is why this felt bigger than one rejection. It felt like an indication that I wasn't good enough. That I would never make it in this field.

She gives me a sympathetic look. "Having thick skin is good, but it's okay to be upset about this."

"Trust me I am. I usually don't get my hopes up about these things, but this one felt different…"

"Your research proposal was exactly what they were looking for. I wonder what their concerns were. Have you had time to look at your reviewer comments?"

"Not yet. Once I saw I was rejected, I didn't read the rest."

"Should we go over it together? Or do you need some extra time to process?"

"Let's just do it now. Rip the band-aid off."

Bethany pulls up the email and angles her monitor so we can

both see the screen. Most of the email was the typical fluff. "We had several exceptional applications this year...", "Unfortunately we can't offer you funding...", "Find your reviews below from Drs. Howard, Kross, and Atkins." Atkins. As in Dr. Darlene Atkins. The woman who had torn me apart every day my first year. The woman who made me doubt everything I did. I had hoped I could finally move on from my past, but it had come back to haunt me. "Well, I guess that explains why I was rejected."

Bethany's face is tense. "I don't know what the fellowship committee was thinking. She should have never been allowed to review your application. She must not have disclosed her conflict of interest."

"I guess it was something they never considered." *Or maybe they did.* Maybe they were just too scared to stop her. It wouldn't have been the first time that other faculty members chose to ignore Dr. Atkin's abuse of power out of fear. She was practically untouchable at this stage of her career. Pissing off a world-renowned researcher who brought in millions of dollars for the school was a risky move. One that I had chosen to take a few years ago, and was still paying for today.

"Maybe I can reach out to the department chairs and ask them to review your application again?" Bethany offers.

"No. It's fine. I don't want you to get in trouble."

"I'm your mentor Violet. It's my responsibility to ensure you're supported and treated fairly."

"I really appreciate you wanting to stand up for me. Trust me I do. I just don't have it in me to go up against Dr. Atkins again. I'm still trying to move on from what happened years ago..." My eyes start to sting, and I know I'm dangerously close to crying. Wouldn't be the first time Bethany saw me cry, but I know if the water works start now, they won't stop, and I still had two discussion sections to lead after this. "I don't want to fight this." *I don't know if I have another fight left in me.*

"It's your decision, Violet. But if you change your mind, I'll support you."

I give her a tight smile that she returns, along with a firm hug and words of affirmation that everything will be okay. I want nothing more than to believe her but the only thing I can think is how every time I get close to moving forward, I find myself drowning in the past.

forty-three

. . .

Mason

I FORGOT how fast my old agent worked. One second, I was on the phone with Marty asking if the offer to play in the European pro league was still on the table, and now I'm looking at a round-trip ticket to the Czech Republic in my inbox. In a couple of weeks, I'd go through their training camp, meet with their coaches, and hopefully sign a three-year contract. Marty mentioned their doctors would take a look at me, but he didn't seem worried about me gaining medical clearance. I was going to be a professional hockey player again. Words I never thought I'd be able to say when I took that hit so many years ago.

Hopeful feelings aside, I'm dreading breaking the news to Violet. Long distance would suck, but I know we'll pull through. I devised a plan for managing the six-hour time difference as I made dinner. By the time I was done cooking, I was feeling excited about this next phase in my life, and I was thinking Violet might be excited too. I hear the door open, and I step out of the kitchen to greet her.

"Hey Vi, how was your—" She looks defeated. "Angel what's wrong?" I remove her backpack and coat, opening my arms to her for a hug and placing a soft kiss on her forehead as she melts into me.

"Just a really shitty day." She mumbles into my chest.

"Do you want to talk about it?"

"Not now. Maybe later."

We walk over to the dining room table where I had laid out dinner for us — chicken and saffron rice, a sweet and savory dish her mom had taught me to make. The sight of the familiar dish makes her smile. It's a sad, "Wow I really needed this" kind of smile. Not the kind of smile you want to rub in good news to.

"How was practice today?" Violet asks as she finishes the last bit of food on her plate.

"Practice was fine…"

"Uh-oh. That doesn't sound good."

"Eh, the practice itself was fine. The conversation I had with Coach Jameson afterward…not so much."

"What happened?"

"He told me he's not renewing my contract after this season. He doesn't feel like I am a good fit." Even the abridged version of our conversation stung like hell.

"Oh Mason, I'm so sorry. I know how hard you worked to prove yourself. I can't believe he didn't see that." She takes my hand into hers giving it a tight squeeze.

"Yeah, I was definitely caught off guard."

"Well, whatever you choose to do next, I'll always support you." Violet leans over the table to press a kiss on my cheek.

"Do you really mean that?" I need her support more than anything.

"Of course I do."

"Even if it meant me going to Europe?"

Her eyebrows scrunch together. "That's oddly specific…"

"I reached out to Marty, my old agent. He thinks I have a shot at working for the pro league in the Czech Republic. He approached me about it when we were at Connor's award ceremony. I blew him off at the time…but I don't think I can turn this offer down, Vi." I sit on pins and needles, trying to read her face as the words settle over her. She looked pleased, I think.

"That's amazing Mason. But are you sure you don't want to look for a coaching position closer to home first? Maybe at Boston U? Or Even Northeastern?"

"I'm not going to Europe to coach, Violet. I'm going there to play."

"What do you mean?"

"Marty thinks I will clear their medical requirements. He thinks I have a real shot at playing again."

She rolls her eyes, letting out a laugh. "Marty is a shark. You could have one working brain cell and he'd try and pitch you a job. You're a money sign to him."

"Okay? That doesn't make the job opportunity any less real. I have to try."

Violet sucks in a deep breath. "Mason, no legitimate doctor is going to let you play again with your concussion history."

"C'mon Vi, what's in the past is in the past. I'm fine now."

"So, the migraines you get every few weeks are a fluke? Or what about the fact that you feel unsteady whenever you get out of bed too fast?"

Shit. I had no idea Violet had even noticed those moments. But what hockey player didn't have lingering aches and pains? "I'm fine."

"No, you're not. And any team willing to sacrifice your health to make money isn't worth your time."

"You said you would support me no matter what," I remind her.

"I said that when I thought you were looking for other

coaching jobs. I didn't think you would be dumb enough to try and play again."

"Just because I'm not getting my PhD doesn't make me dumb," I snap back.

"I didn't mean it like that. I just meant that you don't want to make any rash decisions after getting bad news. Give it some time. We'll figure something else out."

"Give it time? Like the time we wasted waiting for you to forgive me? I should wait three years to make a decision?"

She crosses her arms and looks away from me. When she looks back, she looks like she's trying to collect herself. "Yes Mason. Time can be a good thing. Like the time you took to forgive your dad. When something or someone hurts us—"

"I'm not one of your psychology experiments. I don't want to hear this." I stand up and lean against the counter.

"Well maybe you should, since I'm clearly the only one thinking rationally right now."

She didn't understand. She was smart and incredible and could accomplish anything she set her mind to. She wasn't like me. She didn't put all her eggs into one basket and now had nothing to show for it. She didn't know what it felt like to have everyone look at you with pity. To have everyone know you peaked years ago. My spot with the Czech team could be my second chance.

And I should've told her that. Should've come clean about my insecurities. Instead, I let my frustration get the best of me. "You know what Violet? I really wasn't asking for your permission. I was keeping you informed." I regret the words as soon as they come out.

"Well if you want to ruin the rest of your life, I guess that's your choice." Violet's tone is clipped, clearly hurt. "I'm going to stay at my apartment tonight." She stands, starting to collect her things.

"Let me get my keys, I'll drive you—" I search around the kitchen as she cuts me off.

"No need. I've already called an Uber." I watch as she shrugs on her coat and grabs her backpack.

I should have stopped her. Should have ran outside and begged her to come inside and talk this out. Instead, I stand frozen in place, staring at the door Violet just slammed shut behind her. Flashbacks of Chicago flood my mind. My chasing after her never slowed her down, she just fled faster. I just hope that this time, she comes back.

As I roll around in bed trying to fall asleep, I wonder if the only time we would be together again would be in my dreams. Sleep evaded me. My thoughts were plagued with whether I had lost the best thing I ever had because I couldn't let go of my past.

forty-four

Violet

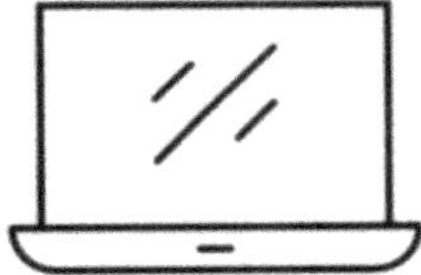

I REPLAYED my fight with Mason in the shower when I got home, all night as I rolled around in bed, and this morning when I woke up. I had many regrets about the things I said last night. I knew a fight was inevitable, no couple can stay in the honeymoon phase forever, but I never would have guessed we'd fight over him playing hockey again. I couldn't think straight as soon as he said he was going to be playing. I kept imagining him getting hit and landing on his head. Kept seeing him on ice, laid out, unable to stand up. Those thoughts petrified me.

I know leaving wasn't the most mature thing, but I was scared my temper would get in the way of my concern for him. And after my temporary time out, I feel much calmer. I planned to go to his office and talk things out, but after last night I think we could both use some caffeine. So I'm at the Beanery, waiting to order some apology lattes. The Beanery is surprisingly crowded for an early Saturday morning, and it feels like an eternity before I make it to the cashier.

I pull off to the side impatiently waiting for my drinks while refreshing my phone. I haven't heard from Mason beyond the text he sent me last night asking if I got home safe. I debate texting him now to apologize, but I know we need to have this conversation in person. That doesn't stop me from checking my phone repeatedly hoping for an olive branch. The barista's yelling grabs my attention. "I have a medium iced chai latte and a small americano."

"That's mine!" I call out, at the same time as another patron.

My eyes are fixated on Mason as I watch him weave through the crowd. I trail behind him catching him off guard as he collects his/my order. His eyes soften as soon as they meet mine.

"Hey." He looks relieved to see me.

"I have another medium iced chai and small americano, for Violet."

I gave Mason a sheepish smile. "Looks like great minds think alike." We grab our drinks and I jerk my head, gesturing for him to follow me outside. We walk double fisted with our drinks, waiting for the other to break the tension. We both take a deep breath before blurting out, "I'm sorry" in unison. He gives me a nod to signify I can go first.

"I'm sorry I snapped at you last night. I should have never brought up your dad or called you dumb. I never want to hurt you, or make you feel like I'm not in your corner. I'm not trying to make excuses, but I completely freaked out when you said you were going to play again. I just kept imagining all these worst-case scenarios in my head. I love you so much Mason that the thought of losing you scares the shit out of me. I can't handle it. I can't handle the thought of you getting hurt." I let out a small sob, and Mason quickly sets his drinks and mine on the ground and reaches out to hold me.

He rubs soothing circles on my back while kissing my temple. "I love you too Violet. And I'm so sorry I snapped at you last night. My conversation with Coach Jameson just really messed with my head. He called me out on my lack of confidence as a coach, and I kept thinking how I would never have what it takes to do his job. That my skills were best put to use as a player. That's why I called my agent. I got so caught up in getting my old dream back, I lost sight of the new dreams I have right in front of me."

I pull back from him and look him in the eyes, so he can see I mean it when I say, "Coach Jameson's wrong. Westchester is a whole new team after the changes you made. Look at Jake! He was one assignment away from becoming the Zamboni driver. Now he's a C student. You did that. You are an amazing coach. And no one can take that from you, Mason."

He gives me a sad smile. "Thanks Vi. Do you think you can forgive me?"

"Only if you can forgive me for all the shitty things I said last night?"

"Done."

"Done." I lean in for a kiss, which he gladly accepts.

In this moment, I know it's safe to tell Mason about my rejection. He knew exactly what it felt like to have open wounds that still haven't scarred years later. Rather than feeling ashamed, or worried about the pity, I know Mason will make me feel supported and remind me that my worth is not tethered to my work. I know this simple fact, but it helps when someone reminds you. "It turns out the old professor I used to work for was one of the people who reviewed my fellowship application. I got rejected. That's why I was in such a bad mood yesterday." Mason's arms tighten around me, holding me together.

"Fuck Violet. I'm so sorry. That's such bullshit." Mason trails his hands up and down my back, comforting me.

"Bethany said I could talk to the department chairs about it, see if they can fix this. I just don't know if I have another fight in me."

"I get that. If you do want to fight this, I'll have your back. And even if you don't, I'll also be here. Always."

Embraced in his arms, my neck tucked under his chin, I felt so cherished, loved, and understood. We grab our drinks, and head into my office. As we sit down, Mason's phone rings.

"Hey Coach what's up? Oh shit…What do you need from me? Are you sure? No. No. Don't leave the hospital. I can handle it. Trust me. Take care, Coach."

"What's wrong?"

"Coach got in an accident. Broke his leg. He's scheduled for surgery tomorrow, which is also the first game of the Hockey East tournament."

"What are you going to do?"

"He asked me to take over as Head Coach for the time being. Got any tips for tackling imposter syndrome?" He smiles nervously.

"About 1,000. But you're not an imposter. You can do this."

"I should probably go talk to the rest of the staff. We have a lot to figure out now." He places a kiss on my forehead before standing to leave. He hesitates for a moment as he steps into the hall. He turns around to face me. "What if I fail Violet?"

"You won't Mason. Win or lose, that's for your players to decide. You only fail if you don't go out there and be the best damn coach you can. And that I know you can do."

forty-five

. . .

Violet

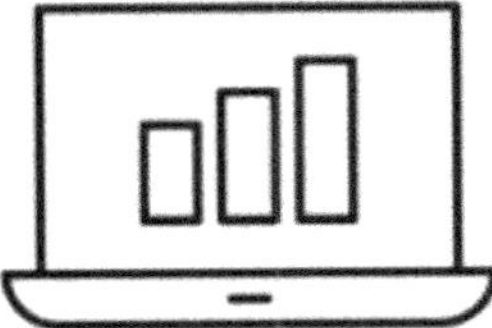

WATCHING Mason step up and lead his team inspired me. If he could tackle his insecurities and confront his past demons, then so could I. After he left, I emailed the department chair, Dr. Wayne. His assistant responded immediately saying he had a last-minute cancellation, but the meeting time aligned with the start of Mason's game. I debated asking for a later appointment, but I knew the longer I put this off the more I would talk myself out of doing it. I knew Mason would understand.

A few hours later I'm sitting outside of Dr. Wayne's office, bouncing my leg up and down, on the verge of a panic attack. It's not lost on me that I was in this exact position two years ago when I reported Dr. Atkins for stealing my work. I remember the way my hands shook as I presented all the evidence of her abuse. The way Dr. Wayne gave me a sympathetic look. Most of all I remembered how unsurprised he was. It was then that I realized I was one of many students she had harmed over the years.

"Violet, nice to see you. C'mon in." Dr. Wayne's voice snaps me out of my flashback, and I take a seat across from him. His office looks the same.

"Thanks for seeing me on such short notice."

"Of course. Now what brings you in?"

"I recently submitted an application for the department's Dissertation Award. It has come to my attention that Dr. Atkins was involved in reviewing my application. My application was rejected, and I would accept this decision, however, all my other reviewers stated my proposal was exactly what they were looking to support. I'm here today asking for a fair review." I hand over the stack of documents for him to see, which included the feedback from my three reviewers.

He takes his time reading through the documents. I try to stay calm and remind myself that I'm not on trial. Even someone who was unaware of our volatile history could see that her comments were unsubstantiated. He finally breaks the silence. "I'm sorry you've been put in this situation, Violet. Her conflict of interest was a large oversight on the part of the review committee."

I nod in agreement.

"Unfortunately, there isn't much I can do at this time. The person selected for the fellowship already accepted their offer. And asking for all applications to be reviewed again would invalidate our review process."

"So, she gets away with mistreating students again?" I summarize.

"What I can do is inform all future fellowship committees that Dr. Atkins is not permitted to review your application materials. Frankly that's what should've happened in the first place. I can't reiterate how sorry I am about this oversight."

"I see. Well, I appreciate you taking the time to speak with me."

I leave his office feeling deflated but proud. Violet three years ago would have been devastated by the events of the past few days. She never would have stood up for herself the way current Violet just did. Current Violet wasn't knocked down as easily. Even if I didn't get the outcome I was hoping for, I wouldn't live as a shell of myself anymore. Dr. Atkins had taken enough of my joy, and I refused to let her take any more of it.

I sent Bethany a quick email updating her on how my meeting went. She provided some words of encouragement that further fueled my desire to push past this. Starting tomorrow, I will compile a list of all the other fellowships I could apply to. Tonight, I had a hockey game to attend and a partner, who I loved more than anything, to cheer for.

Though Mason tried to put on a brave face this morning, I knew he was petrified heading into this game. Monroe had texted me earlier saying she corralled our parents, as well as Mikey and Bradon, into coming out to the game in support. I decided to keep that bit of information to myself. He was already feeling the pressure of not letting his team down. Knowing all his loved ones were also in attendance would stress Mason out even more.

I check my phone as I walk over to the Hockey arena, hoping for an update from Monroe. I had tasked her with sending me regular texts about the game. When I make it inside the arena, I can hear the crowd gasp loudly followed by a large groan. *Maybe that was just the UCONN students.* Fans of the away team usually showed up for major tournaments like these.

I tried to stay positive but that got harder as I climbed up the stairs toward the friends and family suite. My heart drops when I enter the room and see pained expressions on everyone's faces. We were in a three-goal deficit as UCONN scored a fourth in the last three seconds of the first period. I looked down at the players bench just in time to see Mason snapping his clipboard on the bench as the team shuffled back into the locker room. Monroe reaches over to squeeze my hand, neither of us having the strength to voice what we were thinking. Short of a miracle happening, Westchester's season was over. And Mason would be known as the coach that was responsible for the biggest choke this season.

forty-six

. . .

Mason

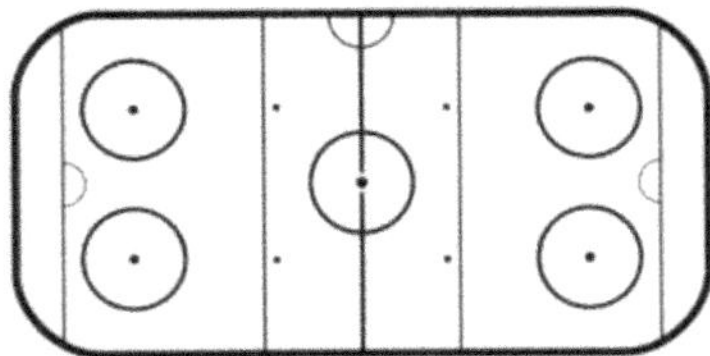

I **SEE** red as I enter the locker room. I have never seen such a cluster fuck on the ice. Being down four goals is a fucking nightmare. The only thing that gives me hope is that some of the greatest comebacks happen when the team's back is against the wall. All they need is a great speech and some fucking passion. Time for our *Miracle* moment.

"What happened out there cannot and *will not* happen again. Do you understand me?" It's my first time yelling at them, and it feels cathartic. I have so much bottled-up energy watching from the sidelines. This is why coaches break things (RIP my clipboard), we have no bodies to crush or pucks to slap.

"Dylan, Tristan, we practiced that drill with Adam and Jake hundreds of times. If I see you cower away from the UCONN defensemen one more time I will make sure your asses are benched next season. Adam, Jake. Drawing penalties and starting fights every thirty seconds isn't helping. Three out of UCONNs four goals were during a power play. You're captains for fucksake. *Act like it.*"

"We can still win this game, but only if you want it bad enough. Only if you *choose* to fight for it. Because as much as I want this team to win, you have to want it twice as much. I want to remind you boys that you have beaten UCONN before. You're the ones who put an end to their win streak during the regular season." I take a pause, letting my words sink in. "They probably view that loss as a fluke. That we got lucky. But it wasn't luck that beat them. It was skill. Skill and patience and determination. We stayed locked in, and persistent. We didn't cave in to their cheap hits or let the fact that they scored some goals rattle us. We went out there and made sure they never underestimated us again. And now they have stepped their game up. But we *can* beat them again. We *are* better. You just have to want it bad enough."

I leave them alone for the rest of the break, hoping my speech lit a fire under them. Like them, I need to get my head on straight and stay focused. I'm as fired up as they are, but I have to keep my eyes on the bigger game, and help my players adjust accordingly. Good players make good teams. Good teams make history with great leadership.

The second period starts, and it feels like we're a brand-new team. The players skate onto the ice like soldiers charging and primed to win a war. Gone were the miscommunications or the half-assessed attempts at carrying out plays. Dylan starts off strong with a big hit on UCONN's captain. He sends the puck toward the boards, and I watch as it ricochets. Adam is right there to pick it up and slide it through the goalie's legs. 1-4. Not even a minute later, Jake intercepts a pass and skates like a mad man toward our goal. Try as they might, none of UCONN's players can catch up to Jake as he sends the puck into the top right corner of the net. Our entire bench goes crazy as they celebrate his breakaway goal. My players keep the same intensity throughout the period, and we end the second down one goal.

The hunger and desperation to keep our season going is palpable as I enter the locker room. "Everything you just did out there, I need to see it again. The next twenty minutes may be the hardest twenty minutes you've ever played in your life. UCONN is desperate now. They're going to try some of their dirtiest tricks, going to do everything they can to get in your heads. Don't let them. We know their game. We know how they play. And we know how to beat them. Keep your heads on straight and we'll win. It's as simple as that."

The third period starts off with UCONN's captain trying to rile up Jake. My heart races as I watch a smirk come over Jake's face, the same look he gets when he's about to drop his gloves.

"Control yourself, Keeley!" I shout across the ice and watch as Jake clears his head and gets in position. He wins the face off and passes the puck over to Dylan who skates down center ice before he takes a nasty hit that sends him flying. The arena goes quiet as Dylan lays there limp, and his teammates go to check on him. He manages to get himself back up on his feet but he has a look on his face that I'm too familiar with. "Dylan, head back and see the trainers now."

"C'mon Coach, don't take me out now! I'm fine."

"You're not fine, you're concussed. And you're not going to win this fight with me either. I won't risk your health for a game. Trainer's room. Now." When I'm done with Dylan I turn my attention to the bench.

They look predatory, hungry for payback. "Everyone listen to me. That was a dirty hit, but we can't let our tempers get the best of us. You want to get even for Dylan? Then you win this game. You take all that anger and you put it toward getting pucks deep and into the net." I look each player in the eye to make sure they understand me. "I promise you no fight will feel as good as winning this game. Don't blow it now when we're this close to beating them."

I get confirmation that my words resonated when I watch Jake and Tristan shake off the verbal harassment being targeted at them. Jake's jaw twitches with every beratement, but he never falters. He takes a shot that's too high and the puck bounces off the glass. The UCONN defensemen are on it immediately pressing the puck against the boards to keep it away from Jake. He's not going down without a fight. It takes a minute for Jake to dig the puck out and pass it to Tristan who delivers one of the most beautiful slap shots I'd ever seen. Tie game.

A glance at UCONN's bench tells me their coach has lost his shit. He calls for a timeout.

"Alright everyone huddle up. I don't want this game to go into overtime. We have two minutes left, more than enough time for one more goal. Adam, I'm sending you out with Jake and Tristan. Run the same drill we've been working on for the past couple of weeks. Jake to Tristian, Tristan to Adam, and then Adam to Jake for the kill—"

"I think Tristan should take the shot," Jake says.

That catches me off guard. "Are you sure?"

"He's on fire tonight. UCONN is going to expect either me or Adam to take the shot. Not some freshman. They won't be expecting him."

"Tristan, that sound good to you?"

He nods. "Let's fucking win this boys. We won't let you down Coach Hayes."

Coach Hayes. That's who I am now. My heart squeezes in realization.

I'm doing my best not to cover my eyes as the puck hits the ice. Adam wins the face off but UCONN's defense is relentless. Adam, Jake, and Tristan, pass the puck back and forth several times looking for an opening they can't seem to get. With thirty seconds left in the period, Jake gets hold of the puck and skates up to the goal like he's going for it. All the UCONN players focus their attention on him, leaving everyone else unguarded. In a Hail Mary attempt, Jake sends the puck loose toward Tristan. The goalie's field of vision is blocked by all the chaos down in front that he doesn't notice the puck sailing past him until the buzzer goes off. The entire arena comes unglued, and a sea of gloves and helmets go flying. We fucking did it. Holy shit.

While everyone shuffles on the ice to celebrate, I scan the arena for the friends and family booth. I see Violet jumping up and down, alongside our loved ones. That moment would replay in my head forever.

———

Leaving the warmth of my bed this morning is particularly difficult given my late night celebration with Violet. I could still hear her delicious little moans as licked her clean and showed her all the ways I was grateful to her for being at my side. There was one more person I need to express my gratitude to, though in a much different way of course.

I'm standing on Coach's doorstep, rehearsing what I'm going to say, when the door flies open to reveal Coach Jameson, standing up on a very unbroken leg.

"Mason? What the hell are you doing here this early?"

"I came to check up on you. See how your broken leg is doing." I give him a pointed look.

"Come in."

He shoves me inside and we sit down in the kitchen. From the corner of my eye, I catch Penny glaring at me for a moment before returning to her breakfast.

"What is going on Coach?"

"I may have embellished a bit. I did have a pretty rough fall the other day, one that landed me in the hospital, but after a few tests they determined I was fine. A sprained ankle that just needed a few days to heal."

"Then why did you lie to me?"

"I'm retiring at the end of this season. My wife and I decided earlier this year it was time for me to call it. So I spoke with Don last week. I told him you would be taking my place."

"You said I didn't have what it takes to be a coach, that I relied on you too much."

"You *did* rely on me too much, and that stopped you from trusting your gut. I knew if you had the chance to step up, you would. That if given the opportunity with you at the helm, that fire would ignite. And from what I hear, it did."

Damn. I was so focused on being the best coach for them, I never once thought about what Coach would want me to do, or what he would say. I was Coach Hayes through and through, no hesitation.

Coach continues. "At first, I really thought coaching was just a filler for you, and I was worried you'd come to resent it because coaching can never replace playing. But I had to know for sure; I had to remove myself from the situation and see how you handled it. If you would take it seriously and saw yourself as more than just the assistant. You took charge and became a head coach for those boys when they really needed it. And damn did they need it what the fuck was that first period? Anyway." He claps a hand on my shoulder, "I believe in you, Mason. The team believes in you."

His words feel like a weight lifted off my shoulders. Sometimes you just need someone to tell you that you are good at what you do. It's hard to find a passion. I once thought after losing mine, all I could wish for was settling. But last night confirmed coaching was what I was meant to do all along, and it feels good to know others could see it too. I was going to lead Westchester all the way to the Frozen Four championships this year, and we'd continue our winning streak for many years to follow.

"Then I won't let you down. You may be retiring, but I promise the legacy you created will live on."

Coach smiles at me, a rare sight. "Good because if you had said no, then you'd have to face the wrath of Mrs. Jameson."

"So, what's retirement going to look like Coach?"

"Not quite sure yet. All I know is I'll have the love of my life with me the whole time."

"Sounds perfect."

"It is, Mason. It is."

forty-seven

. . .

Violet

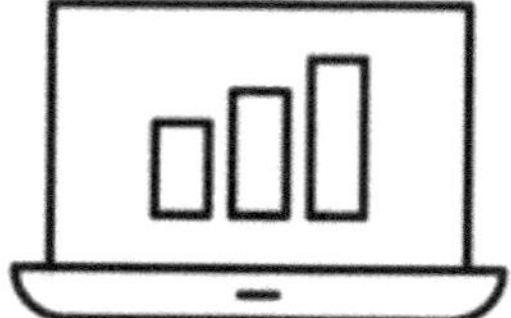

"VIOLET, Angel, it's time to wake up." The sound of Mason's voice, paired with the soft kisses along my neck, stirred me awake.

I stretch my arms wide causing the sheet that's covering me to fall. My face flushes red as I watch Mason's eyes take in my bare chest, as he licks his bottom lip.

"What time is it?" I ask.

"12:30. I just got back from Coach's place. We need to get moving soon if we don't want to be late for lunch."

"If you keep looking at me like that, we'll *definitely* be late to lunch." I counter I head into the bathroom, lock the door behind me, and get into the shower. I hear Mason's laugh followed by him yelling 'Tease!' from the other side of the door. I'd make him pay for that comment later.

I wrap up my shower and get dressed as quickly as possible. The traffic usually isn't too bad on a Saturday, but Castle Harbor is an hour away and I didn't want to keep our families waiting. Mason comes back into our bedroom as I apply various products to my hair. He grabs one of my leave-in-conditioners from the counter, pours some into his hand and runs it through my curls.

"A girl could get used to this," I whisper, as he massages my scalp.

"Good. Because I have every intention of making this a regular occurrence."

I take advantage of the drive up to Castle Harbor to catch up on my emails, one of which grabs my attention immediately.

Today, 11:11 a.m.
To: Violet Amin (aminv@westchesteru.edu)
cc: Bethany Coleman (bcoleman@westchesteru.edu)
From: Psychology Admin (psychadmin@westchesteru.edu)
Subject: Excellence in Mentoring Fellowship Update

Dear Violet,
Congratulations! You have been selected as a recipient for the Edgar R. Johnson's Excellence in Mentorship Fellowship. Recipients of this award were nominated by their primary supervisor and have displayed excellence in mentoring undergraduate research assistants throughout their time as a graduate student. This fellowship will include two years of financial support. We hope that support from this fellowship will allow you to continue your research and mentorship efforts. Please continue to check your email for further updates on accepting your offer.

Best,
Westchester University Psychology Fellowship Program

"Holy shit." This can't be real.

"Everything okay?" Mason places a hand on my thigh.

"Bethany nominated me for a fellowship! For all the work I've been doing mentoring my research assistants, and I got it. It's going to cover me for the next two years so I can focus on my research."

"I am so fucking proud of you, Violet. No one deserves this more than you."

"I was planning on scouring through the financial aid website tomorrow to see if there were any fellowships I could still apply to, but it looks like I don't need to anymore. I didn't even know Bethany had nominated me."

"She did tell you everything would work itself out. Looks like she was right." He places a kiss to the back of my hand. "Now we have two big things to celebrate today."

After the win last night Mikey insisted we all come over to his family's restaurant. Along with promises of champagne, Mikey also wanted to run some new menu items by us, for the grand reopening once he officially takes over for his parents. Despite my late morning, we beat everyone there, with the exception of Monroe. Neither she nor Mikey even noticed that we arrived as they engage in a heated conversation.

"Not happening Monroe. Over my dead body am I going to let you turn my family's legacy into some kind of circus," Mikey states, as he cleans glasses behind the bar.

"Don't be so dramatic! Think of how much publicity this place will get."

"I am thinking. I'm thinking about how none of the locals will want to step foot in this place if there's a whole camera crew hanging around."

"What are you two yelling about?" Mason cuts in, taking a seat at the bar.

"Your best friend is impossible," Monroe groans throwing her hands up in defeat.

"And your sister won't take no for an answer."

"What are you plotting, 'Roe?" I wrap my arm around her shoulder.

"One of my clients is starting a new reality dating show, *Love in a Small Town*. It's going to be based in Castle Harbor and we need a place to shoot our date scenes. This place would be perfect, but Mikey refuses to listen. Even though my company is willing to compensate him *generously*."

"I don't want your dirty Hollywood money."

"We're based in New York!"

"That's even worse."

"Alright, why don't you two agree to table this conversation for now, so we can enjoy this afternoon?" I offer, getting a grunt from both. Good enough for me.

My mom and Melissa shuffle in not too long later, Joe trailing behind them. Mason and his dad had spoken on the phone regularly since Christmas, and while there were moments of lingering tension, overall they've managed to focus on the positive.

"I appreciate you all coming out today. Go ahead and get seated and I'll bring lunch out in a second." Mikey gestures to the table closest to the window that overlooks the harbor. He joins us, placing a large pan of lasagna and a plate of pasta Carbonara in the center of the table. "Dig in."

We do. I can't even stop myself from letting out a moan as all the flavors hit my tongue.

Mason leans over and presses his lips to my ear. "Make another noise like that Angel, and I'll have to take you back to our car and handle our unfinished business from this morning."

I do my best to maintain composure, but Monroe can read all my tells. "Gross Mason, I'm eating. Can you try to keep your bedroom eyes to yourself when I'm around?"

He throws a wink at me, and I look down at my plate as my mom and Melissa shoot knowing looks at each other. If either one of them mentioned grandchildren today I might just crawl under the table and hide there forever.

"I'd like to make a toast," I announce. "To Mikey, for inviting us into your restaurant and bringing us all together today. To Joe and Melissa, for giving me another place to call home growing up. To Monroe, for always having my back from the second we met until now. To my mom, for all the sacrifices you've made for us over the years to make sure we were happy and healthy. And to Mason, how lucky am I to get to spend the rest of my days and nights with you." I smile, blinking away the happy tears that were starting to form as I took him in.

"Nowhere near as lucky as I am." He brings his hand up to cradle my face and press a soft kiss to my lips.

We bring our glasses together and spent the rest of the afternoon retelling our favorite stories. And on the ride back home, I think of all Mason and I had overcome the past few years. All the times life knocked us down to our knees, and how we refused to stay down. Watching the sunset turn the horizon into breathtaking shades of orange, pink, and purple, I started to fall asleep dreaming of Mason and I's future and all the moments that we get to spend together. Forever.

epilogue

. . .

Mason

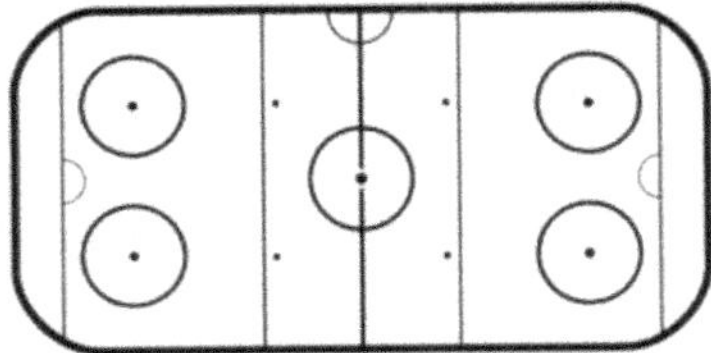

one year later

"ALRIGHT I REALLY NEED YOU TO work with me here," I beg. "Violet's going to be home any minute and I would really hate if this surprise is ruined because you refuse to stay inside this cozy little box I made you." The only response I get is a high-pitched 'Meow' while the small Calico kitten stays a firm three feet away from said box. I placed a little bed inside and planned to cover it with a blanket just for a few seconds so I could unveil this adorable little gremlin to my wife.

If you had told me a few years ago I would've spent the last three months visiting shelters and inevitably falling in love with a small but rambunctious kitten who was only slightly bigger than my hand, I would've laughed in your face. But after a few weekends cat-sitting Penny, and the longing in Violet's eyes each time she had to say goodbye, I knew I had to do something.

Violet had completed her dissertation proposal a few days ago and was under the impression that dinner at her favorite restaurant in the North End and the most expensive bottle of champagne was the main celebratory act. I knew this kitten would steal the show.

Glancing at my watch, I know Violet will be home any minute. I need to take charge of the situation.

"Okay friend. Can I call you that? I saved you from the shelter, so I feel like we're friends." Another small meow comes from the kitten. "Great. So, here's the thing. Your mom, my incredibly smart and talented and beautiful wife, will be home any second now and you're my big surprise. But for you to be a surprise you need to stay, well…hidden. So, if you could just get in this comfy little box—"

I jump at the sound of the front door opening which spooks the little gremlin in front of me. I watch in horror as she jumps off the bed and scurries underneath it. Fucking hell. The Deja vu hits hard.

"Babe, I'm home," Violet calls from the living room. I rush out of our room, slamming the door behind me.

Even after a year of marriage and nearly twenty years of having her in my life, my heart still stops every time I see that beautiful smile. I bring her into my arms and pepper soft kisses on her temple, nose, and finally, her lips. Violet's hands move up my arms until her fingers run through my hair. I relish in how her entire body melts into mine. I would've gladly stayed in her arms for the rest of the evening, but I had a small problem to solve, and I needed to keep Violet distracted long enough for me to fix it. "I was thinking maybe we could order some takeout tonight?"

"How do we feel about Thai?"

"That sounds perfect." I bring her into the kitchen and sit her down on one of the barstools while I pour her a glass of wine. "Let me just run to the bathroom, and we can put our order in."

I try my best to remain calm as I enter our bedroom. The good news is nothing seems to be torn apart or ripped to shreds. The bad news is the kitten is still very much under our bed, and no matter how far I stretch my arms, I can't reach her. "Alright little gremlin. I realize you have all the power right now. I want you to know that I am not above negotiations and bribery." The furball just blinks at me, cowering in the corner. "I'll give you catnip every day for the next week if you come out." More blinking. "Okay fine, every day for the next month—"

"What are you doing?" Violet's voice comes from behind me.

Shit. "Just dropped something underneath the bed."

"And you're talking to it?"

"Nope, just myself." I glare at the Calico kitten, who has now taken to licking her little paw and completely ignoring me.

"Need any help? I can probably crawl underneath."

"Nope. I got it." I swat my hand to grab the thing, but I spook her instead, drawing out a loud screech.

"What was that?"

"I nicked my hand on the bed frame."

"Mason, just let me help you." She crouches down next to me, and I accept defeat. "Now what are we looking for—OH MY GOD."

"Surprise?"

"Mason there's a *kitten* underneath our bed."

"I'm aware."

"No wonder you sounded so stressed." Violet lets out a small chuckle before crawling under the bed and scooping the furball out. "Hello there cutie. How did you even end up under here?"

"She was on the bed earlier," I grumble. "And then she got spooked and decided to hide under the bed." Despite my irritation my heart clenches as I see the little kitten curl up to Violet's chest and let out a small purr. Of course she would immediately fall in love with Violet. Who wouldn't?

"Did she come in through the window? She doesn't have a collar, so I don't know how we'll get her home."

"She's already home." I walk closer to Violet and smile as the little kitten lets me rub her head.

"What?"

"It was meant to be a much cooler surprise. I had this fun little box I was going to hide her in and give to you, and then the little gremlin refused to play along and ruined the big reveal." I roll my eyes. "It's a good thing she's cute."

"That's what you say about me." Violet looks up at me, tears of joy forming in her eyes. "I can't believe you got me a kitten."

"I'd give you the world if I could. I thought you knew that already."

She steps up on her toes to kiss me. "She's ours?"

"All ours. Do you like her?"

"She's perfect. You're perfect." She steps into my arms and adjusts the kitten so it's curled between us. "I love you, Mason."

"I love you too, Violet." With her head tucked into my chest I know with absolute certainty all I could ever want is right here in my arms.

The End

behind the book

Writing characters who learn how to communicate their complex thoughts and emotions so they can heal — done! Feeling comfortable talking about my own emotions and lived experiences…still a work in progress. I started writing *The Ice Out* as a means to distract myself from the utter turmoil that was my life at the time. Months after moving across the country and leaving the one place I considered home, I found myself in a relationship that was turbulent on a good day and emotionally abusive on a bad day (and there were many bad days). To say my confidence (which was already lacking in the first place) was wrecked would be an understatement. My main saving grace was so many of my friends and loved ones who immediately jumped to support and remind me that I deserved better. Which I did (and if this story resonates with you in any way, I want to emphasize that you, too, deserve better). Once I got out of that relationship, I thought I would be magically fixed and able to go back to the person I was before, but that was wishful thinking. So, I started my mid-twenties by slowly building myself back up, piece by piece. A journey that Violet and Mason can relate to.

As an author, there are many things I've always wanted to include in my books but was too scared to tackle out of fear for how it would be received by others (did I mention I am a people pleaser?) With *The Ice Out* I forced myself not to be afraid. This was no easy feat as someone who struggles with anxiety. While Violet's story is entirely her own, her identity of being an Iranian (or Persian) is one thing we share. With every romance novel I came across growing up I longed to find myself represented in the books that I loved. In many ways I was able to find community amongst stories that featured children of immigrants and/or women of color. In other ways I still felt there was a need for romance novels to include characters from my own culture and background. This was a task I wanted to pursue, that was frankly easier said than done.

Though I knew I wanted Violet to be Iranian, and that I wanted to address the various microaggressions one can experience as a woman of color, I also was incredibly aware of the fact that I couldn't and wouldn't speak for every member of my community. Violet's experience as an Iranian American is closest to my own, but I find it important to note that no culture is a monolith. Violet's anxiety and panic attacks are another thing we have in common. It was important for me to include depictions of Violet's struggles with her mental health not only because of my lived experience with both anxiety and depression, but also because I work in the mental health field. Similar to how people from the same cultural background don't all have the same experiences, I find it important to note that I know that not everyone's anxiety looks the same. Still, I hope Violet can serve as an example of someone who has been dealt some rough cards in life, and though she sometimes struggles in handling those difficult moments, in the end she always persists (and she does so surrounded by love).

Now that I've touched upon the ways Violet is near and dear to me, I think it's only fair I give Mason some love. Mason being unsure if he could be a supportive partner, pushing away loved ones, avoiding the town he grew up in, experiencing imposter syndrome, and making rash decisions because he's terrified he will never live up to his past — let's just say the Venn diagram of what makes me and Mason similar is more of a circle. If I can learn anything from Mason, it's the fact that my worth isn't tied to my work (*the academic in me is screaming*) and that my past mistakes only define me if I let them.

So we've tackled the heavy…how about the fun? I never imagined I'd write a second-chance romance until I heard 'Now That We Don't Talk' by Taylor Swift. This song had me thinking about my own relationships where I went from talking to someone I loved every day to being a stranger in their life. Almost instantly I got the idea for my second book. Except I knew Violet and Mason would get their happy ending…whereas I would continue to blast 'Since U Been Gone' by Kelly Clarkson every time I thought of my ex-boyfriends/ex-friends (I'm a Gemini in case you couldn't tell).

The more I got to know Violet and Mason the more they consumed me. I thought about them as I commuted to work, when I was listening to music, and when I watched my favorite TV shows. When my days were draining, I found myself revived at night typing away at Violet and Mason's stories. From the feet-kicking moments to the ones filled with pain and heartbreak, all of them felt like a privilege to write. I also had entirely too much fun creating the small town of Castle Harbor which is inspired by one of my favorite places – Gloucester, MA. Since I just spilled where you can go if you want a real-life Castle Harbor experience, I think it's only fair to balance it out with a teaser. Not only did V&M consume my thoughts when I was writing *The Ice Out*, but so did many of my side characters. In fact, I hinted at three different couples in this book – each of which will have their own book. Any ideas who?

acknowledgments

This page could probably go on forever, so hopefully I covered most of my bases.

To Sierra, Lauren, and Parker I can't put into words how grateful I am to have met such an incredible group of people years ago, who have now helped me bring this book to life. Your friendship and support mean the world.

To Kelly, my best friend then, now, and always. Thank you for always having my back, listening to me vent, and being my biggest cheerleader. Love you loads.

To Alexis for always being there to listen to my anxiety-driven thoughts, chaotic ramblings about plot ideas, and hot bookish takes.

To Alexa for being the person I can spoil all my secrets too (both writing related and otherwise). Thank you for always begging me for tea about my books. If not for you I would be blabbing to the world.

To Sammy for always understanding me, and for inviting me to Gloucester many moons ago and allowing it to become my second home. Castle Harbor exists because of you.

To Michelle, for the never-ending kindness and support you've show me in some of my lowest points this past year. The world is brighter with you in it.

Lastly, a massive thank you to all my incredible readers who decided to spend their days/nights/weeks supporting me. I can't tell you how much it means to hear all your excitement about *The Ice Out* and theories of what's to come. Every time I doubt myself when I'm writing, I think of you and how you've changed my life.

With Love,
  Mina